Praise for the

Murder in the Tattoo Parlor

"Murder, motorcycles, and tattoo parlors are unlikely settings for a group of senior citizens. But if you're a fan of the Bucket List Mystery series, this is exactly where you would expect to find Francine and her friends! The ladies are crossing more items off their bucket lists while solving a murder and getting into trouble in the most entertaining ways. The suspicious death of a tattoo artist will be the toughest case yet for the Skinny Dipping Grandmas, while Francine is working on her own mystery involving her family inheritance. Elizabeth Perona continues her mastery of the cozy mystery genre and you won't want to miss this hilarious entry in the series." —*Jeff Stanger, Amazon "Hot 100" Bestselling Author*

Murder on the Bucket List

"Bubbly characters keep this cozy debut lively as you search through the red herrings for the big fish."—*Kirkus Reviews*

"A well-crafted mystery." —*New York Journal of Books*

"Do yourself a favor and treat yourself to Elizabeth Perona's charming debut, *Murder on the Bucket List*. This warm and witty caper features delightful characters, hilarious antics, and a celebration of friendship. *Murder on the Bucket List* is this year's must-read for fans of amateur sleuth mysteries. Don't miss it!" —*Julie Hyzy, New York Times bestselling author of the White House Chef Mysteries and the Manor House Mystery series*

"Elizabeth Perona mixes murder, mystery, and a charming cast of characters to concoct an engaging and fun read. High on ingenuity and imagination, low on gore, *Murder on the Bucket List* keeps the reader guessing. Looking forward to many more stories from this promising new author." —*Mary Jane Clark, New York Times bestselling author of the Wedding Cake Mysteries and the KEY News Thrillers*

ELIZABETH PERONA

Murder Under the Covered Bridge

"Perona crafts another clever adventure … with a magical ending, and the feisty and smart seniors are an engaging lot and will appeal to Agatha Raisin fans." —*Booklist*

"Cozy fans will enjoy spending time with Francine and friends." —*Publishers Weekly*

"A wonderful cozy … This is one group that no matter what your age, you will want to join up with and have a whole lot of fun." —*Suspense Magazine*

"The second in this series spices up Perona's usual recipe with a little fantasy." —*Kirkus Reviews*

"Plenty of fun … After reading *Murder Under the Covered Bridge*, you'll have a new appreciation for these seniors who have plenty of rev left under the hood." —*Mystery Scene*

"If you miss getting new episodes of *Murder, She Wrote* every week, you should definitely check out the Bucket List mystery series. Thank goodness Perona has given these senior sleuths long bucket lists, so we can hope for many more adventures with them." —*Donna Andrews, author of the Meg Langslow series*

"The skinny-dipping grandmas are back, and what a joy it is to see their return. This second in the Bucket List series is perfect for curling up on a chilly afternoon with a spot of hot tea and no distractions." — *William Kent Krueger, New York Times bestselling author of the Cork O'Connor mystery series and the Edgar Award winning novel Ordinary Grace*

Murder at the Male Revue

"Mirth and murder make for a winning combination in this cozy whose sleuths are as quirky as the suspects." —*Kirkus Reviews*

"Readers who want their cozy mixed with a lot of slapstick humor, shouldn't miss this one." —*Sharon Magee, Mystery Scene Magazine*

"They're feisty, they're over fifty, and they're back on the case! I love the members of the Summer Ridge Bridge Club and their crime-solving ways. Murder at the Male Revue is another fun-filled read in the Bucket List Mysteries by Elizabeth Perona. It struts its stuff!" — *Molly MacRae, National Bestselling Author of the Haunted Yarn Shop Mysteries and the Highland Bookshop mystery series*

Murder in the Tattoo Parlor

A Bucket List Mystery
ELIZABETH PERONA

Murder in the Tattoo Parlor © 2021 by Perona LLC. All rights reserved.

No part of this book may be used or reproduced in any manner whatsoever, including Internet usage, without written permission from the authors, except in the case of brief quotations embodied in critical articles and reviews

Cover design, illustration, and book formatting by Teri Barnett/Mystery Cover Designs, www.mysterycoverdesigns.com

PRINT ISBN 978-1-956685-07-7
EBOOK ISBN 978-1-956685-06-0

This is a work of fiction. Names, characters, places, and incidents are either the product of the author's imagination or are used fictitiously, and any resemblance to actual persons, living or dead, business establishments, events, or locales is entirely coincidental.

To all the fans who encouraged us to keep the Bucket List mysteries going even after Midnight Ink closed up shop and left us hanging—this one's for you!
—*Tony*

To all our readers—you are the absolute best! I appreciate you!
—*Liz*

ACKNOWLEDGMENTS

As always, I first and foremost thank God for everything. His continued blessings in all things, including this gift of being able to write novels, are way beyond my expectations and in no way related to anything I deserve. His lovingkindness is overwhelming.

Second, also as always, I appreciate the support and contributions of my co-writer, my daughter Liz. It's great fun to be able to do this 'Elizabeth Perona' gig with her. And I appreciate the support of my wife Debbie and the rest of my family. Without them, I wouldn't be a writer.

As it relates to this novel, there are a number of people I want to thank for their help: the Plainfield Police are always a great resource, and I especially want to call out Lt. Gary Tanner for his thoughts on the various scenarios I tossed out at him and how they might be handled. I also appreciate the time Penny Lutocka spent with me giving me a primer on forensic accounting. Elizabeth Gilbert, Teri Barnett, and several others shared with me their experiences and reasons for getting tattoos, and Bradford Smith, a tattoo artist extraordinaire, answered endless amounts of questions from me about the craft. (But I still don't want a tattoo!) No mistakes in this manuscript are attributable to them; Liz and I do our best to treat things as realistically as possible, but sometimes we veer out of ignorance or for the sake of the story. We hope it still comes off well.

The name of Joy McQueen comes from a reader who entered a contest many years ago and won a character named after her. Joy, I hope you are continuing to find it fun to follow the adventures of the ladies, especially the one named after you.

Finally, my novels and short stories wouldn't be possible without the help and support of the Indiana Writers Workshop, an incredible group of writers I've been privileged to be a part of since the mid-1990s. Thank you!!! I also appreciate the support of two wonderful organizations for mystery writers, Mystery Writers of America and Sisters in Crime, especially their local chapters.

--Tony

First, I'd like to thank God for everything that he's given to me, including this opportunity to work with my dad.

Second, I'd like to thank my dad for asking me to do this with him several years ago! I can't believe we're on book four. It's been such a blessing to spend extra time with you creating. Thanks for asking me!

Next, I appreciate the support of my husband, Tim. Thanks for holding down the fort so that I can write, edit, do events with Dad, and for encouraging me to do this in the first place. Finally, thanks to my kids, Lucy and Isaac for being so excited about the fact that their mom is an author. It really is an encouragement to keep this going. Also, thanks for getting older, sleeping more and becoming more independent, it makes this much more doable (I kid, kind of ;))

—Liz

CONTENTS

Praise for the Bucket List Mysteries	1
Acknowledgments	9
Chapter 1	12
Chapter 2	18
Chapter 3	25
Chapter 4	34
Chapter 5	46
Chapter 6	57
Chapter 7	64
Chapter 8	74
Chapter 9	84
Chapter 10	91
Chapter 11	102
Chapter 12	113
Chapter 13	123
Chapter 14	135
Chapter 15	142
Chapter 16	152
Chapter 17	164
Chapter 18	175
Chapter 19	185
Chapter 20	196
Chapter 21	207
Chapter 22	215
Chapter 23	224
Chapter 24	233
Chapter 25	239
A Note from Liz and Tony	245
Sneak Peek: Murder at the Karaoke Bar	247
About the Authors	255
Books by Elizabeth Perona	256

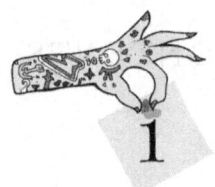

1

"I don't bleed anymore," Eric said. "When I get a cut, even a deep one, it heals on the spot."

Francine McNamara tried not to telegraph her reaction, that deep down she was scared. She had her hand on her knee, gripping so it so tightly she could practically feel the weave of her jeans. It trembled anyway. "I don't understand. Why are you telling me this?"

Eric Dehoney had called her two days ago, and asked to see her. Though he hadn't said why, Francine had been pretty sure whatever it was would not be good. She had taken a big risk to help him when he'd needed it most, and now she might have to deal with the consequences. Eric had been friends with her youngest son Chad in high school. She'd been "Mom" to half the football team, Eric included. That had been sixteen years ago. Now thirty-four, Eric had returned to Brownsburg, Indiana several months back as the owner/principal dancer of the Royal Buckingham Male Revue. A secret in his past led to him being seriously wounded by a gunshot not too long after his return.

Because Francine had been there and had a moment alone with him, she'd been able to save him. Thinking him to be delirious at the time, she presumed he wouldn't remember the tiny vial of Formula #58 she'd given him. And what choice did she have? Let him die? But now it looked like he'd recovered some of that memory.

She wasn't certain what, if anything, she could do about it. Admitting what she'd done, however, was nothing she wanted to consider. Not now. She needed time to think about it. Desperately.

Eric's hazel eyes looked imploringly at Francine. "You were there when I was shot. You held me. I remember that. Didn't you … give me something?"

She continued to feign puzzlement. "Like what?"

"Something to drink. My memory of it is dim, like a dream you get just before you wake up. Mostly it fades but a small part of it hangs on. You wonder if it was real. You know?"

She tried her best to look obtuse. "You said you were thirsty. Cass ran to the kitchen to get you a glass of water." Cass was his girlfriend then, now his wife. "She passed it off to me and I held it to your lips and you drank it."

Eric bit his lower lip. "Yes, I remember that. Vaguely. But the memory I'm talking about is one I had before that—I know it sounds crazy—that you gave me a sip of something. Like you pulled it from a necklace?"

Francine was glad she'd stopped wearing a necklace. She self-consciously fiddled with the top of her purple tee near the neckline. *Maybe he'll see I'm not wearing a necklace.* "I guess I'm just not following you, Eric."

He dropped his head, dejected. "I suppose it was a long shot. I had to ask. This whole thing is just so mysterious."

Francine pushed a plate of brownies toward him. After he'd made the request to see her, she'd extended an invitation to her house. She'd wanted to control the environment, which she couldn't do if she visited him and Cass. She hoped that sitting in her dining room around the old-fashioned Tell City maple wood table would bring back warm memories of the days when he and other members of the football team met there for breakfast on game days. That he wouldn't doubt her. That she couldn't possibly be any different now than the woman who fed them and cheered them on then.

Eric looked at the brownies and shook his head. "No thanks. I'm sure they're delicious, but I don't exercise those calories away like I used to." He looked off into space. "Too bad this healing condition doesn't cover excess calories."

"I assume you've been to see your doctor about this?"

Eric stood. He was taller than Francine's six-foot husband Jonathan by three inches. Though Eric was still in excellent shape and could have continued as a male stripper, he'd taken over his aunt's much less-physically-demanding consulting business. "Yeah, Dr.

Eisenbarger. He called it 'paranormal healing.' He said he's never encountered it until now, but he's heard of cases like it in Eastern medicine."

Francine shivered to think his physician was Dr. Eisenbarger. He'd also been a football player but for one of the competing high schools. His reputation had been that of a ruthless individual who would stop at nothing to get what he wanted, which he'd proven on numerous sports fields. "Dr. Eisenbarger?"

"Oh, I know what you're thinking. He's changed a lot since high school. I wouldn't go to him otherwise."

Francine had her doubts. Kids like Daniel Eisenbarger rarely underwent personality changes. They just became better at hiding their motivations. She stood and walked him toward the front door. "Does he seem concerned about it?"

Eric gave a self-conscious roll of his eyes. "No, he said I should be glad I heal so fast! But he hasn't seen *how* fast. You know, I can't get a tattoo. My skin heals before the dye even gets in. It just runs off my arm. An hour later, and you can't tell the skin was ruptured."

"Maybe your body is telling you a tattoo isn't a good idea." Francine held the opinion that a tattoo never looked good on anybody.

"Well, Cass is a tattoo artist now, and it's kind of weird that I can't wear any of her designs."

"I hadn't heard she started doing tattoos."

"Part time. You probably never knew this, but she was an art teacher before Brownsburg Schools moved her to phys ed. She was licensed for both. She's very talented."

They stopped at the entryway. Francine observed Eric's navy blue short-sleeve t-shirt, the kind that was fashionable these days, with the sleeve short enough that it stopped mid-bicep. Eric's muscular arms were covered with tattoos. Francine didn't remember them from the time he was a stripper, which wasn't all that long ago.

"It looks like you've managed to get 'sleeves' tattooed on your arms," Francine remarked, puzzled. "That must have happened recently."

Eric's grin had a frustrated element to it. "It's a temporary. Cass's mentor, Lucas Monet, has a side business with tattoo transfers. He's really good. Quite the artist. Mail order tattoos are becoming a larger part of his income."

"Is that for people who don't want to go through the pain of getting a tattoo?"

He nodded. "Or for those who don't want something permanent."

Francine demurred. She imagined that would fit a number of people. "How temporary are they?"

"Very. I'm lucky if I get two weeks out of mine."

"Do people notice it's temporary?"

"I don't think so. I get the same tattoo design, and Cass re-applies it in the same spot, so unless someone is super-observant, I'm getting by. If you know anyone who wants to get a tattoo, be sure to give Cass a call. Even a temporary tattoo. She can supply those through Lucas."

"I will," Francine promised. She watched him walk to his black Chevy Equinox parked in the driveway.

When she was sure he was gone, she called Jonathan. He had left just that morning for a week-long convention in Washington, DC. It was an annual thing, something to do with his accounting practice. He'd been going to it since before they were married, and she knew it was important to him. He didn't answer the phone but texted back that he was in training and would call her after dinner. When he did call later, they talked for nearly an hour about the predicament and how to handle it. But they never did reach a conclusion, other than to carry on and hope it all died down.

The next day was a Sunday, and after attending church services, Francine made the hour trip from Brownsburg to Parke County, to the home she and Jonathan had built on the 300 acre property she'd inherited from Zedediah Matthew. Their private retreat, nestled into the wooded section that faced the county road, was a cozy, three-bedroom cabin. They used it to escape whenever they felt a need to get back to nature.

But the property also held the one secret they kept hidden from everyone.

Francine parked the car in the garage and after a quick lunch, uncovered the all-terrain vehicle they'd moved from the greenhouse. Though the cabin was remote, she checked to make sure she didn't see anyone hanging around. When the property had belonged to her ancestor Zedediah, he'd had some issues with treasure-hunters who were certain the original owner, Doc Wheat, had buried his fortune somewhere on the property.

There was a treasure; it just wasn't what people expected.

Francine sped off on the ATV, crossing from meadow to a back section of woods, using a narrow, hard packed path that could only be found if you knew where in the woods to look for it. From there she steered toward the ridge overlooking what they'd taken to calling "De Leon's Desire." She parked the ATV in the woods and walked to the summit of the ridge, surveying the canyon below before she descended.

The fact that it was a dry summer made the impact of this view even greater. De Leon's Desire was a breath of spring protected from winter's cold and summer's heat. The rounded end of the canyon, which was below her, had bushes lush with green growth and trees whose tops never strayed out of the canyon walls. A spurting geyser, which they'd named "Perpetual Spring," had just begun its routine eruption in the grotto. She breathed in the heady scent of pine and earth, heard the chatter of the birds, and felt the cool dampness rising out of the canyon, dissipating as it mixed with the arid breeze that swept past her. In the background she listened for the light ping of the geyser's spray hitting the copper collection basin. In the midst of her uncertainty regarding what was surely a blessing, the sights and sounds of the canyon reassured her.

She pushed through a line of pine trees to the hidden path that descended into the grotto.

This was it; this was the treasure so many had searched for, most notably Ponce de Leon. A fountain of youth, one that had sustained her family in past times but one she had been unaware of until just a year and half ago, when the long-lived Zedediah Matthew revealed the secret of his land and bequeathed the property to her, his great-grandchild. The waters were restorative, and mixed properly with other ingredients, could even be life-saving. Doc Wheat had proven that. She had, too, when she'd treated Eric for his bullet wound.

She sat on a large stone and closed her eyes. She breathed in and out, trying to clear her head. Instead of peace, she felt like someone's eyes were on her.

Her eyes popped open. Turning backward, she glanced up at the top of the canyon. Her eyes scanned the lip of the overlook checking for movement. She saw none. She held her gaze for a full minute, but nothing stirred other than the leaves in the breeze.

She turned back to the serenity of the scene and pulled a knee to her chest, hugging it. She wished Jonathan was home, though she knew it wouldn't change anything. The twin problems of what to do about Eric and what to do about Daniel Eisenbarger would still be there. She and Jonathan had talked the day before and had agreed they'd have to monitor that situation closely. But how to do it without being obvious? That was yet to be determined.

An idea came to her.

Though she had no desire to get a tattoo, she knew someone who did. And that might get her close to Eric's wife Cass, which would enable her to stay in the loop of what was going through their heads. Yes, she thought, that might work.

Francine nodded sympathetically as her friend Joy McQueen spun out a story about her fiancé Roy Stockton, former sheriff of Parke County, and the symbol of love he'd just made for her, a symbol that Joy thought required some kind of reciprocation. Joy sat across the kitchen bar, perched on a stool, with her legs crossed over black capri pants. She nervously nibbled the homemade Chex party mix Francine had set out in a small, hand-thrown pottery bowl she'd bought at a library fundraiser.

"How interesting that his first wife's name was Jody, and yours is Joy, just one letter less," Francine said. "I don't remember you ever telling me that."

"I knew it, of course, because he doesn't hide that he was married before, but he also doesn't talk a lot about her around me. I suppose that's natural. It was difficult for him when she died. Still is, eight years later. He says he didn't think he'd ever get married again. He didn't even date for a long time. Then I came along."

"You knew about the tattoo?"

"It was high up on his shoulder, so the first time he took off his shirt, I saw it."

Francine suppressed a smile. This was a sign that Joy was getting better. Until six months ago she had an anxiety attack every time she even thought about a naked man, let alone saw one. The unfortunate situation had been brought on a decade earlier by her ex-husband Bruno's leaving her for another man. The group's effort to get her over that fear of nakedness with men had involved Eric Dehoney's male dance troupe, a fund raiser, and a catered event. While successful, it had also led to yet another murder investigation. The women, all in their 70's, had navigated that, too. "It must have been difficult for the tattoo artist to eliminate the letter "d" in the tattoo. I mean, I would think it would be easier to *add* a letter."

"Roy knew a guy who was good at covering up mistakes. Not that "Jody" was a mistake. But you know what I mean. Tattoos that didn't age well or ones the wearer had come to regret."

Francine nodded. Though she had no personal experience with it, she could imagine how that could happen. "And now you want to get a tattoo?" She paused. This was incredibly convenient. She'd looked through Joy's bucket list, fairly certain she'd remembered something about it. Sure enough, it had been there, #26. But still, she had to make sure Joy knew what she was in for. "You don't do pain well."

"I've looked into it. I've talked to the same guy Roy used. He says he knows what it's like to be sensitive to pain and will walk me through it. Getting a tattoo is on my bucket list, you know."

"Now that you mention it, I do remember."

"Roy's birthday is at the end of the month. This is a chance to show him how much I love him and check the tattoo off my list. If he went through all that to get his tattoo changed over, it can't be too much longer before we set a date."

Francine had to smile at Joy's earnestness. The only downer was that she seemed to have already chosen the artist.

Joy leaned forward. "I need you to be there to help me through the tattoo. Can you do it?"

Maybe this was her chance to suggest Cass Dehoney. "Do you already have it scheduled then?"

Joy nodded. "Tonight, right here in Brownsburg! That new set of shops on 56th Street."

"You mean Tattoo You Two, the nail salon, tattoo parlor, and piercing studio? That's where Charlotte and I have been getting our pedicures! Though I've never strayed into the back offices where the tattoo artists are."

"Yes! That's where Lucas Monet has his studio. He's the tattoo artist Roy used."

"Monet?" Francine blurted out. She remembered the name as the artist Eric had said was Cass's mentor.

Joy laughed. "I know, like the famous artist. I had the same reaction. I'm sure it's just his pseudonym."

That wasn't why she'd said it, but Francine was relieved Joy had misinterpreted it. "If that's his real name, it could explain why he's become an artist, of sorts."

"Anyway, it's at 11 o'clock tonight."

"Tonight? At eleven? That's really short notice—and eleven seems awfully late!"

"I need to get in as soon as possible, and this was the quickest way to do it. I was going to suggest everyone come with me tonight after Bridge Club, but then it got cancelled."

"Delayed, not cancelled. We moved it to tomorrow night."

"You know what I mean. I don't want to move it to tomorrow because I begged and cajoled him two weeks ago just to get this appointment tonight. Besides, how do I know Bridge Club won't be cancelled again? Look how easily tonight's meeting got cancelled. Mary Ruth had yet another date, right? And with a different guy! She's got to stop dating people she finds on the internet. She could meet a crazed killer!"

Francine wasn't sure that would happen, but she agreed Mary Ruth had met some odd characters.

"And it wasn't just her," Joy continued. "Charlotte had to cancel because of her motorcycle class. I hope she never succeeds in getting her license." Joy rolled her eyes. "She has no business riding a motorcycle. She's going to hurt someone, most likely herself."

Francine had to admit it was getting harder and harder to schedule Bridge Club. "Alice's evening real estate deals are becoming a scheduling nightmare, too."

Joy put her hands to her hips. "What's gotten into us? We didn't used to be this way. So many different directions we're headed in! Not that we were ever a placid group of biddies. I fight that notion every time I create a segment for *Good Morning America*. Just because someone reaches her seventies doesn't mean she—or he—is ready to be put out to pasture. But we used to have regular Bridge Club meetings. Now it's catch as catch can."

Francine pushed the bowl of Party Mix away from her. Joy's

complaining was a case of the pot calling the kettle black. Joy and Roy had become a fixture at charity events in Indianapolis. It was hard to miss them in the society pictures on social media. Roy always wore a white Stetson.

But as for why the Bridge Club members were acting more and more like younger versions of themselves—well, she certainly didn't want to discuss that right now.

"I could call everyone and see who can rearrange their schedules for 11:00 tonight," Francine offered.

Joy looked relieved. "And remember to tell them to keep it on the down low. If it gets back around to Roy that I was at the tattoo parlor, it won't be a surprise."

Francine briefly wondered if Joy wanted them there as much as for peer pressure not to back out as it was for getting her through it. In general the women tried to keep their efforts to accomplish everything on their Sixties List – their "bucket lists" of the sixty things they most wanted to do before they died – quiet and away from their husbands, boyfriends, family and the curious public. But it didn't always work.

And Joy may have that in mind. She'd shown she wasn't averse to broadcasting their bucket list accomplishments in her reporting. The attention was not always welcomed by the rest of the group. But if it was Joy's intention, then it would have to come after she revealed the tattoo on Roy's birthday, which would give Francine time to figure out how to use this connection to Monet to get chummy with Cass Dehoney.

"Eleven o'clock it is, then!" Francine said.

Joy left and Francine made the phone calls. Charlotte said she would no doubt be up for a wild night after practicing on a friend's 'cycle (pronouncing it 'sickle'). She said she would meet Francine there.

After debating with herself, Francine decided not to involve Alice or Mary Ruth. The more who were there, the less likely it would be she could make a connection with Lucas Monet.

And she really felt she needed to take advantage of the situation if she was going to protect her secret.

At five minutes till eleven, Francine pulled her Prius into the quiet, eerily vacant parking lot. The Tattoo You Two nail salon and piercing studio was at one end of the strip mall, with a seafood restaurant, a mortgage company, a doggie bakery, and a chiropractor filling out the rest. None had their "open" signs lit. The large logo signs above the storefronts were dead, and no lights were on inside any of the buildings save a single office light in a back office at Tattoo You Two. The light shone out in the hall.

She wondered where Joy and Charlotte were. She didn't want to get out of the car and stand on the sidewalk in front of the store. It creeped her out to be there so late at night with no one around. It had the makings of a bad horror movie.

She heard the noisy rattle of an engine approaching and saw Charlotte ride up on a motorcycle. In the light of the street lamp she'd parked under, she could tell it was red and maybe just a little too much motorcycle for Charlotte's five foot frame. Francine wasn't sure her feet could touch the ground while the bike was upright.

The motorcycle came to a stop next to the Prius just as Francine got out of the car. Charlotte, on tiptoe, removed the helmet and white scarf she'd wrapped around her neck like a World War I fighter pilot. She gave Francine a thumbs-up sign. She tried to throw the kickstand, missed, and the bike would have dragged her down had Francine not been there to grab onto it. It took a lot of grunting and straining but the two managed to wrestle it back into standing position. On her second try Charlotte was able to engage the kickstand and get off the bike, though not gracefully.

"Are you sure you should be riding this thing?" Francine asked. "I thought you were taking lessons to get your license."

"I got a learner's permit. And before you go telling me it's illegal for me to drive at night as a learner, well, I already know that."

There was no sense arguing a point Charlotte already admitted knowing.

Francine gave the bike a skeptical appraisal. "What kind of motorcycle is it?"

"It's a Kawasaki," she said. There was no denying the eager enthusiasm in her voice. She wrapped her arms around the handlebars. "An older model. I just love this thing."

Francine let out a sigh.

"Where's Joy?" Charlotte asked. "I thought this was her gig. You don't suppose she's chickened out, do you?"

As if on cue, Joy appeared around the side of the building. She motioned them toward her. "I don't get it. The back door is locked. Lucas said he'd have it open so we could go in behind the building."

"Lucas who?" asked Charlotte.

"The tattoo artist, Lucas Monet."

Charlotte smirked. "His last name is really Monet?"

"We're thinking it's an alias," Francine said. "It's too weird to be true."

Joy waved it off. "Don't know and don't care. Roy says he's that good."

Francine strode over the front door and pulled on the handle. "It's open. He must have meant the front door."

"No, I'm sure he said back door." Joy insisted. "But let's go in anyway."

Emboldened by the presence of her friends, Francine entered first and once again noticed the odd stillness that seemed to permeate the evening. She perked up her ears, hoping that she might hear someone —anyone—in the building.

"Lucas!" Joy called out. "We're here." Despite the loud pronouncement, there was no sound from the back, only a faint echo that seemed more ominous given the darkness of the front office and the late night hour.

"Lucas?" Joy put a hand to the side of her mouth as if she wanted the sound to go further, even though she'd said it softer this time. "He doesn't seem to be here," she said. Her voice quivered.

Francine was having the same misgivings she could hear in Joy. "Maybe we should come back another time."

"Nonsense," Charlotte said, starting toward the back. "He might be back there."

Francine gripped her by the shoulder. "And not answering? Why would he not be answering?"

Charlotte swiveled toward her. "If he's not here, we'll at least turn off the light to save energy. Shouldn't you, long-time owner of a Prius and now newly-installed rooftop solar panels, be pleased that I care about that?"

Francine frowned at her friend. "I don't think that's why you want to go back there."

Joy cleared her throat. She put on a brave face. "Look, Charlotte is right. We're all creeped out, but he said he would be here to give me the tattoo. There's a light on. We should check it out. Maybe something happened to him."

"Precisely," Charlotte said. She lurched forward out of Francine's reach, then took one slow step at a time past the reception desk and into the manicure and pedicure area as if she were sneaking up on someone.

Behind the large area devoted to nail care, the Tattoo You Two salon divided into two sections with an aisle in between, a smaller set of two cubicle offices on the left and a bigger expanse to the right which served as the hair salon and piercing studio. Both areas were identified by signs hanging from the ceilings. The lone source of light they'd seen through the front plate glass window was coming from the further of the two tattoo cubicles. Francine presumed it was Lucas's workspace.

Charlotte crept past the first tattoo office. "No one in there," she whispered, moving on the next. As Francine passed by, she looked in and saw a mechanized chair that reminded her of the type you'd find in a dentist's office. Because the office was dark, the oversized chair was the only thing she could really make out.

The trio advanced on the second office. A red exit sign above the back door to the building put a red cast on the hallway. Time seemed to halt for a moment as Charlotte reached the entryway first. Even she appeared hesitant to continue. There was a brief pause as they all took a collective but un-orchestrated breath.

Charlotte bustled her way in and backed out immediately. "Call 9-1-1," she said.

"What is it?" Francine asked.

Charlotte pointed, her hand trembling. "You're the nurse. You better check him out."

The first thing Francine noticed when she entered was the smell of vomit. The sickened man, she presumed Lucas Monet, had a few traces of it splattered on his black t-shirt. A bit more lay around the chair as if he had not bothered to get up when the urge had come. Francine put her hand on his neck and checked for a pulse. There was none, but the body was cool, not cold, so he hadn't died that long ago. After a quick debate with herself as to whether he was too far gone to try CPR, her medical training kicked in. Even as a retired nurse, she couldn't let herself give him up just yet. She spotted a box of disposable gloves, grabbed two, and put them on. Hurriedly assessing the buttons and levers on the chair, she lowered it so he was below her hand level. Once she cleared his mouth of vomit she began pumping his chest.

"He looks dead," Charlotte said.

"And he probably is, but his body's not cold yet," she said, grunting with exertion. "Is someone calling 9-1-1?"

Joy's eyes widened. She nudged Charlotte. "You have to do it. I need to get out of here."

Charlotte gave her an angry glance. "You need to stay until the police come. We all do."

If she'd been nervous before, now Joy seemed positively alarmed. "Why do I need to stay?"

Charlotte stared at her in disbelief.

"Well, if word gets around that I was here, Roy'll hear about it and I won't be able to surprise him."

"That's not ..." Charlotte started, but before she could finish, Joy had turned and dashed down the hall. They heard the front door close.

Charlotte got out her cell phone. "That was a hasty retreat."

"I think ... she's still shaken up ... from finding Camille Ledfelter's body." Francine said in between pumps on Lucas's chest. How long had it been since Joy found Camille stabbed and barely alive at the male revue benefit? A few months, a half-year? She couldn't remember.

"Roy'll be surprised in any event, once he hears his tattoo artist friend is dead and you and me found him. I wonder if he'll start to be suspicious Joy might have been here anyway."

Charlotte's call went through. She identified herself and said, "We have a dead tattoo artist at the Tattoo You Two parlor. Please send help right away. No I don't know the address. It's in Brownsburg. The corner of 56th Street and the Ronald Reagan Parkway." She paused to listen. "I'm pretty sure he's dead. We have someone performing CPR and he doesn't seem to be responding." The voice continued to ask questions, but Charlotte hung up.

"I've got to step out in the hall for a second or I'll gag," she told Francine. "That smell is getting to me."

Francine paused just a second to look around. "He must not have ... had much in his stomach ... really not much vomit ... I've smelled worse." But Charlotte was already out in the hall taking gulping breaths. Francine wasn't sure if her reaction was to the vomit or the fact that it was yet another dead body they'd come across.

Charlotte recovered and stepped back in. "I did tell you the paramedics are on their way, didn't I? You can stop the CPR."

"No, I can't ... not until the paramedics get here and take over ... it's the law."

Charlotte shrugged. She began to move about the office using her cell phone to take pictures.

"What are you doing?" Francine asked.

"Taking pictures of the crime scene, of course. What else?"

"Why? It's not our problem."

"Oh, it'll become our problem. Once that new police chief finds out we're involved, there'll be trouble. Why do you think Joy left so quickly? It might have a little to do with Roy, but more to do with the chief. She's had a couple of run-ins with him recently."

Francine thought about that. Joy had behaved uncharacteristically, for sure. Then a sudden wave of panic washed over her. "What are we going to tell the police? They're going to want to know why we're here."

Charlotte, over by a shelf containing a vast amount of small bottles of tattoo ink arranged by color, clicked off a couple of more photos. "We'll tell them it was me, that I wanted the tattoo. The salesman at the motorcycle dealership has a bunch of them; I think it's kind of cool."

Francine wasn't sure about the wisdom of this lie. "You don't do well with pain ... You'd end up with a couple of squiggly lines ... permanently engraved on your body and quit."

Charlotte put her hands on her hips. "I'll have you know living with that botched knee replacement has meant putting up with a lot of pain. If it hadn't finally straightened itself out, I'd probably be in Colorado toking up on weed."

In spite of the situation, Francine laughed. They were going to need some kind of excuse if they were going to protect Joy. She guessed Charlotte's ruse was as good as any.

Charlotte reached out to touch the ink bottles.

"Don't do that!" Francine blurted out. "It'll leave fingerprints."

"Good thought. I'll put on gloves," she said.

Francine slowed her compressions just a bit so she could study the tattoo artist. His face was just getting age lines. He had grown a beard and mustache that looked scraggly, but would likely fill in given a few more years. She guessed he was late twenties/early thirties, but she might fudge it up to mid-thirties if she could see his eyes. Eyes were the giveaways, in her opinion. She'd always felt she could read the life in them. To her surprise, he had no tattoos on his face or neck.

She scanned the rest of his body. Even before the vomit, the black Five Finger Death Punch t-shirt he was wearing had seen better days. The ends of the short sleeves were tattered, making Francine think it was either old or heavily worn or both. From the photo below the logo, she guessed Five Finger Death Punch was a band. She had no idea what they played, but based on their looks she was willing to predict she wouldn't like their music.

Lucas's left arm hung down off the arm rest of the chair. It was not as heavily tattooed as she would have thought for someone in the business. She couldn't see his right arm to determine how tattooed it might have been because it was pinned between his body and the chair. He wore jeans, not shorts, which seemed curious given how warm it had been lately. Most businesses kept their air conditioning at a temperature too chilly for her, but men seemed impervious to the cold. Certainly younger men. She looked back at the arm being tattooed. Whatever the tattoo design was, it looked incomplete, like the artist had only gotten started.

She stopped momentarily to check for a pulse.

"Any luck?" Charlotte asked.

"No. Do you know CPR? Can you take over for me?"

She pointed to herself. "Are you kidding? Me? I avoid knowing CPR for exactly this reason."

Francine resumed pumping on Lucas's chest. "Well, put your head back in the sand, then … I was hoping to do some snooping before anyone gets here."

"I've been hearing sirens for about thirty seconds," Charlotte said. "They should be here any moment. Probably too late for you. But don't worry, I've done enough snooping for both of us."

"Take some photos of the body … get some of this partial tattoo on his arm."

Charlotte obliged by snapping off some photos. "What do you suppose killed him? You're the medical professional here. I don't see a bullet hole anywhere."

"Based on the lack of blood … and with the vomit …I would guess some sort of poison."

Charlotte held her phone above the waste basket and took a photo. "I'm uploading all these photos to the cloud so we won't lose them when the police confiscate our phones."

"Do you think they'll really do that?"

Charlotte was nonplussed. "Even if they ask the right questions and we give honest answers, I'm pretty sure they will." She poked around in the wastebasket using a small ruler she'd found on a sketch desk. "What's this?" she asked, and pulled out a small cup using the end of the ruler. The cup had a few drops of water in it like it had been rinsed, but there were also traces of ink in it.

The emergency vehicle sirens now blared like they were right outside the shop. The suddenness of it seemed to startle Charlotte. She flicked the ruler and the ink cap dropped to the floor, not back in the wastebasket but behind it.

She bent down to pick it up.

The sound of the front door being jerked open reverberated through the shop. Seconds later paramedics stood outside the office door watching Francine perform CPR.

Charlotte straightened up with the ink cap tucked into her hand.

At least it's gloved, Francine thought. She turned to speak to the paramedics. "No pulse."

Charlotte waited in the hallway while the paramedics took charge. The second one, a tall youth with over-gelled spiked hair, saw the vomit and slipped on gloves before taking over CPR duties from Francine. The lead paramedic, a black woman with a kind smile, asked the questions. "How long have you been working on him?"

"Not long," Francine said, still a bit out of breath from the exertion of the CPR. "Only a couple of minutes earlier than it took you to get here. We called right away when we knew he didn't have a pulse."

She looked at the traces of vomit on the man and on the floor. "Did he do any of this while you were here?"

Francine shook her head. "He was gone when we arrived."

The paramedic tried to find vital signs but it was clear there were none. She put her hand on the forearm of her partner and gave her own head a shake. He stopped the compressions.

The police arrived at that moment. After a quick conversation with the paramedics, they started to separate Charlotte and Francine for questioning.

They tried to move Charlotte first, ushering her toward the other tattoo artist's office. "I wish I'd never said I wanted a tattoo," she wailed. The effort sounded a bit fakey to Francine.

"No talking," said a deep-voiced policeman.

"If it hadn't been so late at night, I'd never have brought my friend with me," Charlotte continued, despite his warning. Francine understood it to mean that Charlotte intended to protect Joy by saying they were the only ones there and that Charlotte was taking responsibility for the tattoo appointment. Francine hated to lie, but it seemed like she should go along and not contradict what Charlotte had already admitted to.

"I said be quiet." His voice was firm. "Captain Judson is on his way here."

Jud. Francine had to smile. Of all the investigators to be on duty, she was glad it was Jud. She'd known him since he played youth sports with her own sons, and he'd overseen most of the investigations they'd been party to. Because, like it or not, the Summer Ridge Bridge Club was beginning to make Brownsburg look like Cabot Cove.

"So, let me get this straight," Jud said, summarizing what he'd learned so far from Charlotte. "Charlotte wanted a tattoo, and of course it needed to be late at night because she was afraid it would be painful and wanted to do it when no other customers were in the shop, and that she persuaded you to come along for moral support?"

They sat in the office behind the registration desk. Francine had been placed in the desk chair that resided in front of the computer by the policeman who'd isolated her for questioning. Jud had wheeled in an office chair from the front registration desk.

"That's right," Francine said. She was trying to focus on just answering the questions and not elaborating, which might cause her to contradict something Charlotte might have said. They'd had no real time to concoct a cover story.

"To tell you the truth, this sounds like one of your bucket list adventures. Where are Mrs. Jeffords, Ms. Burrows and Ms. McQueen? Too busy tonight?"

"Jud, I'm surprised at you. You sound so cynical. You know we don't go looking for trouble when we try to check off a bucket list item. Sometimes it just happens."

"So, is this one of them?"

"I'm not going to answer that. Charlotte's already said she was here to get the tattoo, and I came along for support. Whether or not it's a bucket list item is irrelevant. As for the others, you'd need to check with them to see where they were tonight."

He considered that. "Tell me what you saw when you arrived."

Francine stepped through the night's activities, careful to leave out any reference to Joy. Since Joy had been the last to arrive and the first to leave, she'd not found it all that difficult.

"Did you see or hear anything that would lead you to believe someone else had been here?"

She thought a moment, then shook her head. "The night was so still, and we were a little freaked out because of the late hour, so I feel pretty certain if there had been something, I would have heard it."

Jud made a few notes and then sat back, watching her.

She had the impression he was waiting for her to say more. She decided to take the initiative to question him. "Did you find any evidence there might have been someone here?"

"We've called the building manager. We're going to get hold of their security cameras and check the videos."

Little alarm bells started going off in Francine's head. She'd forgotten about the surveillance that was necessary with any business these days. She hadn't seen any cameras, but then she wasn't looking for them. She guessed if there were any, they'd be pointed at the entrances and exits, not internally. But you never knew.

In any event, it was likely Joy would show up on them. Should she recant their earlier story now, or wait? She'd already lied and presumed Charlotte had, too. Would it look any worse to wait until the lie was discovered? Maybe when they had a chance to alert Joy to the situation and she knew she'd be discovered, she could come in and explain it to Jud. That might exonerate her and Charlotte. It probably wouldn't look too bad.

"Why would he vomit like that, Jud? He wasn't drunk. I smelled no alcohol whatsoever. The only thing I can come up with is poison in his system, but it would have to have been fast acting to knock him out like that." She ran a finger along her jawline, thinking. "He hadn't moved from his chair, yet he had to have been alive to have vomited. And why would someone want to kill him?"

His smile was grim. "It's been my experience that the rationale killers use are varied and twisted, depending on how crazy they are. But no doubt you've reached the same conclusion, haven't you?"

She was not unaware of how pointed his question was. "I suppose we've encountered a few killers."

He nodded.

"But it's not like we run around looking for dead bodies." She thought about how awkward it sounded when she said it, though. Given the late hour, the fact that the shop should have been closed, and the secretiveness they'd sought, it was almost as if they were willing for something to go wrong. Again.

A tall black man in a Brownsburg police uniform stepped into the room. Francine recognized him from some brief articles she'd seen on the Town's Facebook page as being the new chief.

Jud stood up. "Chief Turner," he said, nodding to the man. "This is Francine McNamara. She discovered the deceased. Mrs. McNamara, this is our new police chief."

He stuck out his hand. "Marvin Turner," he told her, emphasizing his first name, though Francine wasn't clear on whether he was implying she could call him by it.

She elected to go the formal route. "Nice to meet you, Chief."

He gave her a smile, but it was a hard one. "I've heard a lot about you." He let that hang in the air, then added, "But more, I suppose, about your friend Charlotte."

Francine wasn't sure how to take that. His facial expression gave no clues. The Chief was a solidly built man with a no-nonsense air. His hair was short. He looked like he'd been a Marine at some point in his career. She guessed him to be in early forties. Without a good sense of his personality, she decided to answer neutrally about Charlotte. Charlotte had a way of rubbing people the wrong way at first. "She does tend to attract the spotlight."

"I want to be perfectly clear in one matter before we go much further, and I've told the same thing to your companion," he said. "We do not need any help finding out who killed this man. I will view *any* interference in a *very* negative light. If I find you are withholding information or obstructing my detectives' abilities to investigate this murder, I can have you charged with obstruction of justice, and I will not hesitate to do so. Do you understand me?"

Francine was taken aback by his seemingly abrupt and vitriolic language. She opened her mouth in puzzlement and then closed it. She looked at Jud to see if he was onboard with his chief's decree. He did not make eye contact. Instead he looked straight ahead with clenched jaw. She took a deep breath and made sure Chief Turner heard the hurt in her voice. "I'm sure you've misunderstood any intentions we've had in past cases …"

He cut her off. "What happened in the past is past. I'm the chief now. I'm talking about procedures going forward. I said, do we understand each other? No interference will be tolerated."

She gulped. "If that's what you want."

"I do. Thank you."

He nodded to Jud and left the room.

After the door clicked behind him, Francine turned to Jud. "What …"

Jud gave her a warning glance that she should say no more. He shook his head. "I might have said it gentler, but those are the chief's orders, and I will be abiding by them. Please help me and yourself by doing what the chief says."

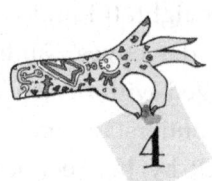

4

Francine and Charlotte decided neither of them could go home and sleep right away, so they drove to the all-night Steak 'n' Shake by the interstate. They got a booth by the window and looked out into the darkness. The moon was hidden by the clouds. All that could be seen were lit signs on high poles advertising the names of gas stations and other restaurants also open at two in the morning. Steak 'n' Shake's logo, cheerily reminiscent of the 1950s, stood in stark contrast to the women's moods.

Francine pulled out her phone and briefly considered calling or texting Jonathan. But then, she didn't want to wake him in the middle of the night with this. He needed sleep so he could concentrate on his training, and nothing would really change between now and morning anyway. She decided she would call him then.

She noticed that she had appointments on her calendar for that day and checked to see what they were. Bingo! She had been thinking she and Charlotte had appointments coming up soon at Tattoo You Two to get pedicures. She had no idea they were so close. "Charlotte! We have pedicures scheduled for later this afternoon!"

Charlotte's eyes lit up, but then her mouth twitched. "We'll see if they're open by afternoon. If the whole place is a murder scene, it could be closed."

"I suppose you're right. But if it is ..." she let the thought trail off.

Francine had no sooner set her phone on the tabletop when Joy rushed in, looked around, seemed satisfied there was no one else in the place but Francine and Charlotte, and came over. Plopping herself down next to Francine, she let out a deep breath like she'd been holding it for hours.

"What'd I miss?" she asked half-jokingly.

Francine glared at her. Charlotte tried to act like this was a completely normal activity, for them to be at Steak n Shake at 2 a.m. and have Joy collapse in a state of nervous exhaustion in the booth with them. But before anyone could answer, the waitress brought ice water and coffee and said she'd return after they'd had a chance to decide what they wanted.

Charlotte waited until the waitress was out of earshot. "Where have you been?"

"Watching from a distance. I gather Lucas Monet was in fact dead, and you were interviewed by the police?"

They nodded.

Joy glanced around nervously again, even though it was clear they were alone. "When I saw Jud's car pull in the parking lot, I said a prayer of thanksgiving that he'd be on the case. That was before the new police chief showed up. What did you think of him?"

Charlotte leaned up against the table so she didn't have to speak too loudly. "Where did this guy come from anyway, and when is he going to take his first anger management course?"

Joy stifled a laugh. "So you have met him."

Francine sighed. "I don't think Chief Turner has anger issues. I think he has control issues."

"I think of it as a personality disorder," Joy said. "When control issues leak into someone's ability to deal with others, it's a personality defect."

"You've had run-ins with him, then?" Francine asked.

"A few. And he's only been here a month! But let's get back to Lucas Monet. What do you think happened to him?"

"Poison," Francine said before Charlotte could pontificate. "There was vomit."

"A lot of vomit!" Charlotte chimed in.

"It wasn't that much."

"It was all I could do to keep from retching."

Joy's nose wrinkled. "I remember smelling it more than seeing it. So he was trying to get it out of his system. I guess he wasn't successful."

"He wasn't successful because I think it wasn't a poison he *swal-*

lowed," Charlotte said, weighing in. "It got into his system through the tattoo."

Joy gasped. "He was tattooed to death?" She looked to Francine for confirmation, who nodded.

"Sounds like the title of a bad cozy mystery novel, doesn't it?" Charlotte said, a bit of delight in her voice. She loved to insult cozy mysteries, though she was known to read more than a few.

"Don't knock cozies," Francine warned. "Somedays I feel like we're living in one."

"But back to Lucas Monet again," Joy said, "so you think there was poison in the tattoo ink?"

"That's exactly what I think," Charlotte said. "While I don't have any idea what poison it was, I bet the coroner will find out fairly quickly."

Francine shook her head. "That will depend on how long it takes to get a blood analysis."

"Someone had to plant it in there though," Joy said.

"Yes, so who did the tattooing?" Charlotte said. "Whoever did it has to be the prime suspect. I mean, a person can't tattoo themselves, can they?"

"A good question," Francine said. "If I try to look at it objectively, he vomited in a few different spots. If Lucas was tattooing himself, he persisted way beyond reason. He would have had to know he was killing himself and wanted to do it deliberately."

Charlotte held up a finger. "On the other hand, if someone else were doing it, Lucas must have gone along with it, because to have generated vomit and not stopped the guy could have meant he was complicit in his own death."

"Or he was drugged," Francine said.

"Here comes the waitress," Joy muttered. "We should order something."

"Good idea," Charlotte said, opening her menu. "But it's too late for a burger. Maybe something breakfast-y. Anyone had pancakes here?"

Francine finally cracked a smile. "I know I shouldn't be surprised having known you for so long, but how you could contemplate a stack of pancakes at two in the morning after the circumstances we've been through …" With the waitress rapidly approaching, Francine did not elaborate further.

"Sorry to be distracted," the waitress said, refilling their coffee mugs. "The night shift drive-through person didn't come in and I have to fill in for him, too. What'll you have?"

Charlotte ordered the pancakes, Joy asked for a breakfast sandwich on a biscuit, and Francine settled on whole wheat toast with jam.

"So what are you ladies doing out so late?" the waitress asked. "The only women we generally get in here this late are the busty strippers from some titty bar in Indianapolis."

Charlotte gave her a withering glance. "We've just come from a murder scene and we're trying to figure out why there wasn't more blood. And why this has strangely made me hungry for pancakes with strawberry syrup."

The waitress looked to Joy and Francine as if she was seeking confirmation that this was a joke. Instead, Joy smile weakly and Francine gave her a palms-up shrug. She beat a hasty retreat to get their orders to the kitchen.

Francine cupped her hands around the warm coffee mug. "Joy, we may be in trouble with the police. When they find out from checking the security cameras that you were there, they'll know we lied to keep you out of this. You need to level with us. Why did you leave so quickly?"

Charlotte leaned against the red vinyl seatback and shook a finger at her. "Not to mention your name is also going to show up on Lucas's appointment calendar. When they find it, you'll be a prime suspect. Next to the killer tattoo artist, that is."

Joy took in a deep breath. "I didn't think of any of those things. I'm in trouble, aren't I?"

"Yes, you are," Francine said. "And us, too."

The women sat in silence for a moment. "So, what made you skedaddle out of there like you were running from the mob?" Charlotte asked.

Joy gave her an annoyed look. "Roy. Just like I said, I don't want him to know I'm getting a tattoo for his birthday."

"I'm not buying that." Charlotte waved her hand dismissively. "It's a birthday gift, sure. But it's not the end of the world if he knows ahead of time. And he won't know what the tat looks like, anyway."

"The tat?" Francine said.

"It's what all the cool people call them."

"Now seriously, Charlotte, when was the last time we were cool? The 1970s?"

"We're coming back around to coolness. Haven't you heard? We've got more in common with the millennials than any other generation. Maybe I should be looking at a hot new motorcycle instead of a used one. After all, I'm the one who claimed to be getting the tat. Tattoos are in. If you're a young person and you don't have a tattoo, you're not boss. I like the idea of looking boss."

Francine rolled her eyes. "Tat, now boss. Really?"

"You'll be jealous when I show up in the news on my new motorcycle looking boss."

"Please," Joy said, interrupting. "Let's get back to my problem."

"Which one?" Francine asked. "That you still need a tattoo or the impending police discovery that you were there?"

Charlotte drew herself up to the table again. "Speaking of the tat, what's it going to look like? Is it going to be outrageous? Is that why you're keeping it a secret?"

"I really hadn't decided yet. Lucas was going to show me some samples. But I wasn't going for outrageous."

The waitress brought their food and refilled coffee cups again. Francine wondered if she'd ever get to sleep since she forgot to ask for decaffeinated coffee. She spread blackberry jam on her toast and took a bite. She watched Joy scroll through something on her phone. "What are you looking at?"

"Earlier Charlotte asked if someone could give himself a tattoo. I'm checking it out. The consensus seems to be 'it's not a good idea.'"

Francine winced. "I wouldn't think so."

"It would appear most artists recommend having another artist do it. It's awkward enough, depending on where the tattoo is on your body, that you can't be assured of getting the precise image you want." She lifted her head from her smart phone.

Charlotte forked up a wedge of pancake she'd cut from her stack. She dipped it in the lake of strawberry syrup on her plate. It really did look like a pool of blood. "The tat wasn't finished. We should have seen a tattoo machine if he was giving it to himself. It would have dropped on the floor when he died." She put the bite in her mouth.

Francine set down her toast. Charlotte's bloody pancakes were suppressing what little appetite she had. "Tattoo machine?" she asked. "What's that?"

Charlotte savored the pancakes before responding. "It's the delivery system for the ink. There are different kinds, but all of them have needles that provide ink to the skin. They're large enough we wouldn't have missed it if it was there."

"How do you know so much about tattooing?" Joy asked. She eyed her in suspicion.

"How do I know about anything? I read a lot. I also watch Ink Master. It's a tattoo reality show on the Paramount network."

"Never heard of it," Joy said, not convinced. "Just watching? Maybe you've already had one done?"

Charlotte gave her a mischievous grin. "I'll just say this. Now that I'm closing in on becoming a motorcycle boss, I'm looking to be 'all in.' That includes getting at least one tat."

While Francine could imagine Charlotte considering it, she didn't think her friend had gotten one yet. She would have let it slip before now. Charlotte wasn't good at keeping things to herself. "So that leaves us with someone else tattooing him and leaving after he was dead. I should probably tell you now that I know someone who Lucas was mentoring."

Both women's eyes widened. "Who?" they asked at the same time.

Francine glanced around. A couple of new patrons had wandered in, but they were several tables away. Still she leaned in and whispered, "Cass Dehoney."

"Cass?" Charlotte said, a bit too loudly.

Francine put a finger to her lips. "Keep it down."

"I thought she was a teacher," Charlotte said, toning it down.

"I think she still is. But she has a degree in art, and being the phys ed teacher at the high school doesn't satisfy her creativity. That's what Eric told me."

"One would think a watercolor or an oil painting might satisfy that itch just as well," Charlotte said.

"Tattoos are art, too," Joy said, somewhat defensively. "But do you suppose Cass did it? What motive would she have had?"

Charlotte shrugged. "If Cass were in the shop tattooing Luke, she'd probably show up on the video surveillance, just like you will," Charlotte said.

"Ouch. Do you have to keep bringing that up?"

Charlotte dredged another bite of pancake through the syrup. "Chief Turner's going to be none too happy with you."

The women were silent for a moment. Joy focused on her food. She took a small bite of the breakfast sandwich like she was taste-testing it, followed by a bigger bite. Satisfied, she went back to scrolling through her phone.

"Now what are you looking for?" Charlotte asked.

"Information about Chief Turner."

"Such a shame we lost our last chief to retirement. He didn't care if we found dead bodies right and left," Charlotte cracked.

Francine bristled. "We do *not* find bodies right and left. We've had a few unfortunate encounters, but that's all. Those deaths would have happened with or without us. We just happened to be there."

"Call it what you will. We find 'em; we solve 'em. You'd think he'd want our help."

Francine was always the first to give others the benefit of the doubt. "We should hold off judgement until we get to know him better and hear his story."

"Well, he came from a Kansas City suburb," Joy said, bent over her cell phone reading the Town's Facebook post. "He was the assistant police chief there for six months before applying for the Brownsburg job."

Francine watched her scroll. "Anything in his bio that would hint at his personality?"

"Not that I can tell. There's nothing about a family, either. Did anyone spot a ring on his finger?"

"No ring," Charlotte said. "He's not married."

"Not every married person wears a ring," Joy reminded her. "Not in this day and age."

"I suppose. I miss the good old days when snooping was easy, when a Miss Marple could detect a cheating husband from an untanned mark on his ring finger."

They all nodded in agreement.

"Once they get hold of the video surveillance, this whole thing will no doubt be wrapped up," Charlotte said pointedly. "We probably have nothing to worry about, except for Chief Turner's animosity toward us, Joy being hauled in for leaving the scene of the crime, and our being forever tainted for lying to the police."

"You forgot about press coverage," Francine added. "Thinking back on it, I remember seeing Channel 8's news van pull into the parking lot. It won't be long before your station gets hold of it, too, Joy. Then the whole 'skinny dipping grandmas' thing'll get resurrected."

"I hate that," Charlotte said. "Makes us sound old."

Francine eased herself into bed and, not being able to hug Jonathan, hugged her pillow. Strangely, she didn't feel distressed. Though she'd performed CPR on the tattoo artist, seen it fail to bring him back to life, been questioned by the police and even had a hostile encounter with the new chief, she felt like she could drift off to sleep. Was this familiarity with death a harkening back to her decades as a cancer nurse, or was it the recent bizarre reality of encountering so many dead bodies? She hoped it was the former. Over the years of being a nurse she'd come to grips with the tough truth that some patients sicken and die with cancer, even after cancer treatments advanced and the odds improved.

That was easier to think about than people wanting to kill others.

She finally woke to the persistent ringing of the doorbell. She glanced at the clock by her bedside. 9:01 am. She clutched a lightweight robe around her and headed downstairs to see who it was. Before she opened the front door, she checked an outside monitor.

Joy stared back, dressed in trendy jeans that no doubt came from Nordstrom's and an eggplant-purple cotton t-shirt. She leaned in closer so her face loomed large in the monitor. She knew where the security cameras were. "Let me in, Francine. I know you're in there."

Francine tied her robe and tried to gather her wits. She ran a hand through her brown hair, hoping it would fall into place and wondering if the roots showed. Clearing her throat, she cracked open the door just enough so only Joy would be able to see her. She worried someone might be passing by on the sidewalk. "C'mon in," she said. She stepped back to allow Joy in, then shut the door behind her.

"Are you just now getting up?" Joy asked. She handed her a bag from Hilligoss Bakery. "I brought a peace offering. I feel bad about leaving you in the lurch last night. And after I begged you to accompany me to the tattoo parlor. I feel awful."

They settled onto stools across from each other on the island in the kitchen. Francine peeked into the bag. "Pecan Danish! That may be just what I need this morning." She pulled out two of the sweet sticky rolls. "Oh! There are some yeast donuts in here."

"Cake, too. I wanted to be sure I could get into your good graces."

"Jonathan's away at a convention, you know."

"Then I have you well-covered for sure."

"I guess the news coverage must be bad?"

Joy shook her head. "Mysteriously, it's not. The reports have absolutely no detail. Police are being closed-mouthed. No one will even confirm that there was a dead man in the shop and who it was."

"Really? I was so sure I saw a Channel 8 reporter there."

"Oh, he was there. He has a distant camera shot of you and Charlotte leaving the building. But with the police not confirming anything, he can't say too much other than show the picture and report that he thought it was you and Charlotte. Still, I was surprised not to find reporters camped outside your house. Unless they've been kept at bay by the police car sitting at the entrance to the subdivision."

"There's a policeman down there?"

"Policewoman, actually. I saw her when I came home from the bakery. Presumably, she's a sentry looking out for the two of you."

Francine cut a pecan Danish in half. "And you, too, presumably. If she let you pass, maybe they haven't gotten hold of the video surveillance tapes yet."

"I'm bracing for that," she said quietly. "Not sure how Chief Turner is going to react. I keep reminding myself that his reputation is he's tough, but fair. That doesn't make him any easier to take."

Francine put the split Danish on two plates and offered one to Joy. "I wonder why he thought it was necessary to post the sentry."

Joy gave a snort of laughter. "Seriously? You have to ask that? After all the times we've been hounded by the press?"

"Yes, but we said we wouldn't reveal what we knew."

Joy shook her head. "Don't be naïve, Francine. He doesn't know you personally. All he has to go on is your reputation, and we've been heroes and goats a number of times."

"Now that you've brought up the subject, seeing as how I'm not supposed to talk to the press, what's your role here? Are you a reporter?"

"I'm here as a friend. Thankfully this particular story hasn't been assigned to me, so you're good there."

The women heard the front door open. "It's me!" Charlotte announced. She came through the kitchen door and made eye contact with Francine. "Guess what I just bought?" She gestured to what she was wearing, an oversized black leather motorcycle jacket with a Harley Davidson logo on it.

Joy turned in her direction. "A Goodwill donation from a heavyweight biker?"

"This old thing?" Charlotte held the jacket open. Underneath was a white t-shirt with "This Bud's for You!" emblazoned on it. "Actually, I've had it for a while."

Joy muttered under her breath. Francine thought she heard, "Worse than I thought," but she couldn't be sure. Joy shook her head in despair.

"I'll pretend I didn't hear that, Joy," Charlotte said. "I bought a motorcycle!"

Francine looked at her watch. It wasn't even 9:30 yet. No motorcycle dealerships would have been open for her to buy it. "The one you had last night?" Francine asked. She got off her stool and went around the bar to greet Charlotte.

"Yep. Want to go out and see it? It was dark last night and I'm sure you didn't get a good look at it."

"By all means," Joy said dryly.

Charlotte had parked the motorcycle behind Joy's car. It was bright red and looked very sporty.

Francine and Joy circled it. "It's not a Harley," Joy commented, looking at Charlotte's jacket.

"Of course not," Charlotte said. "This is a starter bike. It's a Kawasaki Ninja 300! I wanted a 650, with a 649 cubic centimeter parallel twin engine, but my feet could barely touch the ground. So I had to go with this one. It has a little lower seat height."

"It looks a little ... intimidating," Francine said.

"It's not all that heavy," Charlotte said. "It just looks striking. The color is passion red."

Francine could feel the heat radiating from the engine. Since she didn't live all that far away, Charlotte must have been out for some time. "You bought it just this morning then?"

"Yeah. After last night's events, I decided, why not? I mean, Lucas checked out at such a young age. The woman I bought it from was motivated to sell. She wants to upgrade to a fancier bike. I got a good deal on it."

"About last night's events ..." Joy started.

A police cruiser drove down the street right at that moment and pulled into the driveway. Chief Turner got out and walked over to the three women. He eyed Joy and then spoke to Francine. "I thought I told you not to talk to the press."

"Joy's a friend of ours," Francine said. "She's here out of personal concern. Her station got a video of us leaving the building last night and was worried about us. She's been a friend a lot longer than she's been a reporter."

"And she's not all that good of a reporter, either," Charlotte said.

Joy shot her a look.

"I mean, murders are not the kind of stories she gets assigned," Charlotte explained. "She gets the light, frothy stuff."

Chief Turner looked like he was struggling not to smile. "She *is* a reporter, nonetheless."

"Well, I'm not giving up our friendship while you solve this thing, and you can't make me," Francine said. She stuck out her chin in defiance. In daylight, the chief didn't look nearly as intimidating. For one thing, he was only as tall as Jonathan, about six feet tall. Francine herself was five ten.

"Have you had a chance to review the video footage from the tattoo shop?" Joy asked. Francine could hear the nervousness in her voice.

Chief Turner turned to Francine instead of answering the question. "See? These are the exact questions a reporter would ask."

Joy threw up her hands in despair. "It's a fair question that *anyone* would ask, given the circumstances."

"And one I'm not going to answer. I got word from one of my patrol cars that a reporter was spotted here, and I wanted to check it out." He nodded at Francine and Charlotte. "Just remember that you are not to speak to the press about this matter." He got back in his car and left.

Joy's phone rang. She looked at the number and answered it. "Joy McQueen," she said. She listened for a few seconds before she started nodding unconsciously. "Uh-huh. Uh-huh. Are you sure about this? Uh-huh. Okay." She hung up.

"Things just got worse," Joy announced. "The station knows you two were there, and they want to assign the story to me."

5

"He's probably on his way to get the surveillance footage now," Charlotte said. "If he'd already had it, the chief would have hauled your keister into the station to be questioned."

"She's right," Francine said.

Joy paced around the motorcycle. "What am I going to do? I won't only be in trouble with the police, once the station finds out I was there and didn't tell them when they assigned me this story, they'll be angry, too."

"Did you actually accept the assignment?" Francine asked.

"Well, technically, no, but the presumption is there."

"Then you still have time."

Joy waved her arms about. "Time to do what? Incriminate myself?"

"Yep," Charlotte said. "You're in trouble in more ways than one. Once you start reporting on it without disclosing you were there, you'll have crossed a journalistic boundary that could cost you your job."

"Thanks for making me feel better, Charlotte! Don't you think I don't see that? You got a time machine so I can go back and fix this?"

"Let's calm down," Francine said. "You still have time to save face before too much more happens."

Joy wasn't calming down. "Not *much* time! And I don't know how to fix it!" She continued to pace. "I need a strategy to minimize the damage."

Charlotte started following her. "You could always hope there was a malfunction with the cameras. That does happen. I know I'm hoping it did. Don't forget that we stand to get in trouble, too, once it's discovered. We've been lying to protect you."

Joy thought a moment. "Francine! You've got to go to Jud. Find out what's going on. Maybe clue him in on what's happening with me. See if he has an idea how I can come out of this with minimal damage."

"Why me?"

Joy was nearing hysteria. "Because you're clearly his favorite! Your boys played football with him at Brownsburg High School. You were a football mom. The whole team called you "Mom." If he's going to help anyone, it'll be because you asked him."

Francine took a deep breath. Joy was getting out of hand. "Have you just considered letting the station know you have inside information that could jeopardize your reporting integrity? You don't necessarily have to say what it is …"

"Inside access to you and Charlotte is exactly what they're looking for!" Joy said, still not calming down. "I'd have to tell them the truth, the reason why I can't report on it, which is that I was there. Then they'd realize they not only have access to an insider, they have me on their payroll! They'll use me however they can. I'm not saying they'd do anything illegal, but it's bound to come out that I was there."

Charlotte shrugged her shoulders. "I hate to be the Debbie Downer on all this, but if you're convinced it's bound to come out anyway, the sooner you get it over with, the better."

"But *how* that information comes out is critical to me salvaging my career and my good name!" She took Francine's hands in hers. "Please go see Jud. Please. For me."

Francine could feel the cold sweat on Joy's palms. It was uncomfortable, but she dared not pull away. She saw only one way out of this. "All right. I'll go see Jud."

"Right away?"

"No, not right away, I'm still in my housecoat."

Joy and Charlotte looked at her outfit, realized they were outside and it was daylight. Francine's faded blue nightgown was ankle-length, and it stuck out the bottom of her knee length robe. At least she was wearing sandals. They started to laugh.

Relieved the intense mood was breaking, Francine joined in the laughter. "Don't worry. The neighbors have seen this before. I look like this when I run to the mailbox to get the morning paper."

Charlotte donned a black and pink motorcycle helmet with a flip-up visor. "Let me know if you need anything else. Got to practice for my riding test. We motorcyclists *ride*, you know. We don't *drive*." She faced the motorcycle warily, then slipped her leg over the back so she straddled it. While her feet did touch the ground, she didn't have a lot of clearance. "We still on for the pedicure at Tattoo You Two this afternoon, right? Also known as the scene of the crime?"

Francine's hand flew to her mouth. "My gosh! I'd forgotten about that!"

"We are still going, aren't we? I'd like to see if we can get back to Lucas's office for another look."

"If the shop is open today. It might be closed if the police are still processing the crime scene."

"Let me know." She started the motorcycle. "And by the way, Francine, you'll probably find a bunch of phone calls to your phone from Channel 8. They want to talk to us. I'm ignoring them, just so you know." She flipped down the visor on her helmet. "See ya later, alligator."

Francine and Joy watched her go.

"She's going to kill herself," Joy said.

"She needs to stick to just driving—I mean riding—around the neighborhood, but I don't see her doing that," Francine said in agreement.

"She almost seems more interested in getting her license than in the death of Lucas Monet. Don't you find that odd?"

Francine nodded. "I thought that last night, too. Though she did do some snooping before the police got there. Her instincts kicked in during the heat of the moment. She took photos of the crime scene while I was performing CPR on the body. But she hasn't sent out the photos like she said she would."

Something else gnawed at the back of Francine's mind, too, like Charlotte had done something that didn't set well with her. But she couldn't remember what it was. The more she tried to picture last night, the more it escaped her brain.

"Let's get back inside," Francine said. "I didn't get a chance to have a piece of the Danish."

"You also need to get ready to go see Jud."

Francine pursed her lips. "Yeah. That, too."

Joy left quickly and Francine knew it was for the best. She needed to get over the police station in hopes of seeing Jud yet this morning, if he was in the office. It'd likely been a later night for him that it had been for her. She took a quick shower and called the police station. She was relieved to learn he was at the office and willing to see her without an appointment.

The secretary showed her to his door, and Jud stood to greet her. He was dressed in navy blue chinos with a purple polo shirt, purple being the Town of Brownsburg's inexplicably strange official color, given the name of the town.

"Thanks for seeing me on such notice," she said, extending her hand. They shook, but his manner seemed stiffer somehow.

"Glad to, Mrs. McNamara," he said. Francine was taken aback by his formality. He hadn't called her Mrs. McNamara in years. "Please have a seat." He waved her to a chair she'd already sat down in. It made her feel sheepish, that she hadn't waited for the invitation to sit. "Now, what can I do for you?" he asked. "I assume this is about last night?" Continuing to be uncomfortably formal, he sat behind his desk and put distance between them. In the past he would have sat on the edge of his desk and been closer.

"Yes, I …" she hesitated, not sure all of sudden what to say. She hadn't rehearsed how she was going to discuss Joy's leaving the crime scene, and now she was unsettled by his reserved attitude.

"Did you think of something new you wanted to add to the interview last night?"

She looked at him for some kind of visual cue to ease her concern. Jud was his usual handsome self, but his cop-short brown hair revealed something she hadn't noticed before. His hairline had receded a bit. His forehead had more lines, too. *Sleeplessness or age? Or is the job getting to him?* She thought of the horrible things a detective must see week to week. *It would age anyone.*

He finally gave her a smile. It seemed warm. And his hazel eyes were looking at her kindly.

"Can I shut the door?" she asked.

"I'll get it," he said. He rose from behind the desk and shut the door. It had a glass pane so they could be seen, but she presumed, unheard. At least, that had been her experience in the past.

"I was just thinking through everything from last night, and I wondered, did the business have security cameras?"

"In a manner of speaking," he said, leaning against the desk this time so it was not between them. "Why?"

"Well, last night you'd asked if we saw or heard anyone leaving the building, and I hadn't, but the killer must have at some point. So the cameras should have given you a look at that. Right?"

He stopped smiling. She could see his jaw flexing as if he were angry about something. She hoped it wasn't her approach.

"I think the chief made it clear that we don't need your help in solving the crime. If you have something to add, however …"

She decided to apologize. Sort of. "I know it's not my place to be worried about it, but if it was someone, maybe I might recognize him … or Charlotte might … we regularly get pedicures at the place." She let the thought dangle, wondering what would happen if she mentioned she had an appointment there this afternoon.

He closed his eyes. She wondered if he wasn't actually debating with himself over how much to reveal.

He opened them with what seemed to be a resolution. "Unfortunately, the owner of Tattoo You Two didn't see the need to put actual security cameras in the building. They were fake. He says he thought just having props there would discourage any thefts. He didn't think about anything more serious."

"What about outside cameras?"

His mouth turned grim. "That's also unfortunate. Not every building owner wants to spend money to keep up their exterior security systems. Tattoo You Two owns the whole building. The cameras facing the rear weren't working. Whoever did this took advantage of that."

Francine thought about it. Joy must've parked in the back and was therefore in the clear. That was good news. Of sorts. "But our cars were recorded by the front lot's cameras?" she asked to be sure.

"Yes. Though Charlotte was on a motorcycle. Does she have a license for that thing?"

Was this a trick question? While she didn't want to rat Charlotte out for driving at night on a beginner's license, she decided she had better answer truthfully. "She's getting one."

"She's going to kill herself."

At this, Francine had to laugh. "You're not the first to think that." She paused. "So you saw no other cars in the parking lot?"

"No. Should we have?"

So Joy's car didn't show up. But then, I didn't see it either that night. "No. Well, I mean, whoever did this, their car should have, but it sounds like he or she was pretty clever."

"They must have had insider knowledge."

Francine was both elated and depressed by the information. On a positive note, it looked like Joy might actually get away with not being forthcoming. On the other hand, she was bothered that the killer—and Joy, possibly—knew where to park that their coming and going hadn't been recorded.

She looked up to find Jud studying her. It made her nervous. "How do you think he died?" she asked. "I know I said this last night, but I'm guessing it was some kind of poison."

He cleared his throat. She worried he might be getting ready to deliver a lecture, and he was. "Mrs. McNamara, we've had a great relationship in the past, and I think it's worked out really well. I hope that will continue. But the chief views any need to satisfy your inquisitiveness as an impediment to following our policies and procedures. I think I've answered enough of your questions for today."

It hurt Francine to hear that. "As you said, we've worked well together in the past. And that's meant sharing information as the investigation's gone forward. Not that I want to interfere …"

"Your curiosity has resulted in personal injury in the past, has it not? And sometimes almost worse than that. The chief feels—and I've always said this—that you should leave the investigation to the professionals."

Francine wanted to say snarkily that at this point they were almost professionals themselves, but the chief's point was valid. She had been in some tight jams as a result of the situations she and her friends had gotten themselves into. Though they'd come out with their lives so far, there was no guarantee they would continue to do so.

But on the other hand, life was so much more vibrant now. She felt more alive than she'd ever felt. She had bucket list items to achieve, mysteries to solve, unknowns to face. Wasn't that true of the whole group?

The thought kept coming back to her, how much of this might be the water of the Parke County spring?

She shook it from her head. *Later, Francine, later.* "Jud, I understand where you and the chief are coming from. It's not that Charlotte or I or Alice or Joy or Mary Ruth ever want to experience these things, they just seem to happen to us. Don't we have a right to know something about the investigation?"

He shook his head slowly like he was thinking it over. "No, not really. You had no personal relationship with the tattooist, did you? It's not like you're a relative or a close friend, are you? Then even though you were the first to find his body, no, you don't have a stake in the investigation." He leaned in close as though they might be overhead. "Please do me a favor and do as I ask," he whispered. He looked her in the eyes, and she understood he meant a great deal more. She wondered what was at stake. Perhaps his job?

She owed it to him to nod her head, and she did.

He leaned back, apparently satisfied. "So, do you have anything more to add? Anything we need to know about?"

"No, but if I think of anything, I'll be back."

He smiled at her, and she felt it was genuine. "I'm counting on it," he said.

Francine drove home and made a pot of coffee. She poured herself a mug and sat on the loveseat in the living room, staring into space. She was trying to sort out all the craziness that was suddenly going on in her life when the doorbell rang and Mary Ruth came in without waiting for Francine to answer the door.

"It's me!" she called.

Francine set her coffee on the end table and went to the door to find Mary Ruth tugging down the hems of her narrow-legged jeans. She wore them tighter now that she was down to a size ten. "I saw on the news that someone was found dead at the Tattoo You Two parlor last night! Police won't confirm who it was pending notification of relatives. It was on Channel 8 this morning. They also reported that you and Charlotte were seen leaving the building, though no one seems to want to confirm it. What happened? And what happened to Joy? I thought getting a tattoo was on her bucket list, not Charlotte's?"

Francine uttered a sigh that was partly out of tiredness for having to repeat it often and partly because it was on the news. "Good old Channel 8. We were pretty sure they'd seen us, but we'd hoped they wouldn't report it since the police weren't confirming anything."

Francine offered to pour Mary Ruth a cup of coffee but she declined. The two went into the living room where Francine went over everything that had happened last night, swearing her to secrecy. She also told her about the earlier visit to see Jud and ask about the surveillance footage.

"So it looks like Joy is going to get away with it."

Francine blew out a breath. "Looks like it, but the stakes are going to get ramped up if Joy starts reporting on it for Channel 6. Charlotte and I think it would be best for Joy to come clean now and not take any chances."

"I can see why. You've already lied to protect her, but it would be better to tell the truth now in case it comes out later. It would protect your reputation."

"I hadn't thought of it necessarily in terms of *my* reputation, but you're right. To get caught lying would be a blow to my integrity.

"By the way, where did *you* go last night? Was it a hot date?"

"Not hot, not even tepid. We made small talk but weren't really connecting. It was painful until our late dinner ended and he suggested we go see a movie, one of those Marvel comic book superhero things. I decided we needed to be honest with each other and told him we didn't seem to have a lot in common. I said he seemed like a nice guy, and I hoped I didn't hurt his feelings, but I felt it would be better if we called it quits now. His look told me he was relieved but also disappointed. I got the impression he'd been told that before."

"Maybe I should have called you and asked to meet us at the tattoo parlor."

Mary Ruth thought a moment. "Maybe it's better this way. Maybe the fact that I wasn't there makes it easier for me to approach Joy and point out the tough position she's putting you in by not being honest with the police."

Francine was suddenly relieved. "Could you do that? And maybe leave out the part about the cameras not recording."

Mary Ruth chuckled at the last part of Francine's request. "Oh, sure. Though I may not be able to get to it until tomorrow. I'm busy all afternoon working on the menu for a catering event Friday, and then we have Bridge Club tonight." She paused. "I don't suppose you have any plans for Friday morning, do you?"

"You need help getting ready for the event?"

"Yes we do, and when I say that, I'm pretty sure I mean just me. Alice hasn't been too reliable lately and it's been putting me in a bind. She has this habit of not showing up for prep, and she even missed the last event. I appreciate her investment in my company, but I need her there physically as much as anything. She used to be good about that."

"Have you told her that you need her?"

"No. I know I should. It's not like I need the money anymore. It's just that her initial investment allowed me to do a lot of fun things like the Food Network competitions and getting my name out there. Now that I've got some notoriety in central Indiana, I suppose I should be more selective about the events I cater; take fewer events but more where I can charge higher fees. But you know, she's a friend as much as a partner. I can't just cut her out."

"A friend should be relied on to fulfill her obligations, and in your case, that means being there. For both prep work and events."

"Maybe you could tell her that?"

"Like your telling Joy about our situation?"

Mary Ruth gave Francine a rueful smile. "Very much like it."

Francine answered obliquely. "Let me check the schedule, but I think I can be there."

Mary Ruth rose from the chair, consciously tugging the jeans down again. She hesitated as though she wanted to say something else, then plunged ahead. "One other thing. Would you be available on Thursday night to be my wingman at a Kitchen and Table cooking class?"

Francine was completely confused. "A wingman? Why? And what cooking class? Are you teaching there?"

"I've got a blind date. Well, not totally blind. His name is Tyler and I know what his profile is on match.com. But that's not always a match, as last night demonstrated. I'd like to have you there so you can rescue me if he's not my type."

"And if he is?"

"Then you can go home, and I'll go out with him after class. Or maybe we'll just schedule another date. It doesn't matter. You're my safety net."

"And you're not teaching this class?"

She shook her head. "It's being taught by my Food Network nemesis, Garrett Stone." She said it like she was spitting out a horrible bite of food. "You remember him? He's the one who bombarded me with cream pies on a Cutthroat Kitchen episode and sabotaged my dish."

Francine remembered the episode. Though she completely agreed with Mary Ruth that it was embarrassing to her, it was also hilarious. The YouTube video of the pie episode alone had nearly a million views in the first few days after it aired. Francine had had to bite the insides of cheeks to keep from laughing out loud in front of Mary Ruth the first time she saw it.

"You're making scones, then?" she asked, knowing Garrett Stone was the self-proclaimed "King of Scones."

"It's more of a biscuit class. We're making scones but also Southern-inspired buttermilk drop biscuits and a sweet potato variation. And something else he's demonstrating for the class."

"But you know how to do those things, and very well."

"Yes, but Tyler doesn't, and it was his idea since he knew I was a chef. I'm in favor of using cooking classes as a trial date. If I'm going to get serious about a guy, we have to be able to cook together."

"Alice can't do it?"

"Three words: real estate deal."

Francine nodded. The hot economy in the greater Indianapolis area had attracted a lot of house hunters. She pulled out her phone and checked her schedule. There was nothing on it and Jonathan was away at his conference. "I can do it," she said reluctantly.

"Great!" Mary Ruth said, ignoring Francine's lack of enthusiasm, if she noticed it at all. She stood and walked toward the front door. "I'll register you. There are still a few openings in the class. Garrett is charging a fortune. So we're still having bridge club tonight?"

Francine, trailing behind her, just nodded. She'd almost forgotten about it.

Mary Ruth seemed to notice Francine's reluctance but misinterpreted it. "Don't worry. Tonight will be fun, and I promise I'll talk to Joy first thing in the morning about coming clean to the police. It won't be too late if I wait to do it tomorrow. What could possibly happen between now and then?"

Francine called Jonathan and left a message before making lunch, but when he didn't call back right away she assembled a plate of cheese, fruit, and a hunk of baguette and took it up to her home office. She sat at the computer wondering what she would find if she searched the internet for information on the Tattoo You Two business.

Maybe she should open an 'in cognito' window on her browser so it wouldn't be traceable. After all, the police didn't want her investigating. But then, if the police ever needed to search her computer, they'd be able to get past that 'in cognito' stuff anyway.

She decided she was just being paranoid. It wasn't like she was doing anything illegal or immoral. She just wanted to know more about a business owner who wouldn't spring for some inside surveillance equipment or keep up his building's outside cameras.

The first thing she noticed was that there were more stores in the chain than the two she had been aware of. The original Tattoo You salon was in a "transitional" neighborhood in Indianapolis, Two was in Brownsburg, and number three was called "Tattoo You Two Too." It was located south of Indianapolis in Greenwood. There was a note about number four coming soon and was to be located in McCordsville, which was on the east side of Indianapolis. No name was listed for the fourth.

The three up and running shops had similar setups as a one-stop shop of beauty services, though only the Indianapolis shop had multiple floors. There, manicures and pedicures were on the first floor, a hair salon existed on the upper floor, and tattoos and piercings were relegated to the basement. An annex next door provided the opportunity to get one's eyebrows threaded. The only photo was of an older building whose exterior looked like it had been fixed up. For the neighborhood, it looked prosperous. She assumed the inside looked even better.

The Brownsburg and Greenwood stores were located in fairly new strip malls so all services were located at ground level. Once again, only exterior shots were provided.

Francine focused on the original Tattoo You studio. She clicked on the tattoo section and three artists came up. She gulped when she saw that Lucas Monet was one of them. *He must've toggled between the two studios,* she thought. Clicking on him she was able to look through his portfolio. There were a lot of photos. She could tell he was definitely an artist of sorts, but that didn't mean she wanted one of his designs on her back, leg, neck or shoulder. Seeing a ultra-realistic tarantula gracing the shoulder of a client gave her pause. Shoulders. If she understood Joy correctly, Roy had gone to him because he could turn the shoulder tattoo of "Jody" into "Joy." A quick search through the portfolio turned up no "befores" and "afters" of altered tattoos, so she wondered how Roy had known this was a specialty of his.

She opened a second window on the browser and checked on the Brownsburg shop. She found Lucas was listed there, as was Eric's wife Cass. And there was a notice that they would like to add a third artist.

She returned to the original shop. Two other artists were listed, a man named Snake whose portfolio seemed similar to Lucas's, and a woman named Sang who specialized in permanent makeup and post-mastectomy breast nipples. Francine thought the latter was commendable. She'd known a lot of cancer patients in her time that had undergone mastectomies. Regaining that look on the breast had helped them feel feminine again.

Next she checked the manicure and pedicure specialists and followed that up with the hair stylists upstairs. Other than the owners seeming to rely heavily on immigrant labor, she didn't see anything that she wouldn't expect to see at another salon. The addition of tattoo services seemed a bit unusual, but not out of line.

Her cell phone rang and it was Jonathan.

"Hey, I'm sorry I wasn't able to talk earlier. I was taking an Uber to the airport."

Francine recognized the background noise of boarding instructions being announced on the intercom and passengers shuffling past him. "I thought you weren't coming back until Saturday."

"Something's come up at the office. We have an urgent project and Peter can't handle it with everything else going on."

"I'm not sorry you're coming home." She went on to tell him what had happened in less than twenty-four hours.

"Wow!" he said. "This is at Tattoo You Two?"

"You recognize it?"

"No," he said quickly. "I mean, I recognize it's the place you regularly go to get your nails done. Right?"

"I get pedicures there."

"Toe nails *are* nails."

"Yes, that's the place." She thought about telling him she and Charlotte would be getting pedicures today there at two, but he asked her a question before she came to a decision on whether that was a good idea. She didn't want him to worry.

"It was just you and Charlotte and Joy? Where were Mary Ruth and Alice?"

"Alice was busy with a real estate deal, and Mary Ruth had a date."

"Both of them are doing a lot of that lately."

"Tell me about it." She gave him the rundown on Mary Ruth's visit earlier, that she'd agreed to be wingman for her friend's cooking class on Thursday night and help with food prep on Friday morning.

"You know you can't be the solution to everyone's problems, don't you?"

Francine looked at the time and knew she needed to get her lunch eaten. She scooped up a spoonful of the cottage cheese. "True, but then I enjoy helping Mary Ruth because I love cooking." She put the spoon in her mouth.

"It's not just Mary Ruth. You're covering up for Joy's lie, giving Alice an out by helping Mary Ruth, and enabling Charlotte to continue with this crazy notion that she can be a hip motorcyclist when she's just going to hurt herself."

"I'm not enabling her. I'm just not saying anything."

"Okay, you're *allowing* her to do it by not speaking up."

"What if I'm responsible, Jonathan? It's been over a year now that

I've been using the water from the spring in the group's tea. At first, I didn't really think about it. It was just water and I wasn't sure it could keep us from aging anyway. But especially now that Formula #58 cured Eric, and given that it's gotten Eric and Dr. Eisenbarger's attention, it must be real. Right? The group is so full of energy we're splintering. They're all pursuing things they would have done earlier in their lives if they'd had the opportunity."

"So that's good and bad. They seemed to be fulfilled by what they're doing."

"It's the recklessness I worry about," Francine said. "They don't have a sense of moderation. Can you imagine Charlotte *not* investigating a murder? She seems to care more about this motorcycle thing. She hasn't done anything with the photos she took at the crime scene last night. She said she uploaded them to the cloud in case the police took our phones. Which reminds me that I need to text her about that." Francine pulled out a notepad and jotted down a reminder.

"Hang on a second." She heard Jonathan jostling around on the other end. "I'm trying to eat a sandwich before we have to board." He got quiet, so she presumed he'd taken a bite. Finally, he said, "So Charlotte's gone from the reckless pursuit of criminals to a new reckless pursuit. I'm not sure I see a difference."

"It's like her personality has changed. And when has Alice been so interested in real estate? She was always Larry's right hand woman, handling mostly office duties because she didn't want to sell. But now she's outselling him."

"He's mostly retired. He's probably glad she's doing the heavy lifting."

"To the exclusion of everything else. You've heard how she's treating Mary Ruth."

"Do we really know the water does what we think it does?" Jonathan asked, his voice guarded. "It'll be a long time before we have our own proof . All we have right now is Zedediah's claim about how old he was."

"What about De Leon's Desire, where the spring is, and the green growth that never dies, even in the winter?"

"It's located over a hot mineral spring."

Francine shook her head. "No, I'm certain Zedediah's concoction cured Eric."

She heard Jonathan take another bite of his sandwich. Eventually he said, "Keep in mind I'm playing devil's advocate here. Doc Wheat was famous for those concoctions. What's to say the formula had anything to do with the water from the spring?"

"It was in his notes."

"But you can't decipher everything that's in it, and we don't know the source of the second spring he claims to have taken water from."

"You might be right, but in my heart I feel like the water is the real thing."

He bit into something crunchy on the other end. Francine was betting it was a carrot. Jonathan generally ate healthy, even when they were on trips. "Whether the water does anything or not," he said, "it alarms me that you've gone from being the source of reason in the group to desperately wanting to be involved in solving this murder."

Now she was glad she hadn't told him about the pedicure at two o'clock. "That's not true."

"Really? Look who's complaining about Charlotte not sharing the photos. I don't see anyone else in the group concerned about the murder."

"Joy is!"

"Oh, sure. That's because the story got assigned to her and she's gotten herself in to a jam by lying."

Francine sat up tall on the stool. "I am not obsessed with the death of Lucas Monet!"

He paused. "By a curious bit of coincidence, I happen to know a few things about the Tattoo You businesses. Would you like to know what I know, if you agree not to ask me where I got the information?"

At first she was puzzled. Jonathan was good at client confidentiality, and she knew there were things about his clients or his work he never told her, but he'd never asked Francine before not to ask the source of his information. Then Francine laughed. "Is this a trick question? In either case I don't get to find out how you know what you tell me, if you tell me. And if I say 'yes,' you can claim I'm obsessed with the murder. If I say 'no,' then I won't find out what you purport to know."

"Up to you."

She imagined him in the airport, shrugging. Maybe even a bit smugly. "Yes, I want to know," she said.

His tone became guarded again. "For starters, the owner is the son of a convicted drug dealer."

"Hmmm." She looked down at the remaining baguette she hadn't eaten and tore off a piece. "Is that necessarily relevant?"

"It could be, if Tattoo You was ..." his voice got very soft " ... primarily created to launder money."

Francine gasped. "You don't *know* that, do you?" She chewed the piece of baguette. "Is Tattoo You a client of yours?"

"You know I would never take on a client like that."

Hmmmm, she thought silently to herself. *It has to be accounting related in some way.* "Are you speculating or know for sure?"

He didn't answer right away. *Of course,* Francine reminded herself, *he could be eating, not avoiding the question.*

"Mostly speculation," he eventually answered. "Try to conjure up reasons why the original business was located in a dicey part of Indianapolis, but their expansions were located in affluent suburbs. What if the goal is to build legitimacy?"

"But you can't tell me how you know that, about the convicted drug dealer?"

"I asked you not to ask me that."

"True. Would you know how they got their Brownsburg shop approved?"

"It's a tattoo parlor that's a hair and nail salon in addition to tattoos. That's general business. If zoning laws don't prohibit a type of business from settling in a general business district, they have every right to do so provided they meet any standards that are established."

Francine wondered if she shouldn't go ahead and tell him about her afternoon appointment. It wasn't like it was something she could or should hide. He might even get home from the airport before she got home from the appointment, depending on how fast the flight was. Boarding sounded like it might be imminent. "My experience is that it's a nice place, and Charlotte and I have pedicure appointments at two today. Before you ask, they're standing appointments, not something I scheduled after last night."

"Are you still going?"

She answered with a comment designed to make him smile. "Of course. Wild horses couldn't keep me away."

"Is it even open to customers today?"

"We'll find out at two. I don't want to know ahead of time. I want to show up in person to see it."

"Aha!" he said. "Gotcha! You *are* obsessed with this case."

"No. I said that on purpose."

"I knew that."

There was a pause between them.

"Should you be investigating this any further, Francine?"

"I only want to keep all of us out of trouble." She used her right hand to cross her heart, even though she knew he couldn't see the move. "Cross my heart and hope to die," she said flippantly.

"Francine, please don't use that expression, even in jest. You've come too close in the past."

She heard an announcement over the intercom on his end of the call.

"I have to go," he said. "They're boarding us. Promise me you'll be careful this afternoon. Don't do anything rash."

"I won't."

She just hoped she could hold to that promise.

It was just past one o'clock and their appointment wasn't until two, but Francine reasoned it wouldn't hurt to get to the salon early, especially since they were hoping to do some snooping. She drove the Prius over to Charlotte's. When she pulled into the driveway, though, she wondered if she had come too early. The blinds covering the window in Charlotte's home library were closed tight. The only time Charlotte didn't have them open was when she was asleep or wasn't home. Otherwise, she used the window to spy on her neighbors.

Francine parked the car, stood on the front step and rang the doorbell. No answer. *Guess I'm too early,* she thought. She rang it again. Same result.

Charlotte was the one who reminded me of the appointment just a few hours ago, so she couldn't have forgotten about it, could she? Francine pulled out her cell phone and called her.

"Can't talk right now, Francine," Charlotte said. "I'm at the Urgent Care Center."

"Are you okay?"

"Just being checked out as a precaution. I had an accident on the bike. Really, just a few bumps and bruises. Don't worry."

Like she wouldn't be able to worry. "Do you need me to come get you? Do you need a ride home?"

"No, I'm covered. They just called my name. Gotta go."

"I'm still coming over."

"Don't. You still have the pedicure at Tattoo You Two, don't you? Go there. Find out what you can. I'll fill you in later about the accident. Nothing to worry about. I'll see you at Bridge Club tonight."

Francine started to say more but Charlotte disconnected. She stared at the phone until the screen saver made it go blank. Then she placed it back in her pocket.

The motorcycle must still be ridable, she reasoned, *or Charlotte would need a way home. Who would Charlotte have called for help other than me? I'm her best friend.* She returned to the Prius and started it up. *She really must be okay. And she did say she wanted me to investigate Tattoo You Two. That sounds like the Charlotte I know.*

Francine parked her car in the lot and studied the building. The store front looked completely normal. The large plate glass window bearing "Tattoo You Two" in olde-English style lettering obscured whatever activity was going on inside, just like usual. No crime scene tape was strung across the door like it had been last night when they'd left. No police cars were in front with flashing red and blue lights. In fact, it looked like nothing had happened there. Francine was pretty sure that's what the management was hoping for.

There was, however, one difference. A large hand-lettered sign advertising "Now Hiring – Apply Inside" was taped above the section of the window where the store hours and a list of services were displayed. Francine couldn't recall having seen that before.

It made her wonder how long it would be before the management could replace Lucas Monet. Would Cass Dehoney be the logical choice? Would she want to continue to teach if she could successfully take over his business full time? Cass was Lucas's apprentice, but was apprenticeship a formal thing in the tattoo world? Maybe she would just take over the space.

Would anyone want a space where a murder had been committed?

She checked her watch. She had twenty minutes before her appointment. She exited the car and went into the salon.

Tattoo You Two was bustling. At least the front part was, where manicure and pedicure services were offered. The back cubicles had hair stylists, piercing specialists, and of course, the tattoo artists. She wasn't sure about them.

But she was going to find out.

She dodged several customers milling around the front desk hoping to check in. For whatever reason, there was no receptionist to greet them. That also meant there was no one to stop Francine from heading toward the back to see how the police had left the space formerly occupied by Lucas Monet. If she could get in at all. There might be crime scene tape at that door. She wouldn't cross that line.

She figured the crowds were there for the same reason she'd encountered crowds after other murders: once they learned about it, they couldn't resist wanting to see where it happened.

As she threaded her way across the crowded waiting area, she couldn't help but think of all the amateur detectives she admired in the cozy mystery novels she read. With her recent experiences, she even considered herself one. Would any of them waver in the face of this opportunity? Taking a deep breath, she breezed past the waiting clientele and the employees too busy to notice her. She took a sharp right turn at the pedicure station and marched down the hall, shoulders back, acting like she knew what she was doing and where she was going. On the right she passed the two hair stylists who shared a large space. They had clients in the chair and clients waiting. Across from them was an empty tattoo studio. The next one down would be Lucas's cubicle. No crime scene tape, Francine happily noted. The light was on. She ducked into the space without hesitation.

And found herself startling a man who had the office in disarray. He was shorter than her by a couple of inches, so she was guessing five-foot-seven, and in his mid-thirties and skinny. The short-sleeve black "Tattoo You" t-shirt he wore revealed thin arms heavily tattooed with sword-and-sorcery designs. From the look of the Aztec-type symbols peeking out of the top of the t-shirt, his chest was fully tattooed as well. She recognized him from the search she'd done earlier in the day on the Tattoo You Too website, but she couldn't remember his name.

He jerked his head up from an open sketchbook he appeared to be studying as she plowed through the doorway. "Not open yet," he said. The hoarseness in his voice fell somewhere between Kim Carnes singing "Betty Davis Eyes," and Satchmo singing "Hello, Dolly," but more guttural.

"I, uh," Francine stammered, "I didn't know someone would be in here." It sounded like a lame excuse, even to her ears.

He closed the sketchbook quickly, opened a drawer and shoved it in. "Better than finding a dead man in here, isn't it?"

Francine wasn't sure if that meant he knew she was one of the people who discovered the body or if he was simply referencing the murder. She presumed the latter. "I was looking for Cass Dehoney."

He tilted his head in the direction of the empty cubicle she'd passed. "Next studio back. She's not here, though. Not out of school yet, her other job. Not sure when she'll be in again."

Francine wondered how he could be moving in so quickly. She wasn't sure how to ask it though, so she asked a different question. "I guess you've had a lot of people back here wanting to see where he died?"

He gave her a smirk. "I'm hoping it might lead to me getting additional business." He looked her up and down and then squinted. "Probably not you, but here's my card anyway."

Francine took the card handed to her. "Snake," she said, reading his name aloud. She remembered him now. He was apparently a single-named artist, like Cher. *Was Snake a rock-star tattoo artist?* She gave him the same once-over he'd given her. *Perhaps locally.*

"That's me," he said. He put out a hand, and she shook it. His palm was cool to the touch, but the handshake was firm. She could tell by the click of something against his teeth when he said "that's," that his tongue was pierced.

"I'm surprised they found someone to take his place so fast," she said. "It seems …" she couldn't figure out how to say politely say it was pretty crass to not even wait twenty four hours before replacing him.

"I'm a friend of Lucas's." He paused. "Or was. I'm working on packing up his stuff for the next of kin. Or maybe for Cass." Francine wondered what he meant by that. Was Cass set to take over Lucas's business?

Snake continued once he saw her thinking. "Still can't believe what happened to him." He leaned against the back wall, his eyes downcast momentarily. "We'd worked together before. I was hoping to join him at this shop, just not in this way."

Francine glanced at the open cardboard boxes around the small space. He'd packed up some wall posters, now rolled and rubber-banded and sitting upright in a box with plaques and awards. Next to it was a box with several ink bottles in it. She decided to reveal her connection to Lucas. "I'm the one who found him last night," she said.

He straightened up and raised an eyebrow. "You were here to get a tattoo? I'm sorry, then. I misjudged you."

She fidgeted. "Well, I was here with a friend who was getting a tattoo. Moral support, you know."

"I had heard there were a couple of women who found him." He paused, as though considering what to say next. "If you don't mind my asking, what kind of tattoo was it your friend was getting?"

"That's a curious question," she said.

"I'm a curious person."

"My friend wanted the name of her fiancé tattooed on her shoulder." Francine didn't go into more detail lest she accidentally give up Joy's name.

"Then it was a pretty standard tattoo, I guess." Snake rubbed the back of his neck.

Francine leaned forward. "Did you ask that because you think it had something to do with the murder?"

He shook his head, but then chose his words carefully. *Maybe too carefully?* "I just wondered, you know, what brought you here at that time of night. Wondered what the last tattoo of his career would have been."

Francine shrugged. "I can't really say much more. I never saw the design. As far as I knew, it was just his name."

Snake pushed himself off the wall with his hand. He resumed putting Lucas's ink bottles away. She glanced at her watch. If he was hinting she should leave, Francine wasn't ready to do that yet. *He'll have to ask me to go*, she thought. *I still have ten minutes before my pedicure.*

"I would have thought the police would take the ink bottles," she said.

"Why?"

Now she was in a quandary. How much should she reveal? *I may have to give up some information to get some from him.* "It looked to my friend and me like he might have been poisoned. Like there might have been something in the ink."

"Really? Why would you think that?"

"There was some vomiting, which might indicate his body was trying to get rid of a substance that was hurting it."

Snake seemed to consider that. He reviewed the bottles in the box, then stood next to the white cabinet where Charlotte had studied them the night before and did the same. "That could explain the absence of some blacks and blues I would have expected to see."

"Did he have any next-of-kin?"

"A sister, Gabriella. I don't know that they got along or even saw each other anymore. He rarely mentioned her, so I didn't ask about their relationship."

Though Francine didn't have any brothers or sisters, she knew that her boys were close even though they lived in different states now. She wondered how other siblings came to be so distanced, what conflicts separated them. Perhaps Gabriella had been in competition with Lucas. "Was she also in the ink game?"

He snorted. "Not hardly. If I remember correctly, she's a CPA. She probably won't want his stuff. But you never know."

A CPA, Francine thought. She wondered if Jonathan might know her. "Was she from around here, too?"

He again stopped his sorting and turned his full attention to her. "Last I heard she lived up north, Fort Wayne."

"Not that far away, then," Francine said. "A couple of hours."

"If she still lives there," he reminded her. He crossed his arms over his chest. "You ask a lot of questions."

She bit the inside of her lip. She knew it had been risky to want to see the crime scene again, but not because she'd expected to find a tattoo artist here, especially one who actually knew Lucas Monet. She'd thought it'd be from a manager trying to keep people out. But the end result might be the same: the Brownsburg police might learn that she'd been doing some investigating of her own. Jud, if such a complaint got to his ears, would not be pleased. Especially given his new boss, Chief Turner.

"Sorry," she said, faking a smile. "I think it's just that I can't get it out of my mind since I was one of the people to find the body. I keep wondering why a tattoo artist would be murdered. Did he give someone a bad tattoo and they came seeking revenge?"

"Doubt it," Snake said. He leaned his back against the wall. His left leg came up and bent at the knee, his left foot on the wall, stabilizing his leaning position. "Lucas was really good at fixing tattoos people didn't want anymore. He didn't advertise it, but he was good at it. If he'd botched a tattoo, and that's an unlikely scenario, I think he could have handled it."

Francine remembered it was Roy's tattoo change from "Jody" to "Joy" that caused Joy to want to come to him for her tattoo. "I guess I knew that," she said. "Is that a skill few tattoo artists have?"

"I think most could do it if they wanted to, but original tattoos are easier. You have my card. If you know someone who needs that done, I can handle it. Or is it something you yourself need done? You said you were looking for Cass. Though I don't know if she's up for that yet."

The very thought of being tattooed right then made Francine want to bolt. "No, not me. Never had a tattoo, and honestly, Snake, I don't want one. I'm sure you do beautiful work, but it's just not something I've ever wanted."

He licked his lips, and the mere flick of his pierced tongue before he closed his mouth reminded Francine of a reptile. "If you stay much longer, I may talk you into it," he said. "Don't you want to do something just a little dangerous in your life, just a little out of the mold of your white bread lifestyle?"

Francine didn't say it, but she'd done things way more dangerous than having a tattoo. Danger had nothing to do with it. And if he thought her lifestyle was white bread, well, that was more stereotype than reality.

She shook her head vigorously. "No, I'm good just as I am." She took a step back. Glancing around one last time to make sure she had gotten everything out of this visit that she could, she backed into the hallway. "But if I change my mind, I'll be sure to be in touch. And thanks for answering my questions."

Snake had his hand on the drawer where he'd shoved the sketchbook. "No problemo. I'm expecting to take over this space, so maybe I'll see you around." He seemed to be waiting for her to leave. She obliged him.

Or so she let him think. She moved outside the cubicle's doorway to the point where he couldn't see her, but she could watch his hand. He pulled the sketchbook out of the drawer again and resumed studying it. She wondered what was in it, and why he seemed so secretive about it.

Francine glanced at her watch. She had five minutes to check in for her appointment, though given the crowd she wondered if they'd get started on time. She put on the same confident air she'd assumed coming in and started toward the front desk, again hoping not to be questioned. She had just turned the corner when a customer stopped her. "Are you the manager?" she asked.

Francine stopped abruptly. The woman was forty-ish, frowning, and radiating a "take-no-prisoners" attitude. Francine could only guess that she was an unhappy customer. "Uh, no," she stammered.

The woman pointed an index finger toward the back where Francine had been. "I thought that maybe you were, since you seem to know what you were doing back there. Isn't the manager's desk back there?" Francine noted that the nail on the index finger the woman was using to point had chipped red polish. A nervous nail technician hovered behind her.

Francine's head was spinning. All she wanted to do was check in for her pedicure. "Any manager I've ever seen here is up front, not back there," she said, "I was um, talking to a new tattoo artist. I'm actually scheduled for a pedicure at two."

The woman narrowed her eyes. "Are you sure? I heard they were looking for a new manager. You look like one."

Francine shook her head. "No, I swear I'm not. I don't know anything about the shop looking for a new manager. A new tattoo artist, maybe." She knew she was babbling, but she was trying to figure a way out of this.

The foreign-looking nail technician, who seemed confused by the conversation, tried to help. "She right," she said in broken English pointing to her unhappy customer, "we look for receptionist, and manager, too, maybe. I not sure what difference is. Artists, we have."

The woman ignored the nail technician and continued to examine Francine. "Well, this technician is not very good. Look at the polish on these nails." She thrust a hand in front of Francine's face. "Does this look like a job I should pay for?"

Francine noticed that people were beginning to stare. If this didn't resolve itself soon, someone was bound to recognize her. She didn't need that, especially given Channel 8's report that she and Charlotte had been spotted coming out of the place last night. This was a full shop. All it would take would be for one person to record this on their phone and she'd be answering a lot of questions she didn't want to. Probably some of them aimed at her by that nasty Chief Turner. She couldn't let that happen. It was fight or flight.

Or maybe resolve the conflict. She was good at that. She was the sensible one. Everyone said so. "I'm sure your nail technician wants to make this right. No one wants a dissatisfied customer. These ladies depend on tips for their living."

Francine looked imploringly at the technician, whose hands had now succumbed to jittery movements. "How did you apply the polish? Do you know why it chipped?"

Her head bobbed 'yes' but her blank expression told a different story.

Another technician moved in. She seemed to have better command of the English language. "I know what she did wrong. I can show her how to fix it."

The original technician, still gulping air, nodded her head vigorously. "Yes, I do it right for you. Please."

Francine turned back to the upset woman. "Clearly this is a mistake made by someone who just needs a little guidance to get it right. Would you be willing to give her the grace of another chance if she's supervised by a nail technician with more experience?"

The woman's eyebrows unknitted. She glanced at the number of people in the shop who were now staring at her. "Well, I suppose it would be unkind not to give her another chance." She exhaled a little fussily, but Francine knew she had won the day.

The woman who had been unhappy was led back to the manicure area by the two technicians. The experienced one jabbered to the other in their foreign language, presumably explaining what went wrong and how to fix it. The other patrons in the shop went back to reading and gossiping.

Except one. A woman maybe ten years younger than Francine who stood out because she was dressed nicely for someone getting their nails done or getting a tattoo. That woman was looking at her with interest.

Uh-oh, Francine thought. *I've been recognized.*

With the rest of the shop returning to normal, the woman approached her. She put out her hand. "I'm Aretha," she said.

Puzzled, Francine shook it. "Francine."

"May I have a word with you?"

This was exactly what she was trying to avoid. "I have an appointment at 2:00," Francine said apologetically.

The woman leaned in. She said quietly, "I'll check you in. I'm a manager. I only just arrived from the downtown Tattoo You salon in time to see you handle the customer. Thanks for doing that. The technicians aren't particularly good at it."

Francine was relieved not to have been recognized. She smiled. "I'm glad I could help."

Aretha ushered her toward the front desk. "The pedicure will be on us. Our thanks."

The two walked toward the desk, but Aretha didn't stop there. She went past it and through the door into the office area, beckoning Francine to do the same. Unsure of herself, but with the promise of a comped pedicure, Francine followed.

The office was small and minimalist. The uncluttered desk, the large four-drawer file cabinet, and the chairs all looked to be from IKEA. The walls were a stark white. A single framed painting of somewhere in the Orient was on the wall behind the desk. If it weren't for the painting, there would have been no personality to the place at all. It even smelled sterile.

Aretha indicated for Francine to sit, which she did. Aretha pulled the chair from behind the desk and moved it closer to Francine so they would be on the same side. "I don't suppose you're looking for a part time job, are you?" she asked.

So that's what this was about. Francine grimaced. "I'm not, really."

"The manager here quit this morning after she learned about the unfortunate event last night. Our owner is hoping to find someone quickly to replace her. I was sent here from the downtown store."

Francine tried to look flattered. "I was glad to help out, but I really am not looking for a job."

"Are you retired? Let me assure you, it's only a part-time position. The owners are responsible for opening and closing the stores. It's just afternoons they need someone. We're shorthanded."

"Surely there are enough managers at the other stores to staff this one until they can advertise the position."

Aretha shook her head. "The owners pay well, but they hire very few people outside the family. They're particular about their managers. I've been with them about a year now and have helped them hire for the other stores. I'm confident they would feel good about you. What did you do before you retired?"

Francine wanted this to end but she couldn't bring herself to be rude. *One of these days I'll regret being so well-mannered,* she thought. "I was a nurse."

Aretha handed her a business card. "I was fairly sure you had a professional background. Please think about it."

Francine took the card.

Aretha's smile was wide and revealed straight, white teeth that flashed like pearls against her dark skin. "Now let's see about that pedicure," she said, standing up.

Though she did not like the idea of a having a job again, Francine had a sudden insight: she could get no better information on what was going on at the Tattoo You Two parlor than if she was on the inside. Her hand shook for a moment. Trying not to think too hard about it, she followed Aretha back into the salon. After brief instructions to the nail technicians, Aretha left her in their hands.

At first they seemed to be a little awestruck by Francine and gave her a lot of attention. Mostly they talked to each other in their native language, but they did go out of their way to communicate with her and make sure she was happy with their service. Despite the fact that it was a comped procedure, Francine tried to pay for it, and when they wouldn't accept it, she tipped them the amount she would normally have given for the pedicure. Wide-eyed, they bowed and thanked her profusely. The money disappeared into their clothing.

Next time I come I'm going to bring them some cookies, Francine thought. *I bet they'd enjoy that.*

And just like that, she found herself wondering what it would be like to be a manager at the Tattoo You Two salon in Brownsburg.

Francine was glad to have Jonathan home. They fixed dinner together, and he asked a few questions about her pedicure and if she learned anything. She downplayed the meeting with Snake and didn't mention the job offer from Aretha. She told him about Charlotte's accident and that she was anxious to see her that evening at bridge club. Jonathan seemed distracted, like his mind was elsewhere. She wondered if it had to do with the urgent matter that had caused him to leave his conference early, not even half-way through the week. She knew he enjoyed going every year. She asked about it, but he was vague with his answers. She didn't press him. In time, she figured, he'd tell her about it.

That evening the Summer Ridge Bridge Club met at Alice's home. Alice had a formal dining room where they played cards. It was so formal Francine fought the compulsion to dress up just to play cards in there. The walls were papered in a paisley print with a white-stain wainscotted wall tucked below a chair-rail cap. The elaborately carved dining table was made of cherry wood in an old-fashioned Evangeline style. Leaves had been removed to collapse it to something akin to a square. Francine imagined it went unused unless there were guests.

Larry was just leaving and opened the front door for her. "Headed out?" she asked.

He nodded. "Abandoning the hen house. Just too much estrogen in here."

"Well, there's a man who doesn't understand the physiology of menopause," she murmured.

Larry got into his BMW and drove off. He was no sooner out of sight when Charlotte pulled in. She got out of the Buick gingerly—perhaps too gingerly—and stepped back carefully before shutting the door. When she turned, Francine noticed the bandage wrapped around her right knee and the bruises up and down her calves. She limped toward the house.

"Charlotte, are you all right?" Francine hurried toward her friend, offering her arm for support. "What have you done to yourself? You told me on the phone you were fine."

"I didn't want you to worry. I'm still fine. It's just that I was better before a box truck clipped my motorcycle when I was just west of Pittsboro on my morning ride."

"Let's get you inside. Alice! Can you come help me?"

By the time Francine and Alice had Charlotte settled in the dining room, Joy and Mary Ruth had arrived and they all got to hear Charlotte's story at once.

Charlotte sat on the edge of the chair's embroidered seat so her feet could touch the floor. "I was celebrating getting my license and decided to ride out to the Rusted Silo restaurant and celebrate with a barbeque lunch and maybe a beer," she said. "The box truck must've followed me out of Pittsboro but it didn't make a move to pass me until we were well out into the country. We were maybe halfway to Lizton."

Francine sat on a chair to Charlotte's right and leaned over, examining the knee. "Did he really clip you?"

"He would have, if I hadn't swerved. He was so close you would have thought his truck was trying to mate with my motorcycle. I ended up in the ditch."

"May I look at it?" Charlotte nodded and Francine gently removed the bandage. "Did he stop to help?"

"Nope, just barreled on down the road. I was lucky a group of motorcyclists came by about five minutes later. I could never have pulled my 'cycle out of the ditch by myself."

Mary Ruth was incredulous. "But you still rode it to the urgent care center?!?"

"Well, no. Actually I called a tow truck to come get it."

Mary Ruth wagged her finger. "You should have called one of us for help."

"I had help. The motorcyclists. I rode with one of them to the urgent care center."

Francine was appalled. "You rode on a motorcycle after that accident?"

"I was fine. And before you ask, the urgent care nurse didn't say I can't ride any more. She cleaned out the wound and the scrapes and put ointment on them. She said they'd heal in a week or ten days. But it did something to my knee."

Francine re-covered the wound. It looked more superficial than serious. The nurse had done a good job bandaging it. The bigger issue seemed to be the black and blue bruises up and down Charlotte's calves and, of course, whatever jarring the accident had done to the knee. "What did she say it did? Did they x-ray the knee?"

Charlotte nodded. "She said there wasn't any damage done that showed on x-ray, but that if it continued hurting I should see my orthopedist. They sent me the report if you want to read it."

"Only if you don't mind. Or unless you don't improve. Until then we can assume the urgent care center got it right. Do the bruises hurt?"

"Like someone took a hammer to them. It was a good thing Hank was there to hold my hand in the waiting room." She let this drop like she expected them to react.

Mary Ruth took the bait first. "Who's Hank? I've never heard you mention him before."

"He was one of the bikers who stopped to help. A distinguished gentleman. Bright blue eyes, a salt and pepper beard. Bald as a cue ball. Kind of handsome if you ask me."

Joy gave her a dubious look. "What kind of motorcycle gang is this?"

Charlotte shrugged. "Not a gang. It's a club. The guys might have had a bit of rough look to them. But they weren't mean or unfriendly. And they weren't young. Well, younger than us, maybe a decade or two. They didn't have jackets that said "Hell's Angels" if that's what you mean."

"I'm not sure I meant anything."

"Sure you did. You squinted at me like you do whenever you're getting ready to do a tv interview. Especially when you think that someone is guilty of something. The only thing Hank is guilty of is caring enough to stop and help a fellow motorcyclist."

Joy drummed her left fingers on her right elbow, thinking. "I know there are some motorcycle clubs that raise money for charities. One that's been in the news lately is made up of veterans who raise money for veterans that have PTSD and other problems."

Charlotte nodded enthusiastically. "I'm sure Hank is a member of that kind of gang."

Joy narrowed her eyes at Charlotte. Charlotte interrupted before she had a chance to speak. "See, there you go again, giving me that look."

"I was just going to ask if you're sure he and the others didn't have some kind of logo on the back of their jackets. I'm guessing they were wearing leather jackets?"

"Hank's was sleeveless, but yes, he was wearing a leather jacket. I didn't pay that much attention to what, if anything, was on the back. I was mostly interested in getting out of the ditch and to an emergency room."

Francine brushed imaginary dirt off Charlotte's shoulders, like she'd been the one to have found Charlotte in the ditch. "I'm glad you're all right. Did any of the club members see the box truck or get a license plate number?"

"They showed up about five minutes after I flew into the ditch. A couple of them took off down the road to see if they could find it, but they came back shaking their heads."

The women all nodded in sympathy.

Francine was a little surprised but also relieved that Charlotte didn't ask about how things had gone at the tattoo parlor that afternoon. Surprised, because she would have expected Charlotte to ask, but relieved because she didn't want to reveal too much to the group. Maybe Charlotte instinctively knew that and would ask later. Or maybe with the accident, she'd forgotten all about it. She certainly seemed pleased that the group was fussing over her.

"Before we start bridge," Joy announced, "I'd like to declare a moratorium on talking about tattoos, tattoo parlors, and all things murder related."

The women all groaned, but no one verbally objected. Since there were five of them, they drew cards to see who would sit out first. Francine drew a two of clubs right from the start, the lowest of the lows, so she sat watching the others play first. Alice picked up the deck and began shuffling.

"Hank's taking me motorcycle shopping tomorrow," Charlotte announced. It felt abrupt, even for Charlotte.

"What on earth for?" Francine and Mary Ruth said, almost together. Their words tromped all over each other.

"The bike is damaged, and it's in the shop getting an estimate. I'm lucky I remembered to add it to my insurance policy this morning right after I bought it. Hank says in his opinion it's not worth getting repaired. He says he needs to help me choose a more appropriate bike."

"You're in no condition to test-drive a motorcycle!" Francine said.

"I know that," Charlotte said, the exasperation in her voice as transparent as her desire to be the center of attention. "I'm just looking. He thinks maybe I need a bike I can control better, one I could have steered through the shallow ditch. He says with the right bike I wouldn't have been upended driving into it."

Francine scoffed. "I'd have to see the scene of the accident. I'm not sure any bike would have enabled you to do that. We have to remember that we're getting a little older now, and we have our limitations. Bikes are for people who are younger and taller."

Charlotte gave her an offended look. "That sounded kind of discriminatory coming from you. Easy for you to say. You're tall for a woman."

"I'm just being practical here. I'm not sure I'd be able to control a motorcycle. I've never ridden one."

"But I have. And so has Hank. If he thinks so, shouldn't I give him the benefit of the doubt?"

"Just promise me you won't do anything rash like be in a rush to buy something. Wait until you can test drive it and feel comfortable on it."

Charlotte made a production out of her promise not to rush into anything.

Alice finished shuffling and dealt. Joy, sitting to Alice's left, bid first. "One heart," she said. "And speaking of hearts, just how much do you know about this Hank guy?"

Charlotte had a coy smile plastered on her face. "What sorts of things are you looking for? I'm not a lady who tells all."

"Ha ha," Joy said. "You know what I mean. Is he married, divorced, separated, widowed? Is he looking for love?"

"He didn't have a ring on. The subject of his marital status didn't come up. I thought it was inappropriate to question his intention when he was being so nice." She said it a little defensively.

Mary Ruth, sitting next to Joy, bid two clubs. "So, let me ask you a tangential question, Charlotte. Are you looking for love? I mean, you've never indicated before that you were. I could set you up with some people I've come across on ourtime.com."

Francine was sitting on the other side of Joy. Joy leaned over and whispered into her ear. "Just what we need—another person on ourtime.com."

"I see you whispering over there," Mary Ruth said. "How else are we older singles supposed to meet someone? Just because you met Roy while you were at work doesn't mean it's easy for the rest of us to do that. And Charlotte doesn't work."

Charlotte, who was Joy's partner, bid two hearts. "Maybe the right person just hasn't come along. I confess I've been feeling a little randy lately, you know?"

Francine looked horrified. "Are you sure it's not some kind of latent hot flash?"

Mary Ruth uncharacteristically stood up for Charlotte. "That's unfair, Francine. You're married. You want to tell us about your love life with Jonathan?"

Charlotte's confession about being randy made Francine pause. She'd felt that way, too. Was it another effect of the spring water? But then, she and Jonathan had always made intimacy an important part of their marriage, and neither of them had been shy in initiating it. She knew they weren't as active as they'd been in their twenties, but that was a long time ago. If she compared their love life now to what it was in their sixties, it was certainly just as good or better. But maybe it was Jonathan, not her. She was trying hard not to attribute their active love life to the water from the spring. *Arg! This not knowing is driving me crazy!*

Charlotte became wistful. "I've been thinking maybe it's time for another man in my life. And then Hank shows up. Kismet?"

"Yes," Francine blurted out. "I mean, no. I mean, it's probably just a coincidence."

Charlotte didn't seem at all offended by Francine's outburst. "I would like to think it's not." She held the same expression of unexpected bliss on her face. "So let me have that gift for just a little while, okay?"

The others looked at Francine. "Of course," she said with a sigh. "Just be careful, okay? You know I care about you."

"This isn't officially a date, just so you know. He's just being kind."

Mary Ruth brightened. "Kind of like my date at Sur la Table tomorrow night. Nothing wrong with a tryout."

"I thought yours was an official date," Francine said. "That's the way you presented it to me. I'm your wingman in case it goes badly."

"If it wasn't a tryout, then I'd already know he's okay and I wouldn't have invited you along."

Francine grabbed on to that idea. "Okay, then maybe Charlotte needs a wingman. Joy, how about you? You seem really interested in this motorcycle non-date." Francine didn't want to become the official wingman for all the single women here. And she wasn't going to suggest Alice. Alice's tastes ran to expensive, large, well-equipped vehicles. Motorcycles wouldn't be up her alley.

"I could make myself available," Joy answered. "That is, if Charlotte's okay with it."

The blanched look on Charlotte's face gave away her reaction.

"We're just concerned about you," Francine assured Charlotte.

Charlotte took a few moments to consider it. "Well, I guess it couldn't hurt."

"Glad to hear it. I know I'd hate to see your heart broken."

Charlotte sighed. "In some ways, at least then I'd be sure it's still alive."

Francine wasn't sure if Charlotte was referring to her heart or her libido, but she and everyone else let is pass.

And so it went in the bridge game, too. Everyone passed, leaving Charlotte to make the two hearts bid.

"You bid a heart on *that*?" Charlotte exclaimed when Joy put her hand on the table. She rolled her eyes. "Well, let's see what I can do with it."

Of course, Charlotte had been exaggerating. She had no trouble making the two hearts bid.

9

Francine woke with a start at 8:15 the next morning. Jonathan leaned over her. He was dressed and holding car keys in his hand.

"Good. You're awake," he said. "I was just getting ready to nudge you. I have to get to work. The new project will absorb a lot of time, I suspect. And I may not have a lot of time before it needs to be finished.

"Are you okay?"

Francine felt fuzzy-headed. She'd been having a dream, or maybe it was a nightmare, that Snake was tattooing her. She didn't like the design he'd chosen from the sketchbook he had open, and she didn't like the pain. She recognized the sketchbook as the one he'd shoved in the drawer yesterday.

She kept protesting that he should stop. He assured her not to worry, that the tattoo was free since she was an employee.

She shook the nonsense of the dream from her head. "Just groggy from a dream. I'll be fine." Still, she wondered about the sketchbook.

He gave her a kiss. "I won't be home for lunch. Don't know what you had planned for dinner, given that I was supposed to still be in Washington. But if you weren't planning on something that can be easily stretched for two, we can go out."

Francine couldn't remember what her plans were for the morning, let alone for dinner. "I'll let you know."

"Okay." He kissed her again and left.

She laid her head back on the pillow and dozed involuntarily until she heard a buzzing sound. It seemed to get louder and more annoying. She looked to the clock at her bedside, swatting at it with her hand trying to turn off the alarm clock until she realized it wasn't the alarm. She sat up. "Where's the phone?"

Getting out of bed, she put on her glasses and traced the sound to the dresser. The number lighting up her phone was Eric Dehoney's.

"Hello?"

"Francine, this is Eric," he said. "Cass and I would like to meet with you this morning. Would that be okay?"

Again Francine tried to remember what she had going this morning. "I just got up. Let me check my schedule." She grabbed a robe and headed downstairs to the kitchen where she and Jonathan kept their schedule.

"Sorry to have wakened you. I thought you'd be up. It's just, we … have a problem."

Francine guessed it had to do with the death of Lucas Monet, but she decided not to ask. Better to let them bring it up, she thought. And she wanted to have breakfast before she tackled any meeting with him.

The calendar confirmed she had no appointments that morning.

"I can meet," she said. "Do you want to come here?"

"Or you could come here," he said. "Just somewhere not out in public."

Eric had moved into Cass's house when they got married. It was on the far north side of Brownsburg out in the country in a secluded area. Though Francine liked the controlled environment of having them come to her, privacy would be easier if she went there. "I could be at your house around ten."

"That's great. We'll see you then."

Cass was waiting by the door and opened it when Francine arrived. She wore hip-hugger jeans, a beige short-sleeve top embroidered with blue cornflowers, and a jade necklace. She gave Francine a brief hug. In her slight Southern drawl, she said, "Please come in. Make yourself at home. Eric and I really appreciate you comin' by."

Eric stood behind her looking business-casual in slim-fitting jeans and a button down plaid shirt, like he'd just come from seeing a client. The smell of bacon was in the air.

"Have ya'll had breakfast?" Cass asked.

"I have. Thanks anyway." Francine was ushered in and directed to an upholstered love seat opposite a big screen television above a fireplace in the living room. An ESPN talk show was on, but Eric picked up a remote and turned it off. Sensing the tension in the room, Francine perched herself gingerly on the edge of the loveseat. Cass sat down on the fireplace hearth and stared at her with a worried look on her face.

"What seems to be the matter?" Francine asked.

Cass looked to Eric as though she didn't know how to start. Eric sat next to her and put his arm around her. "We need your help. We know you found Lucas Monet dead in the Tattoo You Two parlor Monday night. Cass is one of the police's chief suspects."

"She is? How do you know that?"

Cass seemed eager to continue once Eric stated the reason she'd been invited. "I've already been questioned as to my whereabouts. They made it pretty clear I'm high on their list."

"What do they have on you?"

She sighed and looked down at floor. Her voice was filled with pain. "I was his apprentice. I was the last one to see him alive, at least that they know of. When I left the buildin' at 9 p.m., he was expecting a client. I just wanted to get home to Eric."

Francine's stomach was starting to growl. The bacon aroma was getting to her. She was beginning to think she should have had more than a carton of yogurt and a piece of toast. "Do you know who the client was? It would seem to me whoever it was would be a more reasonable suspect."

She shook her head. "Lucas could be secretive sometimes. When I was at work and didn't have a client of my own, I was either watching him tattoo or performing under his supervision. Those clients I knew. But there were others he didn't name, not a lot, but a few. They were mostly booked late at night. I had the impression he didn't want me or anyone else to know about them. He always had an excuse for me to leave before they came."

"Did you ever ask him why?"

"I didn't think I should. He was being nice mentoring me. And he implied that he was going to start referring clients to me."

Francine still hadn't heard a good reason for the police to suspect her. She took a moment to readjust her seating, easing herself into the throw pillows up against the back. It seemed like she was going to be here awhile. "Was he so busy that he needed to offload clients?" Francine couldn't picture that, but she wouldn't get a tattoo no matter what.

"He was busy, no doubt of that. But what a lot of people not into tats didn't know was that he was an extraordinary artist. His side business was creating temporary tattoos, and his designs were becoming hot. He was starting to make substantially more money from his internet business. Orders were coming in from all around the country."

"Okay," Francine said. "But if he was going to refer clients to you when you got up to speed, and his business was becoming so profitable that it was likely he would start doing that soon, why would you want to kill him? It would be like killing the goose that laid the golden egg."

Cass looked to Eric, and Eric nodded. "You know that I'm an artist, too?" she said. "Lucas liked that about me, that I was formally trained in art, that I had a degree. He said I knew true beauty, and that was important in producing body art."

Francine continued to nod encouragingly. This had to be going somewhere. "And?"

She drew a breath before answering. "And it turned out he left the business to me. The temporary tattoo business. He had mentioned it one time, but I thought it was more an off-the-cuff comment. Like it had just crossed his mind. Like he might consider it, but not really. I mean, who thinks about death when you're in your thirties, right? Who makes a will? Maybe if you have kids.

Anyway, because of it being a homicide, the police obtained a warrant and searched his apartment. They found a copy of his will, which he'd recently written. He may have left some stuff to his sister, but to me, he left the one thing he was becoming known for. A big profitable thing."

"Can you prove you didn't know about it?"

She threw up her hands. "How do I do that? He only mentioned it once. It's just going to come down to my word versus anyone else's that he never really talked to me about it."

"Has anyone else mentioned it?"

"Not that I know of. The way the police are lookin' at me, though, I'm kind of thinking his sister Gabriella might."

Francine remembered that Snake told her Lucas seemed to be estranged from his sister. "Do you know anything about his sister? I've heard she's a CPA. It would seem to me she wouldn't know what to do with a business like that. Why would she even want it?"

Cass was not taking the questioning well. "I don't know. I don't know the answers to all these questions. I just need help." She put her head in her hands.

Eric rubbed Cass's back affectionately. He kept his voice even when he spoke. "It's okay, Cass. Just answer what you can."

Francine sat in silence waiting for Cass to say something. When it was apparent nothing was going to come, at least not soon, she asked gently, "What do you want me to do to help?"

Cass finally lifted her head. "Find the killer, of course. That's the only thing that's gonna clear me. Prove that I didn't do it by finding the person who did."

If Charlotte were here, she'd tell me, "Well, isn't that a pip of a dilemma? The one thing the police don't want you to do." It almost made Francine chuckle to think it.

But this wasn't a matter to chuckle about. "The police have made it clear to me they want me to stay out of it."

"Look," Eric said, "if it's a matter of money ..."

She didn't chuckle but she did smile. "Eric, Cass, I'm not a private detective. You can't hire me. I don't have the experience ..."

"Yes, you do," Cass insisted. "You've solved several cases. You're a regular Jessica Fletcher."

Francine forced a smile. She liked the comparison. Found it flattering in fact. But she had to be realistic. "That was television, not real life. Look, I'll help as I can. I promise to keep my eyes open for anything out of the ordinary, and you do the same. You're still working at the tattoo parlor, aren't you?" Cass nodded. "Make sure you let me know about anything suspicious. And if the police question you some more, let me know what they're asking you. That way I have some sense as to where their investigation is going. But that's really all I can do."

Eric hugged Cass as if to reassure her. "Then please do it," he said, looking at Francine. "We appreciate whatever help you can give us, don't we, Cass?"

She nodded silently, but her eyes blazed. Francine did not think she agreed with what Eric said. Cass looked like she expected more. And maybe it was understandable. Of course, she wanted someone to clear her.

Francine stood. "I'll do what I can."

Eric stood, but Cass remained seated. "I'll walk you to the door," he told Francine. Which he did, but he also followed her outside. When they were out of earshot, he said, "You've helped me before. You solved Aunt Camille's death. It revealed some not-very-nice things about her, but still, you figured out who killed her. And you saved my life. I trust you."

Francine felt a bit of a chill. Saving Eric had come at a cost, as she was learning. "Anything more about the way your body is mysteriously repairing itself?"

"Dr. Eisenbarger has cautioned me not to talk about it to anyone, but since you already know ... he's running blood tests on me. He wants to see if the ability is transferable, if it can be learned by another person's body through blood transfusion."

Her eyes widened. Francine knew there were instances in which antibodies from one person's blood could be used to cure an illness in another person's body. Some of that had come into play in Africa during the Ebola pandemic. But she'd never heard of a person's body taking a cue from what was found in another person's blood. In all the instances she'd read about, the receiving body never figured out to produce the antibodies itself. It could only rely on what antibodies were being shared.

It scared her a little to think of the ramifications. But what had Eric's body "learned" from the formula she'd given him? She still didn't know what it was that was causing his body to repair itself so rapidly. So it might be that the healing properties were transferable.

More worrisome to her was what Eisenbarger might do with it if it was.

10

Francine hurried to her car. Once inside, she took some deep breaths. This was becoming a nightmare. She couldn't turn down Cass and Eric's request to help. For one thing, Cass was a solid connection to whatever was going on at Tattoo You Two. Francine was still worried her lies to protect Joy could come to light, so the sooner someone figured out who murdered Lucas Monet, the better. Whatever she could do to keep that moving along, she would do, whether or not she was overtly trying to solve the mystery. Plus, she absolutely wanted an excuse to keep in contact with Eric about the developing investigation by Dr. Eisenbarger. She needed to stay on top of it. She didn't like where that was going either.

Yes, a nightmare. Just like she'd had last night about Snake tattooing her with that hideous design. She started the car.

Something tugged at the memory of her nightmare.

Lucas was in the process of being tattooed when he died, she thought. Yet she couldn't recall any specifics about the tattoo in progress. Was it possible whoever had killed him was trying to make a statement? Could what he was tattooing on Lucas's arm be that statement? And what about the sketchbook Snake had tried to hide from her? Snake, at least for the time being, was a "person of interest" to her, if not to the police.

Charlotte had taken photos of the crime scene, photos that hadn't been sent around yet. She stopped at the end of the driveway and placed a call to Charlotte so she could talk to her while driving.

"Hello, Francine," Charlotte said when she answered the phone. "I love Caller ID. Have I mentioned that before? I know it's old technology since it's been around so long, but it's still a kick to answer the phone knowing who's on the other end."

"Charlotte, I need to talk to you about the night of the murder."

"Which one?" she said, snickering. "Just kidding. I know you're talking about the *latest* murder. What about it?"

"You took lots of photos of the crime scene, but I haven't seen them yet. I texted you about that yesterday, but maybe you didn't see it. Would you please email them to me?"

"Sorry. When your text came in I was at the urgent care center and I had forgotten about it by the time I was released. What're you looking for?"

"Did you by any chance take a photo of the tattoo that was on Lucas's arm, the one that was in progress when he died?"

"Let me check." Francine could hear Charlotte either talking to herself or ranting at the phone. "No, that's the *camera* app, not the *photos* app. No, I don't want '*albums*'." Finally she told Francine, "Let me call you back."

"It's okay. When you hang up, just send me every photo you have."

"Will do."

"How are your bruises today?"

"Better. I'm looking forward to meeting up with Hank today and going bike shopping together. Is Joy really coming to chaperone? Because I think she's going to be a *kill*joy, not a Joy."

"Haha. Don't you think it's for the best, though? You don't really know anything about him."

"That's what a date is for."

"You told us last night it wasn't a date."

"You're exhausting to talk to, Francine."

There was a bothersome buzzing noise on Francine's phone. It went on and off. She pulled the phone away from her face and looked to see what it was about.

The alarm on their new home in Parke County was going off. Was someone breaking in?

"Gotta go, Charlotte. I'm sure I'm over-worrying about Hank. Date or not, let me know how it goes."

Francine called Jonathan right away. He answered on the second ring. "I see it, too," he said. "The house in Parke County. I'll call the sheriff's department and ask them to check it out."

"Does one of us need to go out there?"

"Let's hear what the sheriff has to say. And no, I don't want *you* going out there. I can leave here if I have to."

"Thanks," she said. "I know you're trying to get your project done. Let me know what you hear from the sheriff."

Jonathan agreed and disconnected.

Francine looked up and realized she hadn't even left Cass and Eric's driveway yet. She was still poised to pull out on the county road. She took a cleansing breath in and then let it out slowly. "This is getting to be too much."

Francine arrived back home and checked her email. No photos yet from Charlotte. Maybe Charlotte was having difficulty sending them all. She reminded herself that Charlotte was technically challenged and she had taken a lot of photos. Surely they would come soon.

Half an hour later Jonathan called.

"The Parke County sheriff's department says it looks like someone jimmied the lock on the back door, so other than needing to fix the lock, no damage was done, not like a broken window or anything."

"What did they take?"

"I gave the sheriff permission to enter. He made sure there was no one there, then he checked for anything that was out of place or obviously missing. He said it all looked fine to him."

"Maybe the alarm scared them away."

"Anyone would know that the sheriff couldn't get there for a while. There would have been time to go in and grab something. It's odd."

Francine would have felt better if they'd taken the television off the mount in the main room. At least it would have given the impression of a random burglary. This news was more disturbing. "Not odd," she told him. "It means they were looking for something specific and they didn't find it."

"What are you thinking? That some people are still looking for Doc Wheat's buried treasure, and now that we own the property, they've targeted us?"

"Yes. But you and I know what that treasure really is. Let's hope whoever broke in is still thinking it's money or jewels."

"I'm going to grab a late lunch and head out there to get the lock fixed. The sheriff was still processing the scene, so for the moment the house is protected. He said he'd block the back door and exit out the front to secure it before he left."

"Any clues as to who might have done this?"

Jonathan's voice sounded grim. "The sheriff said they don't have much to go on. No tire tracks or footprints."

Francine thought about it after they hung up. Not only was the thief looking for something specific, he—or she—was smart enough to know how to jimmy a lock and leave nothing behind. The whole notion that they were being targeted sent chills down her spine.

Joy blew through Francine's front door around 3:00. "I have information," she said. That she came in without knocking was not unusual, but her gleeful announcement was. Of late, Joy had been rather secretive about everything.

Francine looked at her watch. "About Charlotte's date?"

"Oh, yeah," Joy said as if it wasn't the main reason she was there. "The date you signed me up last night to chaperone. That too."

That too? Francine wondered what else Joy could be referring to that would make Charlotte's date the dismissive information. "As I recall, you didn't put up much resistance. I almost thought you were interested in purchasing a motorcycle given your lack of opposition to the idea."

"Perish that thought." Joy stood impatiently in the entryway like she expected to be invited in.

"Would you like to come in and sit down?" Francine asked. Normally she would have indicated the kitchen, where she and her friends frequently gathered, but Joy's demeanor seemed to call for something more comfortable than stools around the kitchen bar. Plus, Francine wanted to make sure Joy covered whatever information was in addition to news of Charlotte's new boyfriend.

She walked Joy into the great room. Joy eased onto the couch with care. Francine sat in the rocking chair that had belonged to Jonathan's mother, facing Joy.

"So what was Hank like?"

Joy cocked her head. "In some ways what I expected; in other ways, not."

Francine waited but ended up prompting her. "Expected how?"

"Well, he looked the biker part. He was dressed in a sleeveless black leather vest with a big logo on the back. Kind of like Charlotte had described him at Bridge Club. He's bald but has a beard and mustache, mostly gray. Neatly trimmed. Charlotte's guess that he was in his sixties was a good one. I quizzed him about his background and found out he was in junior high school when the Beatles put out "Abbey Road," so he's probably in his early sixties."

"Impressive that you got him to reveal his age in such a subtle way."

Joy nestled her back into the couch cushions with a satisfied smile on her face. "Interview skills," she said.

"How was he not what you expected?"

"He is actually quite well educated. Bachelor's degree in physiology and later a master's in physical therapy, back when that was all you needed to get a license. He was career military but retired as soon as he was eligible and did the physical therapist thing. So he's had two careers. Very well spoken, too."

"So you think he's legitimate?"

"You mean legitimately interested in Charlotte?"

Francine laughed. "Yes, I guess that's what I mean."

"I'm not sure, but I wouldn't rule it out. He was patient with her when we looked at all the motorcycles at the Harley dealership first and then at the BMW dealership second."

"You went to two?"

"He was advocating for a BMW model smaller than what you generally find at a Harley dealership. Charlotte was the one who wanted to go Harley."

"Figures."

Joy thought a moment. "I would say he walked a fine line between wanting to be helpful so that she got what he felt was the right motorcycle, but caring enough that his intention could be interpreted as interest. I'd say he's checking her out as much as I was checking him out."

"At the end of the day, could you see the two of them together?"

Joy leaned forward with a big smile on her face. "You remember how unconventional Philip was as a judge?" Joy asked, referring to Charlotte's deceased husband.

Francine nodded. Though she hadn't known Philip and Charlotte at the time they got married, reputedly he'd insisted they exit down the aisle to "In-A-Gadda-Da-Vida" after the ceremony.

Joy continued. "Hank has that same kind of spirit. So, in that way, the two of them are a match. But I'm still reserving judgement at the moment."

"Why?"

"Call it a vibe he gave off. Kind of like he wanted something, and this was how he was going to get it. And I don't mean wanting Charlotte; I mean something beyond Charlotte."

"Does the age difference bother you at all?"

"With all the years that are behind either of them, does that really matter? Probably not. But I do think as long as he's in the picture, she's going to buy another motorcycle."

Francine grimaced. She'd been afraid of that. "We all know how bad a driver she is in her Buick. I can't imagine how dangerous she would be on a bike. I hope she waits at least until she heals."

"They didn't make any promises to the salesman other than they might be back. Hank said something to Charlotte about having a biking date together soon. This was after we all went back to Charlotte's house. I didn't stick around but made my apologies and came over here right away."

Francine pulled off her glasses and gave Joy her best "you can trust me" look. "What's your other news?"

Joy let her head fall back against the couch head rest pillow. The question seemed to make her tense. "I could use a drink," she said, head still in laid-back position.

Francine glanced at the grandfather clock in the hall. It was barely

3:15. "I could make you a hard lemonade, I suppose." The drink had somehow become her specialty. She supposed it was because she kept freshly squeezed lemonade in her fridge during the summer months.

Joy sat up a little straighter. She rubbed a hand on the back of her neck. "Only if you're making yourself one, too."

"I'll have a virgin one," she said. "If I have any alcohol this early in the afternoon I'll just get sleepy, and I'm going with Mary Ruth to a cooking class tonight."

"Oh, that's right. I forgot. You're her wingman this evening. You brought it up when you talked me into going with Charlotte on her date."

Francine blushed. "I hope Mary Ruth's date turns out to be as uneventful for me as Charlotte's was for you."

"You can hope that. Garrett Stone's teaching the class. You know they're rather volatile together."

'Volatile together' was a euphemism. They couldn't stand each other. Garrett was an attractive older man twice divorced who thought very highly of his skills as a pastry chef, not to mention himself. Plus, his condescending manner often put people off or brought out their worse competitive nature. The latter had happened with Mary Ruth on an episode of "Cutthroat Kitchen" in which she and Garrett appeared. The premise of the show is that four chefs are given $25,000 each. They can then spend that money to help themselves in each cooking round or they can use their money to sabotage the other chefs. If they have any money left at the end of the show and win the final competition, they get to keep that money.

Francine never thought of Mary Ruth as the kind of person who would steal ingredients, seethe in anger over being forced to use improper utensils, or squeal in glee when emerging victorious over another chef, but she had seen MR at her worse on the episode with Garrett. That he got the best of her when he 'bought' Alton Brown's pie-throwing machine and forced her to make pie dough while battling cream pies thrown at her face severed the last bit of composure she had. It resulted in a disastrous but hilarious-looking banana cream pie that was judged the worst by guest judge Antonia Lofaso causing her to be eliminated. Garrett was eliminated in the final round, so he hadn't fared much better. Still, Mary Ruth never forgot or forgave him. Francine wondered how tonight's blind date would go.

Momentarily lost in thought, Francine stared past Joy.

"The hard lemonade?" Joy prompted.

"Yes, sorry." She headed into the kitchen with Joy not far behind.

Joy settled into a stool. Francine rummaged through the refrigerator and then the liquor cabinet, finally placing the drink in front of Joy. She put out a tray of crackers and little cheese squares.

Joy popped a couple of crackers in her mouth, chewed, and then took a gulp of lemonade. "These are peppery!" she said. Still, she eyed the tray and selected another one. "But addictive."

"New recipe from Mary Ruth. Try them with the Monterey Jack cheese. Takes a bit of the heat out."

Joy did as Francine instructed, then repeated it several more times.

"Motorcycle shopping apparently makes you hungry."

"I had to skip lunch. Meeting at the station. Rumors are out there we might be sold."

"Oh, no!"

"Oh, yes. Management is saying this is part of media in the new decade. Revolving ownership. They didn't deny the rumors, either. Most of them have their resumes out already. There could be cost-cutting that rivals bloodshed."

Francine sat on a stool across from her. "Would you lose your ABC affiliation?"

"Depends on what stations the new owner has and wants to keep. They won't reveal who the new owner is until the deal goes through so we won't know." She shrugged. "Look what happened to WISH-TV. They lost their CBS affiliation in their last sale and had to align with the CW."

"But you're tied to *Good Morning America*, Joy! You could lose your correspondent status with them."

"Don't think I haven't thought of that. I'm getting my resume in order, too." She fingered a piece of cheese before making the move to put it on a cracker. "You know, there could be even better opportunities out there for me."

Francine frowned. Like her, Joy was in her early seventies. She didn't want say it, but realistically, how many opportunities were out there for older feature reporters? Joy had gotten the gig on GMA thanks to how well she'd done during the difficult interview the women had when they were the "skinny dippin' grandmas" who'd discovered a dead body in the pool shed. It had been sheer luck and circumstances. But was that novelty wearing off? Joy had done a good job reporting on senior citizen activities since then for GMA, but Francine wasn't convinced the network couldn't find another older reporter who could do the same thing.

Judging from Joy's reaction, though, she was more worried for Joy than Joy was for herself.

They sat in silence sipping their drinks. "You said something earlier about 'information' ... " Francine prodded, letting her voice trail off. She didn't think the station's potential sale had been it, but Joy could always correct her if she was wrong.

Joy gave her forehead a tap as if her brain needed to be jump-started. "Yes, I forgot to tell you. Lucas Monet has a sister. Her name is Gabriella Cayman."

"I found out yesterday he had a sister, but I didn't know her last name was Cayman." Francine briefed her on the conversation she'd had with Snake the previous day. "How did you find out?"

Joy smirked. "Actually, I didn't even go looking for it. The obituary is in today's paper. But once I knew that, I checked up on her. She's a CPA. And here's the kicker. The name of the accounting firm for Tattoo You is Cayman and Lawman."

"Wow." The news made Francine sit up straighter. "She's a partner, then."

"Uh-huh."

"Indianapolis?"

"No, Fort Wayne."

"A couple of hours away, then. Anything suspicious about them? Are they reputable?"

"I don't know any different, so I have to assume they're clean. The interesting thing is that they only *recently* started handling Tattoo You's accounting. Like a year ago."

"And you're wondering if there's a connection."

She nodded. "I wondered if Jonathan knew her. Maybe I could get an interview."

"I'll have to ask him when he gets home. He's working on some kind of hot project now. He had to leave his accounting convention in Washington to come back and work on it."

Joy polished off the remaining hard lemonade in the glass with a flourish. "Well, I feel a bit more settled now. Better get back to my house and change into something nicer. Roy is taking me out tonight."

"Glad things are working out with him. You said something the other day about it not being too long before you set a date…?"

The sides of her mouth tightened. "I'd like to hurry him up." She slid the sleeve of her t-shirt up to show a still-bare right shoulder. "I'm hoping the tattoo'll do it, but now I need to find another tattoo artist. What about this Snake guy you met? Although," she said, thinking it over, "maybe I need to find someone with a less intimidating name."

"What about Cass Dehoney? She was Lucas's apprentice."

Joy's face became expressive, like she was delighted with the idea. "I didn't know he had an apprentice. Does she work out of Tattoo You Two?"

"She does."

"By the way, what were you doing at Tattoo You Two? Do I want to know how you met him?"

Francine laughed. "I was there legitimately! I was getting a pedicure. But I did arrive early to do a bit of investigation."

"Despite what Chief Turner said, huh? You've been busy for someone who's not investigating the murder."

"Talk about the pot calling the kettle black! You did some snooping on Gabriella Cayman."

"Yes, but my investigation is bigger than Tattoo You Two."

"Bigger? In what way?"

Joy shook her said. "Sorry, can't say."

In some ways, Francine was taken aback by Joy's refusal to tell her what she was investigating. After all, she and Charlotte had lied to the police to protect her. That had to count for something. And Joy had never been that secretive around her before.

Francine remembered Mary Ruth's promise to talk to Joy today in an effort to get her to admit the truth. "Have you seen Mary Ruth today?"

"She called this morning, but I was busy. Working on my big story. I needed to get some background and I knew I wouldn't have much time this afternoon, what with crashing Charlotte's date with Hank." She said it pointedly.

Francine stared at her. "Am I the only one who's worried about Charlotte?"

Joy raised an eyebrow. "She's your best friend. I get the sense you don't want things to change, and you fear they will if she gets involved with Hank."

As much as Francine wanted to reject Joy's assessment, she was afraid Joy might be right. She bit her bottom lip. "I guess I need to think on that."

Joy nodded. "Well, I probably best be going." She got up from her stool but gingerly. She slowly straightened her back. "I might be a bit sore from test driving one of those bikes."

"Wait! What?"

She smiled. "The things I do for Charlotte. Really."

Despite encouragement from Francine, Joy said no more and left.

Francine blew out a breath. While she was curious to learn if Joy had actually test-drove a motorcycle, she was more interested in something else Joy had said.

What did she mean, that her story was bigger than that? What was her story about, if it was not tied to the murder of Lucas Monet?

11

Late that afternoon Francine finally received Charlotte's photos from the murder scene. She was examining them for the first time when Jonathan came in the back door. She was bent over her iPad using her fingers to blow up a photo, one where she could get a good look at the partial tattoo that was on Lucas's forearm.

She glanced up from the iPad. "Anything new from the break-in?"

"No. It was very much like the deputy described. I walked through the house and saw nothing out of place."

"What did you do about the door?"

"I went to the Ace Hardware in Rockville and bought a new one. They had the names of several people who do handyman jobs so I arranged for one of them to install it. It should be done next week. In the meantime, I put in one of those doorbell video cameras."

"It still makes me nervous that the new door won't be in until next week. Are you sure the house'll be safe until then?"

Jonathan shrugged. "I nailed a piece of two-by-four to the floor so the door can't be pushed open. Nothing was disturbed. I can't imagine whoever did this *didn't* walk through the whole house. If they were looking for anything, I guess they didn't find it."

"What do you think they were after?"

He rubbed his chin in thought. "Hard to say. Given what we know about the property, it would be easy to become paranoid and believe someone is after our secret treasure. But I'm trying not to go there. In any event, if they didn't find it this trip through the house, why would they try again?"

Francine found herself taking nervous, shallow breaths. She thought about the property and the changes they'd made since the fire had burned the original house Zedediah had built. They no longer stored jars of the special water in the greenhouse. They weren't stored anywhere on the property. Instead, they'd brought them back to their house in Brownsburg.

What if someone knew about the jars and was looking for them? They hadn't put an alarm on the greenhouse. If someone had discovered they weren't there, the house would have been the next logical place to look.

"Did you by chance check the greenhouse?"

He nodded. "It didn't look like it'd been broken into."

"Does that mean the perpetrator was only interested in the house, or were they only interested in the house because they were looking for something they knew wasn't in the green house?"

"What are you getting at?"

"Just thinking out loud. When Zedediah left us, he indicated he was going away and not taking any water with him, that he was ready to die. But what if he wasn't ready? Maybe the water is addictive, and he came back."

"If he came back and found we weren't storing the water in the greenhouse anymore?"

She nodded.

"Well, he knows where it is on the property and how to collect it. Or he could just contact us. It's not like we parted enemies."

His words calmed her down. Jonathan was right. It probably wasn't Zedediah. Nor was it likely whoever had gotten in would be back before the new door was installed. He'd left the place as secure as he could. She trusted his instincts.

She looked down at the iPad where her fingers had enlarged one of Charlotte's photos. Jonathan, next to her on the couch, was watching her. "What's that you're looking at?" he asked.

"It's a photo from the night of the murder. Charlotte finally sent them. This is the tattoo that was being inked on Lucas's arm." She handed him the iPad.

He studied it. "It looks very incomplete."

"Well, he died before it could be finished."

"I wonder if it would have been finished if you hadn't come in."

She contemplated it. "You mean before Charlotte, Joy and I blundered in, the murderer had planned to complete it, even if Lucas was dead? You think there might have been some kind of message there?"

He nodded. "Lucas died for a reason. Why kill him while tattooing him? Seems an odd choice. There had to be easier ways. My guess is there's a connection between *why* he was killed and *how* he was killed. Maybe the tattoo would have provided the link."

Francine knew there was a way to do a reverse image search with Google. She'd seen Joy do it before. "Have you ever performed a reverse search image on the internet?"

Jonathan gave her a crooked smile. "No, but I bet between the two of us, we're smart enough to figure it out. Let's use my computer upstairs, though. I think we'll have better success than using the iPad."

Jonathan's home office was more elaborate than Francine's. While hers was a convenience since she no longer worked, his was created for function and comfort. He did accounting work at home, not just instead of going to the office but sometimes in the early morning hours if he couldn't sleep.

The office had been crafted out of one of the boys' bedroom. The room had a side window facing west with airy white draperies and mini-blinds to keep the sun out. Jonathan's desk faced a dark gray wall bearing two Escher prints mounted in black frames. His computer was a midsized Dell with dual screens and a keyboard setting atop a natural wood desk with black, wrought-iron legs. Everything in the office had modern lines.

Francine pulled up a chair so she could sit next to him. He Googled directions on how to perform a reverse image search while Francine forwarded the photo to him. When they finally obtained the results, though, they were disappointed.

"There must be fifty thousand images here that fit the little bit of tattoo the murderer was able to ink on him before he died," Francine said. "Is there a way to narrow it down?"

Jonathan tried to filter it to established tattoos designs, but it yielded no better results. "If we knew what kind of symbol it was supposed to be, that would help," he said. "Like, if we knew it was a flower, we could search flower tattoos."

Francine leaned in and took control of the mouse. "Yeah. It's a shame the killer didn't leave a sticky note with the image on it so we would know where he was going with it." She scrolled through the first hundred images. "You're right. This is impossible."

Jonathan leaned back in his chair and put his hands behind his head. Francine continued to scroll. "Let's back up a moment," he said. "Could this have happened anywhere but Tattoo You Two?"

"Lucas's death?"

He nodded. "Why Tattoo You Two in Brownsburg?"

She looked up from her now mindless scrolling. "It wasn't a random killing. Whoever did this targeted Lucas. I suppose it could have happened at the original Tattoo You parlor in Indianapolis. He recently transferred from there."

"Okay. Why did he transfer? Was he afraid? Was coming out here an attempt to escape from a bad situation?"

Francine thought about her job offer at Tattoo You Two. She hadn't told him yet, and she wasn't ready to do it now, but she couldn't help but feel that if she were on the inside, she'd have access to some answers. "I'm intrigued by your question. What if the answer lies back in Indianapolis?"

Jonathan gave her a cockeyed glance. "Too bad you already had a pedicure."

She smiled back. "I could always get a manicure."

He shook his head. "I couldn't let you go alone. Not that I think you're in any real danger, but …"

"I know what you mean. There are just enough things going on that I feel unsettled, too." She brightened. "Maybe you could come with me."

He frowned. "And what? Get a tattoo? I'm not doing that."

She ran a finger over her lips. "I was thinking maybe you could get a pedicure."

His mouth dropped open, then he closed it. "A pedicure?"

"I know what you're thinking. But even some straight men get them. Not a lot, maybe, but it's not unheard of. And I bet that's especially true in Indianapolis."

"I don't have to get a nail finish on them, do I? I don't want rosy red toenails."

"We'll just have her put a clear polish on them. Or no polish at all."

He thought about that. "Well, I've always wondered what you women find so fascinating about pedicures. Maybe I'll find out." But he sounded like he didn't want to do it.

Francine realized that between checking up on the break-in at their place in Parke County and going with her to get a pedicure, he wouldn't be spending time on the special project he'd come home for. "Are you sure you're okay with this? I know it'll take you away from your work."

"Since you'll be Mary Ruth's wingman tonight, I'll put in some hours while you're gone," he said, sounding resigned.

Francine recognized that tone of voice. She knew he'd likely put in more hours tonight than the 'some' he'd indicated. Probably half the night. It was his choice, though. "What's this project about, anyway?"

His mouth twitched. "I can't talk about it right now."

"Not even in the abstract?"

He shook his head. "Not even in the abstract."

"Okay," she said, though it wasn't really. In all the years they'd been married, she could think of only a few times when he'd been so absorbed on a project and mum about what the project entailed. But even then, he'd spoken to her in nonconcrete terms about it. "I guess it's a secret?"

"Of national importance," he said, in mock earnestness.

There was one other secret she knew he kept—how he'd come to own a gun and how he'd learned to handle it so well. This had come to light only a few years ago when he'd been part of the team that rescued her and Charlotte from someone who wanted to kill them. Given the circumstances, she'd been glad for it at the time. Later, when he demurred at providing answers, she'd let it go. The fact that it was still a secret between them, though, tugged at her conscience.

Francine knew she was being a bit two-faced, She had her own secret she was keeping from him, the job offer at Tattoo You Two. The thought about them going to the downtown location tomorrow made her heart skip a beat. Aretha had said she worked there. She might see them. It could get awkward.

But maybe it was worth the shot. Francine'd have the chance to see the original shop, get a feel for how things are, and with any luck pick up on a clue or two. "Let me see if I can get us booked. How about the soonest I can us in?"

"The soonest?" he said with an uncertain tone.

"Carpe Diem," she said.

He stood up to leave. "I guess the more time that passes, the less likely we are to get any clues. Do whatever. I'll make it work."

"Jonathan, I found out from Joy today that Lucas had a sister, Gabriella Cayman. She's a partner in an accounting firm."

He stiffened. "I've heard of her," he said.

"Good or bad things? Joy says Cayman's accounting firm handles the Tattoo You business."

"And you find that suspicious?"

She nodded. "Joy said it's been a recent change."

Jonathan spoke cautiously. "It could be perfectly legitimate. He was only a tattoo artist. If he found out the owner of the parlor was looking for a new accounting firm, he might have suggested his sister's company. That's a perfectly innocent thing. His getting killed may have nothing to do with his sister's connection to the firm."

"So you're not worried?"

"Only that you won't leave it alone." He looked at his watch. "Don't you have to get ready soon for that cooking class with Mary Ruth?"

"Yeah. I've got dinner in the slow cooker. I'll be down in a minute."

Leave what alone? The possible Cayman connection to the murder? He seemed to be interested in any other aspect of it. She shrugged. If he had some inside knowledge about the accounting firm, it would come out eventually.

She was able to get them an appointment at 12:30 the next afternoon, right after lunch. *This is really working out,* she thought. *It must mean good karma. Everything will go just fine.*

"So have you had the chance to speak to Alice about my needing her help with catered events?" Mary Ruth asked Francine while they were navigating the narrow aisles of the Kitchen and Table cookware store in Carmel, Indiana that evening. Carmel was a former bedroom community for executives looking to live outside Indianapolis that had become an upscale, highly desirable city in its own right. If any location could support the high end kitchenware store and cooking school, it would be Carmel.

Francine gritted her teeth. She had totally forgotten. But then, she also knew Mary Ruth had forgotten to talk to Joy. "Um. No. Have you had the chance to talk to Joy?"

Mary Ruth looked away. "I called her but she couldn't talk. I guess I should have tried again."

"Uh-huh."

"I'm sorry, Francine. I have too much on my mind."

Francine wanted to scoff. Have a lot on her mind? Mary Ruth wasn't the one who gave CPR to a dead corpse a few mornings back. She chose to sigh instead. "Me, too."

"I'll get to it. I promise." Mary Ruth sounded sincere.

"Not sure when, but I will too, next time I see Alice."

"And you're still on board to help me with the catering event tomorrow morning?"

"Right."

Francine decided to change the subject. "Only you would schedule a blind first date at a cooking class," she said, shaking her head. "Do you even know what he looks like?"

Mary Ruth fluffed her auburn hair, which Francine knew had recently been highlighted. "Well, on the dating website Tyler is tall and thin, has chestnut eyes, a Tom Cruise smile, and a Clint Eastwood chin. Good ingredients, at least for a first date."

The two scoured the faces of the shoppers more than the kitchen items. "How can you be sure he didn't fake the photo?" Francine asked.

"I can't." Her head swiveled as she passed a guy with a vague resemblance but was shorter and had a gap-toothed smile. More David Letterman than Tom Cruise. "I can't even be sure his real name is Tyler."

"Did you use your real name and photograph?" Francine pressed.

"Of course." She ran her hands down the curves of her hips. "Did I mention I'm down to a size ten?"

Francine wanted to answer, "only several times a month," but she didn't. In truth, she was proud of Mary Ruth's transformation, just tired of hearing about it. Instead, she said, "And you say he suggested a cooking date?"

She nodded enthusiastically. "Brilliant idea, I think. It's neutral territory. Plus, we're both foodies, divorced, and we love scones. Though I wouldn't have chosen Garrett for a teacher." Mary Ruth mumbled the last sentence under her breath, a nod to her not-so-happy history with Garrett. "I'm hopeful I won't need a way out of this date, but I'm glad you're here to provide it if I need one."

Francine looked at her watch. "We should head to class. Maybe we'll see him back there."

They turned out to be the first ones in. Francine scouted the name tags on the table. "I don't see anyone named Tyler," she whispered.

Mary Ruth slipped the white apron over her head with practiced ease and looped the strings around her waist. "You're right. The only male name is Kenneth. Maybe I've been stood up." She stuck her lip out.

More people scurried in behind them and snatched up aprons and name tags.

The cooking school was in the back room of the Kitchen and Table store. It could only accommodate one class at a time, but the room itself was a well-constructed commercial kitchen. There were four stations arranged in a square with four stools at each station. A natural gas cooktop with two burners was available at each station. The kitchen itself had commercial grade appliances across the back wall. Mary Ruth and Francine took their places at the station closest to the side door entrance and nearest to one of the double wall ovens. "Kenneth" was also at their station, but nowhere to be seen.

Garrett entered the room from a side door and everyone hushed. "Good evening, all!" he said with energy. "I'm Garrett Stone, the King of Scones, and today we're going to learn how to make those British delights and more." He passed by them and gave Mary Ruth a playful nudge.

"He's cuter than on television." Francine said.

"That's in the eye of the beholder. I think he's full of himself."

"Hmmm." Francine took a more critical look at Garrett. "Have you noticed he's tall, has chestnut eyes, and a chin that could be described as Clint Eastwood-esque?"

Mary Ruth seemed stunned. "You're right!" She fumbled with the measured-out ingredients at their station. "He does kind of resemble Tyler. You don't suppose Garrett lured me here for a date, do you? Well, if he did, he's got another think coming. All I want is revenge!"

Uh-oh, Francine thought. *Obviously, she's still angry.*

Garrett, oblivious to anything Mary Ruth had said, winked in their direction. "I'm delighted to see that I'm joined today by Chef Mary Ruth Burrows. When I found out I was going to be teaching in Indianapolis, I was hoping we'd have a chance to meet again. Let's hope today goes better than our first date did on *Cutthroat Kitchen*."

"There won't be a second date, that's for sure," Mary Ruth retorted, eliciting chuckles from the class.

He blanched and proceeded with class instructions.

"Do you believe that comment about a date?" Mary Ruth said to Francine. "Like we actually had one! I think he set this up. I think he's Tyler."

Garrett was still telling the class what to do. Mary Ruth dumped the flour and butter into a bowl. Francine was about to hand her the pastry blender when Mary Ruth began to rub the butter into the flour with her hands, creating a breadcrumb-like mixture.

"Class!" Garrett announced loudly, startling Mary Ruth. She spilled half the flour/butter mixture on the table. He had come up behind her while she was working. Francine used the scraper to get the spilled ingredients back in the bowl.

"Instead of using the pastry blender as I demonstrated earlier," Garrett continued, "the classic way to integrate the butter is with your fingers, as Chef Mary Ruth is doing here. Can you gather round?"

"I'll kill him," Mary Ruth muttered under her breath.

"Time to kick into 'star' mode," Francine advised.

"I'll kick him in his star mode."

But Mary Ruth gamely beamed a high-wattage smile. She tilted the bowl toward her classmates with one hand and used the other to demonstrate.

"While we're here," Garrett asked, "would you please add the sugar, eggs, and baking powder?"

The class followed along as Francine dutifully added them to the bowl and Mary Ruth stirred them with a wooden spoon.

"Now add about half the milk," he said.

Mary Ruth complied and stirred.

"Class, you want it to be a soft, wet dough. Be sure to add enough milk until it gets to that state." He dumped the contents onto the work surface and bumped her out of the way. "Now I'll demonstrate how to 'chaff' the dough." He folded the dough in half, turned it ninety degrees, and folded it again.

"Garrett," she said sweetly, "are you sure this has enough milk in it?"

"Quite sure. If anything, it looks a bit sticky."

"Really? I think you should take a closer look."

He bent over. Mary Ruth pushed the back of his head down, planting his face deep into the dough. "That'll teach you to play me for a fool! And I will never date you, 'Tyler.'"

He jerked his face up out of the bowl. "And you're crazy if you think I would ever date a kitchen witch like you," he said nasally. He rushed from the room to clean his face.

A tall, thin man looking very much like the date Mary Ruth described earlier bumped into him on the way out. He grabbed the name tag "Kenneth" as he hurried over. "I'm Tyler. Sorry I'm late. I ran into traffic."

"Tyler?" she said, stunned. "But your name tag says 'Kenneth.'"

"I go by my middle name, Tyler. Looks like they picked up my first name from the charge card. We can still have our date, can't we?"

"Not here," she said. "We need to leave, and quickly. Before Garrett gets back."

"Was that him with the dough on his face?"

"Yes, we had a bit of a disagreement."

"I was looking forward to meeting him."

"Oh," she said. "You wouldn't like him." She gave Tyler a push toward the door. "I can teach you how to make scones. We'll head over to my house."

"What about the ingredients? We should at least grab those."

"The only real ingredient we need for our first date is a getaway car. Let's move."

They fled, leaving Francine to deal with the aftermath.

Francine stared down at the scone dough in the bowl. Garrett's facial features were embedded in it. She put the bowl under the counter and bothered one of the kitchen assistants to replace her ingredients, which they did quickly. Another assistant stepped up to instruct the class until Garrett could return, which took about ten minutes. He was red in the face but seemed composed otherwise. If he knew Francine had come with Mary Ruth, he didn't treat her like it, though he did seem to stay clear of that particular station.

This turned out to be fortuitous as Francine thought to take advantage of her close proximity to the double wall oven and lack of oversight from Garrett. Knowing the scone dough wouldn't rise much and distort the image, she was able to create a special bake when he and his assistants were busy working with other students.

Though she briefly wondered what a baked good bearing the facial features of the King of Scones might for go for on eBay, she decided instead to present it to Mary Ruth the next day.

12

"So what happened with Tyler last night?" Francine asked Mary Ruth. They stood in Mary Ruth's living room. Francine had just come through the front door to find her standing there, almost as if she'd been expecting her. Which, in some ways, she was, since Francine was helping her with a catered event that morning.

"He was nice."

"Just nice?" Francine set her purse down near the coat closet. She hadn't yet revealed the contents of the gift bag she carried. Mary Ruth glanced at it but didn't say anything. Francine followed her into the kitchen. "'Nice' doesn't sound like a major endorsement."

"He tried hard, but I found it exhausting trying to connect with him. Despite his profile, I don't think we have a lot in common."

"Do you think he's just shy or something?" Francine reached into the pantry where Mary Ruth kept several of her pink "Mary Ruth's Catering" aprons on a hook, took the top one off and put it on.

"Maybe." Mary Ruth checked a timer on the top oven in her double wall oven. "But I think he faked his bio." She pulled on oven mitts.

"I have never understood why people would do that."

"Me, either."

The timer went off and Mary Ruth opened the oven door. The inviting smell of baking powder biscuits wafted out, making Francine's mouth water. She checked a pan on the stove and saw sausage gravy warming at low temperature. "Tell me this is a men's group."

"It's not. It's a women's group. Surprised? This is not a diet-restricted, just-came-from-spin-class-and-headed-to-yoga next group. This is a book club that enjoys eating. They read culinary mysteries and love fats, carbs and sweets. You can help by finishing boxing up those Danish over there." Mary Ruth pointed with her oven mitt toward a table at the back of the kitchen where she routinely staged items before loading them into the catering van. The large stainless steel table was near the back door. Francine knew from experience that there would be a check list on it and the list would be the last thing Mary Ruth would go over before leaving the house. In this case the pastries were being neatly arranged in boxes bearing her catering logo. She presumed Mary Ruth was in the middle of doing that when she'd arrived.

The biscuits came out of the oven, and Mary Ruth transferred them to a cooling rack and brushed them with butter. When she turned away from having finished that, Francine said coyly, "I've brought you a present." She handed her the gift bag.

Mary Ruth frowned. "It's definitely not my birthday. This isn't some made up Hallmark occasion like "Friendship Day" or something like that, is it? Because if it is, I missed it."

"Just open the bag."

Mary Ruth looked inside, pushed aside the crinkling tissue paper and found her quarry. She pulled out the deformed scone, now baked. She studied it curiously. "Am I supposed to know what this is?"

"It's from last night. This scone bears the imprint of Garrett Stone's face."

It took Mary Ruth a second to process that. "Seriously?" She seemed bemused.

"Yes, I baked it when they weren't looking. If you were to use it as a mold, you could reproduce his mug."

"And the purpose of that would be …?"

"I bet you could sell it on eBay."

The two women laughed. Mary Ruth ran her hands over the indentions in the scone. "You got a nice bake on this," she said, "despite the imperfections. How was the rest of the class?'

"It was good, actually. And I brought home a dozen savory and a dozen cinnamon scones. If you and Tyler had stayed, I would have had to split them with you."

"Lucky you, then."

Francine washed her hands before taking over where Mary Ruth left off transferring the apricot-glazed Danish to the boxes. "Will you be having another date with Tyler?"

"Maybe. He was insistent about it. And I felt bad since it was my fault we had to run out on the scone class. I felt like he deserved a second chance."

The bite of tires on pavement came from outside the back door. Francine heard the heavy slam of a door shut and figured it must be a truck. The back door opened and Toby, Mary Ruth's grandson, came in. He seemed surprised to see Francine at the table filling the boxes, but then he got a twinkle in his eye. "Hello, Aunt Francine," he said. He'd taken up calling her that. She'd been "Mrs. McNamara" for a long time, but now that he was an adult she'd suggested just "Francine." He said he couldn't go there yet. Countering with "Aunt Francine," they've agreed it was a good compromise.

"Hi Toby."

"Grandma didn't say you were gonna be here. I figured it would probably be Mrs. Jeffords helping out." Apparently Alice and he were still on a formal basis.

"Alice was busy," Mary Ruth said. "Francine came to my rescue."

"Busy again, huh?" Toby said. "I'm here because I got a last minute catering gig. Desperate plea came in yesterday evening. It's a gender reveal party. I don't know who the original caterer was, but they flaked out."

"What do you need? Anything we already have leftover in the freezer?" Toby, who'd received some press as the "Stripping Caterer" thanks to a catering event that had gone very wrong and ended up in a murder investigation, had started up his own business. For the moment, he was sharing his grandmother's commercial kitchen.

"I doubt you have any pink colored cupcakes, but what finger foods do you have I can borrow now and replace later?"

"Actually, I think we have a dozen strawberry cupcakes in the outside freezer. They're gluten free, though."

He brightened up. "Perfect! I mean, it's not enough for the whole event, but it'll be great. They'd requested something gluten free for a celiac relative who was going to be there. I told them I'd see what I could do but reminded them I didn't have much time to pull it together. This'll make me look superhuman. For the big reveal, I'm making a vanilla butter cake with pink food coloring."

Toby and Mary Ruth went to the outside freezer in the attached garage to pull out the cupcakes and discuss what hors d'oeuvres were stockpiled and what he could take on short notice.

Francine finished boxing up the Danish, checked the gravy to make sure it was still warm and not scorched, and looked in the lower oven. Something was baking in it. Francine guessed it was individual egg casserole cups.

When the two caterers returned, Toby seemed flustered. Mary Ruth glanced at the wall clock in the kitchen. "I'm sorry there's not more out there. You should have started earlier. I taught you better than that. They'll just have to take what you have time for. The cake is the most important thing. I'd help you if I had time, but I have an event."

"What time is the reveal party?" Francine asked.

"Afternoon, around two," Toby said.

"We'll be dealing with the book club event this morning," Mary Ruth answered. "Although ... the head of the book club always shows up early and always wants to help. If I let her help this time, it would free up Francine." They both looked hopefully at her.

Her mouth twitched. She didn't want him to start recruiting her, too. It was bad enough that she was starting to feel like a part time employee of Mary Ruth's Catering. But she hated to see him get a bad reputation this early in a solo career. "I can only help until 11:00," she said. "I was going to tell you that, too, Mary Ruth. Jonathan and I have something going at lunchtime that will take part of the afternoon. But until then, I can help you, Toby. But just this once, okay?"

"Thank you, Aunt Francine!" He seemed relieved and contrite at the same time. "I promise I won't make that mistake again. I was just tired after last night's gig and overslept."

Francine raised an eyebrow. Gig? Was he still stripping? She was pretty sure he'd told his grandmother he'd given that up. Maybe he'd meant another catered event.

Mary Ruth put hands on hips. "You were stripping again? Where was it, and why did you do it?"

Toby got defensive. "You know to get out of my contract with the Buckingham Male Revue I had to agree to participate in a certain number of performances. This was an all-female accounting group's party for one of their managers who was turning 40."

Mary Ruth held up her hands. "I get it. Far be it from me to suggest you're being irresponsible. But you and Francine had better get busy if you expect to make it in time."

Toby crossed his heart with a finger. "I promise I won't take another rush event like this, especially if I'm stripping the night before. It's just that Steig is still having trouble recruiting to replace me and Eric."

Francine wasn't so sure Mary Ruth believed him. And in some ways, it wasn't like he'd been irresponsible; he'd just been trying to finish out his contractual obligations with the male revue.

"Oh, so you'd continue to help Steig out past your obligations if he was still having recruiting issues?" Mary Ruth asked.

Flustered, Toby turned red. "No. Well, maybe. I mean, it's not like it's easy to find the right person for stripping. He's trying."

She turned away. "Not hard enough, in my book."

Toby and Francine conferred and decided she would start on the cake while he worked on finger food. He retrieved the recipe for her and she got started. Mary Ruth pulled the egg casserole cups out of the oven and let them cool while she loaded up the van with what else she was taking. She put foil over the casseroles, thanked Francine for her help, and took off.

Francine weighed out the flour, butter and sugar. She tried to be as casual as she could, but she knew she was prying for information and that Toby would see through it, eventually or maybe even right away. "So, Toby, what do you think of your grandmother's online dating?"

Toby was cutting the rind off a couple of rounds of brie. Francine presumed it would end up in some kind of spread for crackers or bread, but she wasn't sure. He looked up from the cheese. "I don't see anything wrong with it. Where else would she go to find someone? It's not like she's a bar-hopper or anything. Or do you think she's too old to date?"

"No, no, no, not too old to date at all. It's just the *internet* dating thing. Don't you think it's dangerous for her?"

"I have friends doing the same thing. And if I were looking for someone, I'd probably start online."

"But she's a public figure. People know her from the Food Network programs and all the local hoopla that's come with that. There may be dishonest people who are only looking at her profile because she's something of a celebrity."

Toby sighed. "Look, she's my grandmother. If she weren't in her right mind or whatever, I'd be worried. But she's doing pretty well as far as I can see. She flies to New York to be on cooking shows, she runs a successful catering business. If anything, she's as vibrant or more vibrant than she has been in years."

Though that wasn't the reason she questioned Toby, his reminder that Mary Ruth was more active now than ever gave Francine pause. Was she responsible for Mary Ruth's renewed vigor, her sudden libido? Or was it circumstance, that the success had made Mary Ruth more alive? "I guess you're right. She seems to be having a good time, and things are turning out all right."

Toby nodded. He set the brie aside and began chopping some dried cherries. "She has good friends like you who keep tabs on her. I know she doesn't hesitate to invite you along if she's got some kind of concern. She calls you her wingman." He gave her a smile before resuming work.

Francine watched Toby chop. She thought she had pretty good knife skills, especially for not having gone to culinary school, but it was always fascinating to watch a real professional do it. His cuts were precise and efficient. "I don't mind doing it, but it can be awkward. I am, after all, a married woman."

"Then have her ask Mrs. Reinhardt to go."

The prospect of the acerbic Charlotte accompanying Mary Ruth to a cooking class that required attention to direction and in which she would also be required to serve as a third wheel for a date amused Francine. It would never work. But if Charlotte wasn't the right one, who would be? Joy? After handling the motorcycle shopping trip with Charlotte and Hank, her disinterest in being a wingman in the future was apparent. That left Alice. Francine was pretty sure Alice didn't approve of internet dating. She'd be a Negative Nelly all evening.

Francine decided to switch topics. Toby had finished the cherries and was now chopping pecans. He was wearing a short sleeved t-shirt and she could see a tattoo peeking out from under the sleeve of his right arm as he moved. "I know it was some time ago, but where did you get your tattoos done and who did them?"

"Honestly, I don't even remember. It was back in my weed-smoking days, and I think some buddies and I thought it would be a good idea late at night and we headed to a tattoo business in Indianapolis that was still open all night. I don't know if it even exists anymore. And I sure don't remember the artist. I remember she was a woman, though."

"Was it painful?"

"Not after a few joints." He laughed at his own joke. "Some places hurt more than others. Not that I have that many. But enough to know if you don't like pain, stick to places where you have a little more substance, like shoulders and arms. At least on men."

"Do you have any tattoos you regret?"

He set down his knife and lifted up the sleeve on his left arm. Francine could see something that resembled a zombie face on it. "This one. You know I was a video game addict for a while there. This was from "Zombie WWIII," quite possibly the worst video game ever. But I got it when it first came out and scored a ridiculously high score on it. I held the record for weeks, mostly because no one else was playing it. Anyway, I had this tattooed on my left shoulder in celebration." He let the sleeve drop and picked up the chef's knife he'd been using. He scooped the cherries and pecans into a bowl and added fresh rosemary he found in one of Mary Ruth's refrigerators. He pulled out some frozen puff pastry sheets.

Toby eyed Francine watching him. "You know," he said, "I *am* in a hurry. I need you to get that cake into the oven as soon as possible because it needs to cool before I can ice it."

"Oh, right. Right!" she said. "Getting right on it." Francine redoubled her efforts. She quickly mixed the dry ingredients and set them aside, turned to the wet ingredients, which included the vanilla bean paste and sour cream, mixed them up and set them next to the dry ingredients. Creaming the butter and sugar were next, which she did according to the directions. But she paused before the next step. "You're sure you want me to add *whole* eggs? Isn't this a white cake?"

"It is, but we're coloring it pink, so what's the difference? Might as well add the eggs. The yolks provide a nice richness to the cake."

Doing as he asked, she incorporated the eggs one at a time, then alternated the dry and wet ingredients. Once she had them in the three floured and greased pans and in the oven, she resumed her questioning. "Have you thought about having that tattoo removed?"

He looked her up and down. "You don't have any tattoos, do you?"

"No, and honestly, I don't have any desire to."

"You think it'd be too painful?"

Francine nodded. "And I don't feel like I need my skin decorated at this point in my life. I don't know what I'd want to put permanently on it. I feel like whatever I'd choose, the fascination would be gone at some point and I'd want it changed. Which means even more pain."

"The thing about tattoo removal is that it takes a bunch of sessions if your ultimate goal is to have it gone, period. If you just want it lightened, or lightened enough that you can put a disguise tattoo over it, then you're looking at lesser expense and a lesser number of sessions it'll take to get you there. Any way you look at it, because of the number of sessions, it's more painful and more expensive than getting the tattoo in the first place." Toby finished with the brie and found room for it in the refrigerator. He pulled a baguette out of a brown paper bag and sliced it into one inch pieces.

Francine thought about the procedure Roy must have undergone to have "Jody" re-created as "Joy." Maybe he'd just had it lightened with a 'disguise' tattoo enshrined over it. Now she wondered what it looked like.

"Do you want me to start on the frosting for the cake?" Francine asked.

"I'm planning a red raspberry curd that will work well with the pink color theme. You can start on that if you like."

Toby got her the recipe. Her mind wandered, though. Between straining the seeds out of the raspberry puree and making the curd base, she thought about Joy. She said she was in a hurry to get 'Roy' tattooed on her shoulder, but then she hadn't done anything about it. The day before, Francine had mentioned either Cass or Snake as tattoo artists for Joy to consider. She wondered if Joy had called either.

"You're suddenly very quiet," Toby said. "I mean, I'm glad you're focused on the recipe and my time constraint, but I've never known you to be so quiet. Is it because it's me and not my grandmother?"

Francine looked up from the curd base. "No, of course it's not you. Just lost in my thoughts, that's all." She glanced at the recipe. She was at the step where she needed to add the puree to the base. "Do you want me to strain this again to make sure the curd is smooth?"

Toby shook his head. "No time for that. When you used the immersion blender, did you pulverize the heck out of the raspberry puree?"

"I did."

"Good. Just add the puree and heat it till it thickens and darkens to a nice aubergine color. Use a thermometer and keep the temperature around 170 degrees."

"Wait. Did you just say aubergine?"

Toby blushed. "Yeah," he said sheepishly.

"Your grandmother taught you well."

"Anyway," he said, clearing his throat and getting back to the task at hand. "I need that curd to cool, so as soon as it's the right consistency, get it in the freezer to cool it down."

"Will do."

"I really appreciate your help. Any chance you could change your plans and help me set up this afternoon? The gender reveal party is at 2."

"I'm sorry, Toby, but Jonathan and I have plans that involve an appointment. It would be bad for us to cancel at this late hour."

"I understand." He paused. "Grandma told me about Mrs. Reinhardt and her determination to ride a motorcycle. I can't picture it. Knowing her, it sounds dangerous."

"Joy went motorcycle shopping with her yesterday. She says it was not fun."

Toby chuckled. "I can't picture that, either." Then he looked at her with concern. "Tell me you won't go riding with her."

"I don't plan to," Francine said.

He gave her a sideways glance. "Yes, but it's my impression that Grandma and the rest of you do a number of things you don't plan to," he said. "Just be careful. Mrs. Reinhardt seems to attract disasters."

"That she does," Francine agreed. "That she does."

At home, thinking back on what she'd learned from Toby about tattoos, particularly about the process to have one removed, Francine wished she could have had a shot at talking to Lucas about his supposed expertise in it. *Was* that something intentional? How had he become an expert at it? Was it a good business? Maybe not, if he had switched to the temporary tattoo business.

Of course, if he were still around to talk to, there'd be no need for her to talk to him.

At any rate, the next best person to question about this would be his apprentice, Cass. Though she figured Cass would make time to see her anytime, being in the shop and watching her work would be instructive.

Time to see if she could kill two birds with one stone. She called Joy.

"Have you scheduled an appointment yet to get your tattoo?" she asked.

"No, but interesting you should call right now. I was just looking up the number for Tattoo You Two to see if I could get in to see Cass Dehoney."

"Would you like me to go along? I'd be happy to. In fact, I have some questions for Cass, so accompanying you would be a good thing."

She could practically hear Joy smirking over the phone. "Still investigating?"

Even though she knew Joy couldn't see her, she shrugged. "What can I say? It's what I do."

"Now you sound like Charlotte." They discussed their schedules, and other than the appointment she and Jonathan had in the afternoon (she didn't tell Joy where she was going), she was free, and she let it be known that sooner rather than later was no problem.

To which Joy snorted. "Yes, you're investigating. But I need to talk to Cass as well for a similar reason. So I'm on board with that, too."

Well, all the better, thought Francine. *Maybe I'll be able to figure out what Joy's investigation is all about.*

Francine disconnected. Jonathan came downstairs with his keys to the car. "Ready to go?" he asked. "I had hoped you wouldn't be late in getting back from helping Mary Ruth."

"I ended up helping Toby with an emergency catering job he was doing."

"Caterers have emergencies?"

"Clients have emergencies, which means caterers have emergencies."

Jonathan nodded. "I could see that."

"I'll be ready to go in a minute," she said. "I need to change and get a sweater to take with us. I know it'll be freezing in the restaurant."

Jonathan had suggested they have lunch downtown ahead of the pedicure, to which Francine had readily agreed. After a lunch on Mass Ave at Mimi Blues Meatballs, the two drove to the original Tattoo You parlor. There was a lot adjacent to the building where a small corner pile of scorched remains made Francine think a building once had been there but had burned down. She presumed the tattoo parlor owners were either renting the lot or had purchased it because signs directed them to park there. The lot was hard packed dirt with an occasional patch of grass or weeds, not ideal, but the few paved spots in front of the building were already taken. The entire property was surrounded by chain link fence with only one entrance and exit.

"Seems secure," Jonathan said as he parked.

The Tattoo You building looked to be a product of the 1940s. Brown brick, two stories tall and solid. A monolith, Francine thought, since it was on a corner lot with a street to one side and the dirt parking lot on the other. Houses could be seen across the street and down the block from the business, but in its immediate vicinity, it stood alone. Though she had expected many of the houses in the neighborhood to be run-down, she found about half of them had been renovated. The ones that weren't stood out, defiant symbols resenting the gentrification encroaching on them. Though she didn't feel threatened, she was glad Jonathan was with her.

They entered the building, Jonathan allowing her to go first. The interior was exposed brick painted light gray. They went past a staircase leading down to the basement with a sign marking it as the direction to the tattoo business. Adjacent to it were stairs leading up to the hair salon, but a sign indicated all patrons should check in with the receptionist first.

Continuing straight ahead, they came to a large counter that separated a small waiting area from the manicure and pedicure stations. There was no receptionist Francine could see, which both relieved and annoyed her. She was worried she would see Aretha, and it would all come out about the job offer she'd made, an offer Jonathan was unaware of. Francine just hadn't figured out how to tell him yet. So in that way, she was relieved. But now that annoyance had set in, she drummed her fingers on the counter hoping to get the attention of one of the women painting nails. They didn't look at her. "Hello?" she said.

One of them glanced toward the counter. She said something in a language Francine did not understand, then called toward the back.

This time a short woman with crooked teeth and a heavy accent appeared. Her name tag read, "Vanessa." "You have appointment?" she asked.

Francine identified herself and Jonathan and mentioned the appointment time. The woman checked a book and said something to the three manicurists who were busy with other clients. All four of them looked at Jonathan, and there was some chattering in their native tongue. Vanessa smiled. A bottom tooth was missing. "Have seat," she said.

She directed them to the small waiting area. Handing Jonathan a menu labeled 'Services,' she disappeared in the direction of the staircase that led to the hair salon.

The plastic chairs looked and felt to have been reclaimed from salvage. Francine picked up a well-read People magazine from the cheap wicker basket next to her. She noted it had a publication date two years previous.

"Look at this," Jonathan said, showing the menu to Francine. "I don't understand what half of these services are."

"If they ask," she responded, "you don't want the manicure. And they will ask. A lot."

"Really? Why would they do that?"

"I'm thinking it's a cash cow. Highly profitable."

"Why are you getting one?"

"Because we're doing research."

A commotion began upstairs. There was lots of shouting, all of it in the language neither of them understood. What they did understand was that someone was very unhappy.

Francine leaned over Jonathan's menu. "These are your color choices," she told him.

"I feel like I'm in a paint store," Jonathan said. "There are way too many hues and I'm not sure I could ever distinguish between them."

Francine found it hard to suppress a chuckle. "You mean you're not sure if you'd look better in this midnight purple or the starry, starry black?"

"I'm not considering either of them."

"Good," she said, "because with your coloring, I would go with the apple red."

Jonathan ran his finger over the myriad of colors. "No polish is still an option, right?" he deadpanned.

The receptionist returned and checked out two of the three clients who had finished their pedicures. The ladies who had done their pedicures went on break, leaving the receptionist to huff. "What you want today?" she asked Jonathan.

Jonathan looked at Francine. Francine told her he wanted a pedicure and she wanted a manicure.

"Remove shoes, please," she told Jonathan. She held a pair of flip-flops in her hand while she watched him take off his shoes. "Hmmm. Big feet," she said, and disappeared, returning with a larger pair of flip-flops. She handed them to him.

"Have these things been sterilized since the last person used them?" he whispered to Francine.

"Don't make a fuss. They're disposable flip-flops."

The receptionist put a tray down on the floor in front of a comfortable, padded chair resembling a recliner in the pedicure area. She changed the liner in the tray and added water. Then she dumped something blue in the tray. "You sit," she said, pointing to Jonathan and then to the chair.

"What was that blue thing she put in the tray?" he asked Francine.

She shrugged. "Something to soften your feet maybe. Or maybe sterilize the water. I'm not certain, but they do it every time and my feet haven't fallen off my ankles yet."

Jonathan sat in the chair. She slid his pants legs up past his calves and put his feet in the water.

"Ahhh!" he gasped.

"Too hot?" she asked.

"Don't be a baby," Francine said.

"No," Jonathan said, recovering. "I just wasn't ready for it." He sat back in the chair and tried to get comfortable.

Just then the receptionist turned on the massage feature. Jonathan began vibrating. "This is aggressive!" he told Francine.

"Too much?" the receptionist asked, then moved away before he could answer. Inexplicably, she headed into the back room.

Francine looked at Jonathan's bare legs. "I should have told you to wear something different than jeans. Good thing you have big calves to keep the jeans from sliding into the water."

The nail technicians returned from break.

The taller one looked at Jonathan, an amused look on her face. "You want manicure?" she asked.

Jonathan looked at Francine. "Say no," Francine advised. "Remember, they will ask you this again and again."

"No." He pointed to Francine. "She has the manicure. I have the pedicure." He lifted a foot out of the whirlpool.

The technician went to her station to get something. "It felt good to get my foot out of there," he whispered to Francine.

"Don't get used to it," she said.

The technician came back and knelt down in front of the tray. She tapped it. She tapped again.

"Why is she tapping the tray?" he asked Francine.

"She wants you to take your foot out."

"I just had it out."

"She wants to start with the other foot."

"Oh."

He lifted his foot out of the tray. She dried it off and examined it. "No polish," she said.

Jonathan turned to Francine again. "What?"

"I think she means that you have no nail polish for her to remove."

"Correct," he said. "No polish."

She cut and then filed the toenails on the first foot.

Meanwhile, the shorter of the two women started on Francine's hands. The two technicians chatted among themselves in their native tongue.

"Do they speak English at all?" Jonathan asked Francine.

"More than they let on. I'm sure they're talking about us. Well, maybe you mostly. They probably don't get many men in here."

"Thanks. That makes me feel real good."

The technician moved on to Jonathan's second foot, cutting and filing its toenails. His cell phone rang. He looked at the number. "It's Peter, my partner. I better take this."

"Yes, Peter," he said. He listened for a moment, but stopped when he felt something dig into his big toe. "Ouch!" he said. He yanked his foot away from the nail technician. "What the hell is that?" he said to Francine. "It looks like a cheese grater!"

"She's filing the warts and calluses off your foot."

"Does she have to do that?"

"You can tell her no. It does look like a cheese grater, doesn't it? I've never thought of it that way before."

"You no like?" the technician asked.

"No," he said.

"Okay." She pulled out a tool that resembled an upside down spoon. Taking his foot back into her hand, she pushed the tool against the cuticles on his big toe.

"Ow!" he said, and yanked his foot away again.

"He doesn't want his cuticles done either," Francine told the technician.

"Oh," she said.

"What's going on there?" Francine heard Peter ask. Jonathan had let his hand holding the phone drop away from his ear.

Jonathan quickly put his phone back to his ear. "Nothing. Just go on."

The two technicians began to talk between themselves again. Jonathan's tech got up and retrieved some samples, which she handed to him. "Smell," she said. She indicated he should lift them to his nose.

"What are these?" he asked the technician.

"What salt scrub you want? What you want feet to smell like?"

"Just a minute, Peter," he said and sniffed the samples. He frowned. He glanced at Francine.

"Just pick one," she said.

"Vanilla," he said to the technician.

"Okay." She got out the appropriate salt and began to rub his feet with the scrub.

"This is the first thing that's felt good," he told Francine, covering the bottom of the phone with his hand as though it were an old-fashioned receiver. He put the phone to his ear again. "Sorry, Peter, please go on."

The technicians picked up their conversation again.

"Where am I?" Jonathan said, echoing a question Peter must've asked. It amused Francine. She wondered if Jonathan would admit he was getting a pedicure. "I'm in a nail salon with Francine. She wanted me to come with her."

"Did not," Francine whispered.

"Shhh," Jonathan said. He listened while Peter asked another question. "They might be Vietnamese. You want me to ask?"

Another pause. Jonathan listened. He frowned. He leaned over the technician then leaned back. "Yes," he whispered into the phone. "Around her neck. I think it's a snake."

Francine checked out Jonathan's nail tech. She'd noticed earlier that both his technician and hers had tattoos, but the white uniforms had starched upright collars that mostly hid them.

What an uncomfortable place to have a tattoo! she thought. *Must have been painful to have it done.* The tattoo wasn't a snake but a dragon, and it made her think of the title of the Stieg Larsson book they'd read in Book Club. *It was gruesome*, she thought, and wondered if the woman's tattoo had been done in response to the book's popularity or had just been attractive to her.

Whatever Peter was saying to Jonathan, Francine couldn't tell. Jonathan mostly said 'uh-huh' and then finally said good-bye. He let the hand holding his phone drop to his side, but he didn't put it away. "What did he want?" Francine asked.

Jonathan shook his head. "Later," he said.

The technicians continued talking. Jonathan's technician rinsed the scrub off, drained the whirlpool tub of its water, and then got lotion out of the warmer. She began to massage his feet and his calves. "Well," he told Francine, "this is the second thing I've really liked about getting a pedicure."

"Doesn't it feel greasy to you?"

"Maybe a little."

"Your legs will be super greasy, trust me." Francine said, not watching her nail technician. Suddenly she felt pain and knew what it was. "Not the cuticles," she told the technician. Turning back to Jonathan, she whispered, "One of the reasons I don't do manicures."

Jonathan's technician finished the lotion massage and got out a bottle of something.

"Smells like rubbing alcohol," he commented.

"It is," Francine said. "She's going to get the lotion off your toes so she can polish them."

"You want polish?" she asked.

"Clear polish," he said.

Francine smirked. "Not apple red?"

"Clear." He sounded definite. Francine rolled her eyes.

The technician giggled. She put foam toe separators between his toes.

"What are those?" Jonathan whispered to Francine.

"They use them to separate your toes so they can more easily paint the nails. Not everyone needs them, but your feet are pretty big with the toes close together. Why'd you ask for clear polish? I thought you weren't going to get *any* polish."

"Later," he said.

The two nail techs resumed their conversation. Francine's finally got to the color step. "You choose color?"

"Atomic tangerine," Francine replied. The nail tech went to fetch it.

Jonathan laughed. "Atomic tangerine?"

"It's somewhere between red and orange," she said, indignant. "It's a good color for summer."

Jonathan's tech finished. She put his feet back in the temporary flip-flops and directed him toward some dryers beside the door. She carried his shoes and socks with her. "Dry feet."

"They're not that wet," he said.

"It's to dry the polish," Francine called. "Don't be obstinate."

"You want manicure next?" the tech asked.

"No manicure."

"You pay now?"

"Sure, and hers, too," he said, indicating Francine.

The dryer whirred, the technician ran Jonathan's credit card, and Francine's tech finished her manicure. Francine came over and shared the drying station with him. She saw him slip his phone into his pocket.

Before she could ask him why he'd had it out, they heard a loud thumping of feet. Both turned their eyes toward the ceiling. A voice that sounded suspiciously like Charlotte's began shouting things Francine couldn't make out. Soon, voices in foreign language erupted and joined the cacophony.

"This can't be good," Francine murmured to herself.

The next thing Francine knew, a hefty young woman she guessed to be in her early thirties thundered down the stairs screaming in English for the manager. A white salon apron covered her clothes. Her hair was noticeably green.

She was followed down the stairs by two hairstylists, one wearing gloves clearly used for coloring hair and a second behind her with hair shears in her hand. With no one at the desk, the technicians headed over to where Francine and Jonathan were. Francine wasn't sure, but she got the impression they wanted others around in case things got ugly. The stylists alternated between broken English and their native language. Francine surmised they were defending their work. No manager appeared, and the receptionist stayed hidden in the back room.

Trailing behind the three of them was Charlotte.

"You turned my hair green!" yelled the woman in the salon apron. Looking around but seeing no manager, she screamed it at the hairstylists. "I asked for a single lock of it to be green, not my whole head. And it's not just green, it's Incredible Hulk green! Do I look like the kind of person who would want to go around with Incredible Hulk hair?"

"No you don't," said Charlotte, standing next to her and trying to be supportive. "No more than I look like a woman who at my age should have jet black hair."

Francine noted that Charlotte did, indeed, have jet black hair.

"This is all your fault," the younger woman said, turning to yell at Charlotte. "If you hadn't been asking so many questions, they would have noticed the hair color was wrong and could have done something about it." Her face turned a shade of red that did not go with the hair.

Charlotte seemed alarmed that the woman was trying to pin the problem on her. She took a step back and appraised the woman. "Honestly, I'm not sure even a single lock of green hair would have been a good look for you anyway, honey," Charlotte said. "Your coloring is at odds with greens. You remind me more of an early Claudia Schiffer. I'm thinking peach, or maybe orange. Why not call it a lucky break and have them bleach it out and start over with the right color this time?"

The shop had mirrors on every wall. The woman pushed by Jonathan and moved to one. She struck a pose, hands on hips, the left hip tilted forward. "Really? Claudia Schiffer? I guess I do sort of have her coloring."

"Of course you do," Francine insisted. "Orange, for sure, would be better than any shade of green. Don't you agree, Jonathan?"

Jonathan, who already looked uncomfortable with his feet still airing under the dryer, reared back in surprise at his name being dragged into the conversation. He stared at the large woman just a few feet away and made a hasty decision. "Atomic tangerine. It's somewhere between orange and red. It's a good color for summer."

She turned to him and looked him up and down. "Said the man getting the pedicure."

No one knew exactly what she meant by that, but fortunately she gamely turned back to the mirror. "But he knows what he's talking about. Atomic tangerine it is! Only ..." she waved a finger at the two hair stylists whose mouths were now wide open, "that does NOT mean I want my hair to look like radioactive fruit. I'll pick out the color and you *will* pay close attention this time."

They nodded and scurried up the stairs. The woman with green hair sashayed behind them, exhibiting a newfound sense of self-worth.

"That was close," Charlotte said.

"What are you doing here?" Francine asked.

"Getting a haircut, what else?" she said.

Jonathan stood with his mouth agape. "Your hair," he said. "It's black. Has it been black all these years under that white wig?'

"No, I just got it colored," she said. "Did you really say atomic tangerine?"

Before he could answer the nail tech cautiously returned with the credit card receipt. She looked around to make sure there were no unhappy customers still lingering. She presented the receipt to Jonathan and he signed it.

The nail tech saw Charlotte standing alongside Francine. "You want manicure?" she asked.

"No, I want to pay for my hair color." She pointed at the ceiling where the hair salon was.

"Okay," she said. She went to the cash register and rang it up. Charlotte paid and Francine and Jonathan decided their nails were dry enough. Jonathan put on his shoes.

When they were back in the vestibule area where no one could overhear them, Francine turned to Charlotte. "So what are you doing here, really?"

"Getting my hair cut," she repeated. "I could ask the same thing of you." She pointed to Jonathan's feet, then gave him a crooked smile.

"Especially you! Since when are you getting pedicures, or is this something you've been doing for a long time and Francine never shared it?"

"Put the wig back on," Jonathan teased. "It's freaking me out to see you without your wig."

"I may not ever wear it again," Charlotte said with some indignation. "I came here for a cut because my hair is filling back in! I can't figure out why it's suddenly growing like it did when I was younger, but I'm not complaining. Hank says he likes the way I look without a wig." Running her fingers through her hair and fluffing it out, she struck a casual pose, like this was the most natural thing in the world. But Francine was pretty sure Charlotte hadn't been out in public without a wig in at least a decade.

Then it struck her that Charlotte had said Hank liked the way she looked *without* a wig. When had he seen that, and under what circumstances had she taken it off? But she reminded herself it was none of her business. "Okay," she said, "I can get that. But why here in downtown Indianapolis at Tattoo You?"

"Because Hank is downstairs getting a tattoo."

14

Francine's mind was whirling. She was having a difficult time comprehending everything that was hitting her right then: Charlotte's hair was growing out and filling in, she had it dyed jet black, and Hank was downstairs getting a tattoo. "Why is Hank getting a tattoo here?"

"Because that's where his tattoo artist is today. He's switching out to the Brownsburg shop, but Hank's appointment was for today."

"Who's switching out, Hank or the artist?" Francine asked.

"The artist. Well, Hank will follow him, of course."

Francine had a sudden insight. "Is his tattoo artist named Snake?"

Now it was Charlotte's turn to be surprised. "You know Snake?"

"I met him at Tattoo You Two. He was packing up Lucas's stuff and moving in some of his own."

"Why didn't you mention it?"

"I didn't know your *boyfriend* would be getting a tattoo from him."

"Don't use that disapproving tone with me when you say 'boyfriend.' First, he hasn't reached that stage yet. Second, you haven't even met him. You're judging him by the fact that he rides motorcycles and has tattoos, and that's not fair."

Francine gulped. Guilty as charged. "I'm sorry, Charlotte. You're right. I shouldn't judge him by appearances, especially since I haven't even seen him."

"So let's meet him," Jonathan said.

Charlotte hesitated. "I'm not sure this is a good time for that. For one thing, it would look weird."

Suspicion welled up in Francine. "In what way would it be weird?"

"That you're here, at the studio away from Brownsburg. Like you followed Hank and me here with the express desire to meet him. Like you're checking him out because you don't trust him. Or don't trust that I trust him."

Though Francine could honestly say she didn't trail them here, she wasn't sure how she would explain their presence without admitting she was investigating the Tattoo You parlors, and she certainly didn't want to do that here. She didn't want it to look like she didn't trust Hank, either, even though she didn't. Not yet. "Okay, I see where it would be awkward."

"Let me be the one to choose the time and the place."

"I can agree to that," Jonathan said, moving toward the stairs leading down to the tattoo studio, "but I still want to go down and take a look around. Don't worry. He doesn't know what I look like and I won't introduce myself."

"Should I be worried?" Francine asked Charlotte when Jonathan had disappeared down the stairs.

"That he'll get a tattoo? No. I'd worry more that he's investigating this. He's never been this interested in a case before."

"He's just trying to keep tabs on me."

Charlotte stared into the basement. "Or stay ahead of you."

"What did you find out upstairs? You apparently asked a lot of questions and distracted the colorist."

Charlotte turned back to her. "I thought sitting out in the waiting area while my color set I'd hear lots of gossip and that sort of thing. About the murder, you know, even though it wasn't at this location. Maybe get into a conversation with another patron. But there wasn't anyone else around. So I sat next to the colorist in the salon while she was working on the young lady's hair. She didn't speak very good English."

"None of them do. You must have kept at it, though, to have distracted her enough to color that woman's whole head green instead of just a lock."

She grinned. "That might have been a minor misunderstanding all around. The woman in the chair was a control freak, always issuing directives at the poor colorist and berating her. The colorist didn't understand her half the time. So when there was a question about what she'd said, and the colorist looked to me for help, I might have made a small error as to the correct shade of green and how much of the hair to color."

Francine cracked a smile. "You devil."

"She had it coming. But I did learn a little more than you might think."

Just then, the door to the entrance opened. They were temporarily blinded by the sudden daylight, but Francine was pretty sure by the height and the way the woman carried herself that it was someone she knew.

Aretha.

Francine froze, unsure what to do.

Aretha appeared to be in a hurry, but as she passed Francine in the vestibule, she did a double take. "Francine?" she asked, stopping to frown in disbelief.

"Hello, Aretha," Francine answered warmly, making a sudden decision not to deny anything. What else could she do? She put out her hand to shake Aretha's and tried hard not to think about how Charlotte might react. She was just glad Jonathan was still downstairs.

"It's nice to see you again," Aretha said. "Are you here about the job?" her voice held surprise.

"Not specifically. I *did* want to check out another one of the locations just to see how they compared, though."

"So, are you ready to take the position?"

If she denied it now, she might not have a second chance. "I think so," she said.

Aretha seemed quite relieved. "Excellent. Can you start tomorrow? Let me rephrase that. I need you tomorrow."

Francine smiled. "Sure."

"Please be there around 1:00 p.m. I'll let the owner know to expect you. He'll train you, unless he wants me to come over and do it. As I said before, he or his wife or one of their relatives opens the shop every day, then we relieve them for the afternoon. You'll get off around 6:00 or 6:30, whenever someone shows up to close at 7:00."

Francine knew the nail and hair salons closed at 7:00, but she was puzzled by how the tattoo artists operated after that. She decided she could ask that question tomorrow. Because, to be honest, that was the reason she took the job. That was the part she was most interested in.

Aretha shook her hand once again. "I'm glad ... oh, let's be honest, relieved ... that you're coming on board." She bustled away.

Francine turned her attention to Charlotte who was staring at her in disbelief.

"You're taking a job?" Charlotte asked. "At Tattoo You Two?"

Francine shrugged. "Aretha offered it to me yesterday. I hadn't accepted. You can't say a word about this to Jonathan. I plan to tell him about it as soon as I figure out how."

Charlotte raised her eyebrows. "Chief Turner is not going to be happy with you, either. It's going to be really obvious you're investigating the murder now."

She blew out a sigh. "Yeah. I guess I'll have to deal with both of them."

Before she could say any more, Jonathan trudged up the stairs.

They both turned quiet. He looked at them suspiciously. "What?" he asked.

"So, did you settle on a shoulder tattoo of a woman with big bosoms?" Charlotte cracked.

He gave her an eye roll. "No. I *did* look in the cubicle with Snake's name on it but didn't stare. I was surprised to see how clean and sterile everything is. There was a receptionist down there, and I was told Snake was transferring to Brownsburg and they were no longer making appointments for him here."

"Bet you were disappointed," Francine said.

"Bitterly. They offered me another artist on the spot, but I declined." He looked around. Though it didn't appear anyone was listening, he still seemed to be concerned. "Let's get out of here before anyone asks me again if I want a manicure."

"I need to wait for Hank," Charlotte said. "You go on."

Francine wanted to question Charlotte about her earlier remark that she had learned something from hanging out upstairs, but since she hadn't brought it up again, Francine guessed she wanted to keep it just between the two of them. Perhaps they both had secrets now to keep.

"Really," Charlotte said with a smirk. "You two run along. But

Francine, why don't you stop by my place later? Maybe 4 o'clock? I know we have a lot to talk about."

As Jonathan drove toward Brownsburg, Francine asked him about the phone call he'd had with his business partner Peter. "What was that all about?"

He was quiet for a moment. "You know he's half Vietnamese?"

She knew, of course. Peter and his wife were a part of their circle of friends. Not close, like their neighbors in Summer Ridge, but close enough. "His mom was a Vietnamese war bride, wasn't she? I guess it hadn't occurred to me because he was born here and English is his first language. Why is that important?"

"He must have heard something from the way the nail techs were talking. He asked me a few questions and then had me keep the line open the rest of the time we were there. I need to find out why."

"That sounds ominous."

"I don't mean it to be. It might be as simple as he recognized the dialect and thought his mom might want to connect with them."

She nodded. "I hope so."

"Or maybe it's kismet," he said obliquely. "Maybe we were meant to be there at that specific time. Maybe we just don't know why yet."

Francine's thoughts immediately shifted to Aretha and the job offer. She'd thought it fortunate he wasn't there when it happened. Was this the right time to bring it up, though?

His hand was on the gear shift and Francine caressed it. "I love that about you. You always see things as being connected, like destiny is simply a part of our lives and we need to live with it."

He glanced her way with a wry smile before shifting his eyes back to the road. "With all we have going on, it feels like we have a lot of destiny ahead of us."

Francine squirmed in the seat. She opened her mouth to tell him about the job but stuttered instead.

"What was that?" he asked.

"Nothing," she said.

At twenty minutes before 4:00 Francine walked over to Charlotte's house. She knew Charlotte wanted to pry into how she came to get a job at Tattoo You Two, but it also meant she wanted to discuss the murder and Francine had questions. She wanted to review with Charlotte all the photos from the crime scene in case she'd missed anything. And she wanted to ask about the ink cap Charlotte had inadvertently taken out of the waste basket. Had Charlotte done anything with it yet? Between shopping for a motorcycle and dates with Hank, Francine had her doubts.

Charlotte's house was a single story brick built in the 1970s. The bricks were a reddish color with variants that ran from dark red to bluish red. Shutters on the house were a colonial blue that matched the paint on the garage door and gave it a retro look. Francine thought Charlotte and her deceased husband had been smart in going with a classic color scheme. Even if it were never fully in style again, it would never be out of style.

At first she simply tried the front door. The women often left their doors open for each other, especially if they knew one of them was coming. Charlotte's door, however, was locked. Francine knocked and knocked, but no one answered. She rang the doorbell. Still no answer.

Francine took a couple of steps off the porch and peered through the glass in the front window. No sign of Charlotte. That didn't necessarily mean she wasn't in, because the front window looked into the living room, which Charlotte hardly used.

She's most likely in the kitchen or in the screened-in porch off the back of the house. While it didn't necessarily explain her not answering the door bell, Francine was not ready to panic. She got out her phone.

I know you're in there, Charlotte, she texted. *Answer the door.*

She stepped back onto the porch and waited. Charlotte finally came to the door holding a brandy snifter with a touch of amber liquid in it. Hank was behind her carrying the same. Charlotte wore motorcycle pants and a graphic t-shirt that read "I never dreamed that one day I'd become a cranky old lady, but here I am killing it." She was wigless.

Francine wondered if she'd ever get used to seeing Charlotte with jet black hair.

Hank was dressed in elastic-waisted jeans that needed a good wash and a sleeveless tee revealing beefy arms and shoulders with what Jonathan called "old man hair growth," places where hair had no real reason to grow but did so anyway when one reached old age.

"Oh, hello, Francine," Charlotte said, acting like this was a totally unexpected visit. "C'mon in. Hank and I were just having a bit of cognac."

Francine raised an eyebrow, but opened the screen door and went in. Despite Charlotte's invitation, she now felt an interloper.

15

"Francine, this is Hank," Charlotte said by way of introduction. "Hank, this is my best friend Francine."

"It's nice to meet you," Hank said, shaking her hand. "I've heard a lot about you."

"I'm glad to meet you as well." She declined to say how much she'd heard about him.

"Would you like something to drink?" Charlotte asked, holding up the drink she was carrying. "It's just a bit of cognac to enjoy with cheese and crackers. We were in the library."

The library was a converted bedroom in Charlotte's house. Nearly every wall had floor to ceiling bookshelves from one side to the other, though a desk and liquor cabinet had been wedged in on the west wall. The library was Charlotte's special retreat, one she shared occasionally with Francine. And now, apparently, Hank.

Francine followed them down the hall until they reached the room. To Francine's amazement, the library had been picked up and cleaned. Charlotte usually left partially read books lying open on the chairs and shelves. There was also often a settling of dust on everything. Instead, the room smelled of furniture polish, like the job had just been done that morning. Which, Francine considered, it probably had.

The liquor cabinet had a pull-out wooden shelf, on which was a tray of pre-sliced squares of cheese in three varieties—Colby, white cheddar, and co-jack, Francine guessed, surrounded by water crackers, rectangular whole wheat crackers, and buttery crackers of some kind. Next to it was a bowl of mixed nuts and a few small plates. The whole thing seemed a bit staged, especially for Charlotte, who drank rotgut brandy up until a year ago when she was given a bottle of Prunier cognac. Now she regarded her palette as more sophisticated. *The cheese and cracker tray is a nice addition,* Francine thought. "I'm good with seltzer water, but I will take a few crackers and cheese." She nabbed a plate and selected some cheese and nuts while Charlotte poured fizzy water into a glass with ice cubes and added a slice of lime.

It occurred to Francine she hadn't seen Hank's motorcycle in the driveway, which surprised her. She wondered if it was in the garage. Asking that question, though, would be awkward. She figured Hank had been there since they'd returned from getting his tattoo, but she wondered how long that had been. Probably not more than an hour. Of course, she couldn't let on that she knew where they'd been.

Charlotte sat on her usual apricot recliner. Hank had taken Francine's usual seat, a rocking chair, so she used a high-back wooden chair in a corner. No one spoke. Francine tried to cover up her uncomfortableness by eating, but she soon had finished what she had on her plate. She almost wished she had taken more. The other two seemed to be content to sit.

"How have you been, Hank?" Francine finally asked.

He responded with the obligatory "fine."

"Done any motorcycle rides in the last couple of days?"

He nodded. "Did one out to Greencastle yesterday with the gang. It was mainly to get pizza at Bridges," he said. "They know how to make great pizza."

Francine had heard of it, although she and Jonathan hadn't been there yet. They made good pizza at home, so they tended to eat ethnic foods when they dined out.

Another awkward pause. For someone she knew to be a physical therapist, Hank was surprisingly quiet. All the therapists she knew were quite chatty.

She tried not to stare at his tattoos, but he had a lot of them. Also, his forearm was wrapped in plastic wrap over the place where he'd been tattooed earlier. Odd, she thought. "Is that a wound on your forearm?" she asked, feigning ignorance. "Did you have an accident?"

Hank chuckled. "No, I'm working on a tattoo sleeve for my arm." He displayed his left arm for her. The right was already sleeved. "My tattoo artist laid down another piece of the artwork today. It needs to be bandaged for several hours afterwards to protect it."

"Hank and I were at the Tattoo You parlor in Indianapolis," Charlotte said. "You should go there sometime. They offer manicures and pedicures in addition to tattoos." She showed off her hair. "They have a hair salon, too. I got my hair done there this afternoon."

"So I noticed," she said. "I've never thought of you as the spiky black hair type, but it becomes you."

"I love how she looks without the wig," Hank offered. "I mean, why would you cover up that good head of hair?"

Francine just nodded like she agreed.

"Speaking of tattoos," Charlotte said, "I was just about to show Hank the tattoo design that had been started on Lucas Monet's forearm the night we found him. I thought maybe he'd seen something similar since he's got a lot of tattoos."

Francine had to cover up her surprise. She was there to talk with Charlotte about the photos taken the night of the murder, but hadn't expected her to bring them up with Hank present.

"You make a good point," Francine said, not sure where Charlotte was going with this. "He probably has."

Hank gulped, his eyes darting away from both women. Immediately he regained his composure and gave Charlotte a smile Francine thought looked half-hearted. "Let's see what you've got," he said gamely.

Charlotte pulled her laptop computer out of a drawer in the liquor cabinet and called up the photos. Once she found the best image of the partial tattoo, she passed the computer to Hank. Francine stood up and came behind him while Charlotte leaned over an arm of her chair.

"There's not much here," Hank said, sounding relieved. "Just a few straight lines that look like they might be the beginning of a stylized letter, judging by the angles they're at." He tilted the phone to the left. "Maybe 75 degree angles. Definitely less than 90 degrees. Maybe something was going to be written there."

Francine could see where Hank's imagination had taken him. It could be a letter. But it also could be a symbol. Or an animal, vegetable or mineral, for that matter. But she played along. "If it were a letter, what would it be?"

He squinted at the screen. "My first guess would be a "P" or a "Z."

Maybe a small 'd,' if the bottom of the small d is going to be a square or a rectangle instead of a circle. Probably depends on the type face."

"Does that make you think of a particular tattoo you've seen?" Charlotte inquired.

He shook his head. "There's so little there it could be anything. But let me look through the rest of the photographs."

Hank used his finger to swipe through the photographs taken that night. He stopped on one showing the contents of the waste basket. He stared at it for a while. "You took a photo of the wastebasket," he said, using pinched fingers to enlarge the image. "I see something in there."

"I took photographs of everything," Charlotte answered, a bit defensively.

"Ink caps," Hank said, recognizing them. "I wonder if the police took those or if they got thrown away."

Francine and Charlotte looked at each other, eyes wide. Francine had planned to ask Charlotte about the one she'd inadvertently placed in her pocket the night of the murder, but not with Hank there. It looked like Charlotte didn't want her to ask about it, either.

"Is there a reason?" Charlotte asked Hank.

"Not really. I thought maybe it looked distinctive. I wondered if it were a hexagonal ink cap."

"Would that mean anything?" Francine asked.

"Not definitively," Hank said, backtracking a bit. "It's just an unusual shape. It has its fans, but it's more expensive."

"Did Lucas use them? I understand he was quite successful. He could have afforded them."

"Probably," Hank said. "Yes, it was probably his. I didn't really know Lucas." He handed the computer back to Charlotte. "Looks like you have the crime scene cataloged."

"I'm sure the police photographer was more thorough," Charlotte said modestly. "I didn't have a lot of time. Plus, I was distracted. Francine kept talking to me while she was giving Lucas CPR."

"I needed the distraction," Francine said. "You try giving CPR to a dead man."

None of them spoke for a while after that. Hank knocked back the rest of his cognac. Francine noted that there hadn't been much left in it.

Hank got out of the rocker and selected more cheese and crackers. The crunch of the water crackers was the only sound in the room.

"So, Charlotte, ready for a trip to another motorcycle dealership?" Hank asked, finally filling the silence. Francine looked in alarm at Hank's now-empty snifter. There hadn't been much in it, and now she hoped there hadn't been much cognac at all to begin with.

"That's a surprise," Charlotte said. "I didn't know we were going to do that. Francine just arrived for a visit."

"It's okay," Francine said. "We can catch up later."

"No," Charlotte said. "I've got a better idea. Maybe you can come with us, Francine."

"Me?"

Hank clearly didn't like the idea. "I'm sure Francine wouldn't be interested in motorcycle shopping at all."

Charlotte wrapped her arm around Francine's waist and gave her a meaningful squeeze. "You wouldn't mind if Francine came along, would you, Hank?" she asked.

"Yes, on second thought, I would really like to go," Francine said. "Charlotte's fascination with motorcycles may have rubbed off on me." It was a lie, but it was the best she could do with little warning. "I think I might want to take a test drive myself. I hear Joy did."

Hank blanched. Charlotte noticed his expression. "Francine, this is one for the books! I would love to see you get one, too. Maybe we can start a female Brownsburg motorcycle club. We can call ourselves the Brownsburg Biker Babes. It's okay for her to come, isn't it, Hank?"

His smile was weaker. "The more the merrier," he said.

"Maybe I'd better drive," Francine offered. "We can't take three on Hank's motorcycle, and you've both had a bit to drink."

"Good idea, Francine." Charlotte moved the three empty glasses onto the tray and carried it out to the kitchen, leaving Hank and Francine alone in the library.

Francine was sure Hank wanted to say something to her. Standing a few feet away with his left side to her, she could see his lips pinch together and she watched him flex his fingers nervously behind his back.

But he said nothing, just turned and followed Charlotte out the door and down the hall.

Francine exhaled, not realizing she had been holding her breath. Saying a quick prayer, she left the room as well.

"Where to?" Francine asked once everyone was buckled in. She'd walked back home, nabbed her car keys and purse, and driven the Prius back to Charlotte's. Though she'd told Jonathan where she was going, he'd been in his office absorbed by what she guessed was his special project. He'd said "okay," but she wasn't sure he'd processed her words. She laughed to herself thinking of what he would do when he figured it out.

Hank and Charlotte climbed in the backseat. "I've never sat in the backseat of your Prius before," Charlotte said. "It's kind of cozy."

"You've never sat back there because you tend to get carsick," Francine replied.

Charlotte was dismissive. "Only when you whip around on those curvy roads."

"You won't do that to her, will you?" Hank asked Francine.

"No," Francine assured him. Under Hank's direction, they drove to the west side of Indianapolis and visited a dealership that handled Honda, Yamaha, and Suzuki motorcycles.

She kept an eye on the two of them through the rear view mirror. Though she was becoming convinced Charlotte was suspicious of Hank and was playing him to find out what his game was, she hadn't had a chance to ask her one-on-one. Francine, for sure, didn't trust Hank. "I feel like a chauffeur with the two of you in the back seat," she joked, trying to lighten up the silence. "Do I need to keep watch on you in the rear view mirror?"

"Don't be a prude, Francine," Charlotte said, chuckling.

Francine pulled into the dealership and parked in a visitor slot, taking her time to collect her things. After a deep, meditative breath, she got out. Hank and Charlotte had already exited. Charlotte was scanning the bikes parked out front.

"Hot dog!" she said. "I bet I can find something here. I like the look of what's on display. I wonder what they have inside?"

Francine scanned the lot with much less enthusiasm. *I can't get out of this*, she thought. *I'm going to have to test drive one or more of these things.*

They headed inside the showroom. The salespeople all looked at each other as if to question which one of them might be best suited to handle such a diversely dressed group of older people. An awkward pause later, a forty-ish woman with big hair took up the challenge and approached them. She smiled and looked from one to the other before finally settling on Hank as the one most likely to be motorcycle shopping. She introduced herself as Lynette. "Can I help you?" she asked.

"My two friends here are interested in becoming full-fledged motorcycle riders," Hank said. "I'm hoping you can show them something that will convince them to take the plunge."

"Something used," Charlotte said. "But with good power. I don't want something that just putt-putts around."

Lynette smiled like she was choking back a laugh.

Charlotte ignored her. "What about that Harley over there?" She pointed to a nearby motorcycle in the pre-owned section. Francine thought it looked big, black and menacing. The back tire was enormous.

"That's a Harley V-Rod," Hank said. "I think it would be a little too much bike for you."

"It must weigh over 500 pounds!" Francine added.

Charlotte stamped her foot. "But its size would keep me safe."

"Babe," Hank said, "you just don't get it." He turned to Lynette. "She had an accident recently. Her doctor advised her not to ride for a while, so maybe she and I could look around while you show Francine something." He indicated Francine with a wave of his hand.

Lynette fixed her gaze on her. "What can I show you?"

"It's my first time on a motorcycle," she admitted. "I have no idea what I'm looking for."

Lynette sized her up. "Can you ride a bicycle?"

Francine took offense, though she suspected Lynette had not

intended it to be an insult. She nodded. "My husband and I ride the trails in Plainfield and Indianapolis," she said. "Long rides."

If the saleswoman detected any hostility, she ignored it. "Great," she said. "You'll find riding a motorcycle is similar in balancing, except you don't have to pedal." She had them step outside to the bikes on display there.

"This is a Yamaha TW200," she told Francine. "It's got a higher center of gravity, which is important since you're fairly tall."

"It looks like it might have too much engine," Francine said apprehensively.

"Not really. We find it's a good beginner bike. Give it a try. You may find it easier to control than you think."

Francine approached it stealthily like she was attempting to ride a wild bull. In her mind, though, it looked friendly enough. The frame and fenders were gleaming white and the seat was a cornflower blue.

"It's okay," Lynette said. "You mount it from the left. Just throw your right leg over it like you would a bicycle."

Francine tried to be confident. She successfully mounted it. "You've probably never started a motorcycle before, have you?" asked Lynette.

Francine chewed her lower lip. "I've seen Charlotte start hers."

Lynette ran through a series of instructions. Francine thought she'd gone too fast, but when she tried the electric start on the bike, it worked. By this time, she was fairly confident she knew what to do next. She'd watched Charlotte engage her motorcycle, so she let the clutch out.

Unfortunately she hadn't anticipated how quickly it would engage, and the motorcycle jerked ahead. "Aggghhh!" Francine yelped.

The motorcycle flew across the parking lot in the direction of the retention pond, which was off the end of the asphalt.

"Aggghhh!" shouted Lynette. She started to run after her.

I can do this, I can do this, Francine thought. *Where's the brake?* She gripped the lever on the right front handlebar. Then she remembered Lynette said something about the right front handlebar being for the front brake. Squeezing it might throw her over the top. She lifted her hand off it. Looking up, she saw she was right on the edge of the parking lot.

"Aggghhh! Now what?" She shouted it out loud though she wasn't sure anyone could hear her over the noise of the engine.

She put her foot back as though it were an old-style coaster bike. Then she remembered where the rear brake was. She put her foot back but missed. The motorcycle jumped the curb and landed on the grass.

Francine tried to collect her wits. *I can steer it*, she thought, *I can still steer it*. She piloted the bike to the right and found herself back on the parking lot heading straight for Lynette.

Lynette's eyes widened. She threw her hands in the air and ran toward the dealership, abandoning the idea of pursuing Francine. "NOOOOOO!"

Francine saw that Hank was running toward her. Charlotte was behind him shouting something. She tried to read her lips but the panic in her head was blocking everything out. Charlotte was now desperately flexing the fingers of her left hand, and Francine took that to be a sign. The clutch. Charlotte wanted her to squeeze the clutch on the left handlebar. She did, and she felt the bike slow.

But it still had a lot of forward momentum, and she was headed toward Hank and Charlotte. Now Hank was shouting something and dancing on his left foot as he indicated his right, which he was holding up. As she zipped by him, she thought she heard him say, "Rear brake on right."

Francine reached back with her foot, but if the brake was back there, she missed. Her eyes opened in terror as she zoomed by Charlotte, missing her by inches.

"Try again, Francine!" Charlotte said. Or at least that's what Francine thought. But she was too pre-occupied with missing the pre-owned bikes lined up like dominos just ahead of her.

She steered the bike back around and headed for the pond again. That seemed safer than hitting a row of bikes or the building.

Charlotte and Hank continued waving and shouting directions she couldn't hear.

Francine jumped the curb and again closed in on the pond. She put her foot back once more and finally found the brake. She applied it and then remembered the front brake. She tried not to apply them too hard and was successful at pulling it to a stop before she got too close to the pond. She dismounted quickly, found herself dizzy, lost her balance and rolled down the banks of the retention pond. She slid into the water, not deep enough to be in danger, but enough that she got sopping wet. From the collar of her jean jacket to the soles of her running shoes, everything she was wearing clung to her.

Charlotte did her best to hurry across the lot. Hank took her hand and helped keep her steady. Lynette, having reached the safety of the building, looked back at the bike sitting precipitously at the edge of the water. She joined Charlotte and Hank in heading to the retention pond.

Francine climbed up the bank. "I'm okay, I'm okay," she said, putting her hands out to stop them from rushing at her.

Hank stopped to look at the bike. "Wow. It's not damaged at all! Maybe a little mud smeared here and there, but you did well. Good instincts!"

Lynette righted the bike and examined it. "Darned if you aren't right! This is way better than I expected." She rubbed a big smudge of muck off the shiny black fender. "We'll have to have our Maintenance guys look it over, but I think the bike survived just fine."

Only Charlotte seemed to care about Francine. She hugged her old friend despite the wetness of her outfit and the mowed grass clippings stuck to her. "I was so worried you'd crash."

"Not sure I didn't," Francine said, shaking. She started to cry.

Two salesmen who had witnessed the event came out carrying towels. They handed them to her. She slipped off the wet jean jacket and wrapped a towel around her shoulders.

A customer rode his motorcycle over. He excitedly showed the screen of his phone to one of the salesman. "Caught the whole thing on camera," he whispered, though Francine was still able to hear it. "This will go viral!"

Francine sighed and shook her head, but she was too emotionally drained to care.

On the bright side, she was alive. And she'd been viral before.

16

Hank had his driver's license with him, and Francine allowed him to drive them home in her car.

"I know it's going to take you some time to get over this," he told her, "but you need to get back on that horse and ride it. If you don't, you'll never know that you have good instincts. You *can* ride a motorcycle."

Francine sniffed. She wore a "Hot Leathers" midriff t-shirt that read, "Spank me, it's the only way I'll learn," given to her by Lynette, while she clutched her wet t-shirt and felt miserable in the rest of wet clothing. She leaned against the passenger side door of her Prius. "I just want to ride a regular bike again. I don't care about motorcycles."

"I bet you've got some dandy bruises on your legs," Charlotte said from the backseat. "You should probably let them heal up before you go riding again."

Francine tried not to whimper. Now that she'd calmed down, she was embarrassed, tired, and hurting. She looked forward to soaking in a hot bath and taking something for the pain. And maybe having a margarita.

She presumed Jonathan was still working at home and would take care of her. Or maybe she hoped he wouldn't be there, because he would surely not approve of her meddling in Charlotte's life to the point of riding a motorcycle to the brink of disaster.

Hank drove back to Francine's house. Jonathan was there. Once Francine was inside and headed up the stairs, Charlotte briefed him on what happened. When he scurried up the stairs to look after her, Hank and Charlotte walked back toward Charlotte's place.

Jonathan drew the bath Francine requested, helped her get her wet clothes off, and eased her into the jet tub.

She breathed in through her nose and exhaled through her mouth. *Think happy thoughts.* Then she noticed the scent in the room. It was perfect. "You put some lavender bath salts in the water, didn't you?"

"Aromatherapy 101," he replied. "And I'll be back with the drinkable kind of therapy in a few minutes."

He closed the door behind him. She heard him pad down the stairs.

Francine told herself not to worry about Hank and whether he was on the up-and-up. If Charlotte had the wherewithal to shout instructions and save her from near disaster in a time of panic, surely he wouldn't be able to put one over on her. She let her mind wander until Jonathan knocked on the door and entered. He set a margarita on the edge of the whirlpool tub near her hand.

He had made one for himself, too. "Cheers," he said, and held his glass out. She picked hers up and clinked his. They both took sips.

"Just so you know, Charlotte told me everything."

Francine closed her eyes. She tried to ignore her stiff joints and concentrate on the feel of the warm jets of water swirling around her. "Is there really a video of my ride?" She opened one eye to see his reaction.

"Haven't seen one, but you know I'm not a fan of social media." He sipped his drink. "Did you get any new information?"

She swished her toes in the water against the back of the tub. "When I first got there, I thought we were going to look at the photos Charlotte took the night of the murder. We did, but with Hank there, it was kind of stilted. There were things I wanted to say that I couldn't. Then Charlotte asked me to come along when they went motorcycle shopping. I did that only because I wanted to keep Hank from getting his hooks into Charlotte. But I think she's wise to him. I don't think I need to worry."

"Good thing you didn't kill yourself doing it, then." He sat on the edge of the tub. "Did you learn anything more from the photos?"

"I'm still wondering about the design being tattooed on Lucas's forearm when he was killed. Charlotte asked Hank if he'd seen anything like it, and he said there was too little there to make any kind of judgment. But he thought it might be the first letter in a word. Maybe a P, Z, or small d."

Jonathan rolled his eyes. "Well that narrows it down."

Francine gave him a serious look. "But it does, really. We did a reverse search on the image yesterday but came up with too many possibilities. We didn't know how to filter the results. If we presume it's a letter, we might be able to narrow it."

"I guess it's worth a try. We just have to hope someone has used that font before in a tattoo and then thoughtfully provided a photo of it on the internet."

Francine could hear the skepticism in his voice, but she wasn't worried. She could always do it herself if he truly wasn't interested. "One other thing that happened … Hank paged through the photos on Charlotte's iPad. I got the impression he was looking for something. He fixated on what was in the trash can in Lucas's office, and then made a remark about the ink cap. Here's the thing about that. Charlotte *has* the ink cap. She picked it up before the police got there and ended up carrying it out. "

"She tampered with evidence?" He sounded incredulous.

"It's not like that! Well, it's kind of like that. She was wearing gloves so she wouldn't leave fingerprints on anything, and she picked it out of the wastebasket, dropped it, then picked it up again just as the police and EMTs arrived. I think she didn't want anyone to know she'd touched it, so she slipped it in her pocket but never found a way to put it back in the waste basket."

"But she still has it?"

"As far as I know. That was one of the things I wanted to discuss with her, but I didn't want to bring it up with Hank there. And then Hank said something about the ink cap, and Charlotte gave me a look that told me not to bring it up."

"What did he say?"

"He wondered if the police had taken them or if they'd been thrown away. When we questioned him further, he said he saw they were hexagonal, which was unusual and expensive."

Jonathan sipped his margarita and gave her a puzzled look. "Is it too much of a coincidence? Is that what you're thinking?"

"Yes and no. As hard as it is for me to think that Hank could possibly know anything about Lucas's murder, I'm starting to see a possible connection between our presence at the murder scene and Hank's interest in dating Charlotte. We were described as being spotted leaving the murder scene by a reporter the next day. That report never got much traction, but it was on the air. Anyone who watched that news segment would know who we were."

"But Hank came across Charlotte only because she had an accident."

"That's where I have difficulty with this. Could Hank have been party to that? Charlotte was forced off the road. We all joke about how Charlotte is an accident waiting to happen on that motorbike, but the truth is, the accident wasn't her fault."

"That's a scary idea. Do you think someone was trying to kill her?"

Francine sat up in the tub. "Maybe. Or maybe they just wanted her to have an accident that would put her out of commission for a while, and she was more skilled on the motorcycle than they thought."

"So, Hank's motorcycle gang came along to either call in a death or a serious accident, but since neither one happened, they improvised, and Hank started a relationship with Charlotte?"

"It feels like too much of a conspiracy, and you know I don't go in for conspiracy theories. But ... it's a possible scenario. I don't think we should disregard it."

Jonathan nodded. "I think you should stay close to Charlotte when she's with Hank."

She sighed. It would mean more awkward situations. "Fortunately she's suspicious of him now. At least I think she is. I haven't directly asked her that question."

"She went home with Hank. Should you call her?"

Francine swirled the liquid in her glass, thinking it over. "If he's with her when I call, it might raise his suspicions. If he isn't, then it doesn't matter. Let's wait until after dinner. Hopefully he'll be gone by then and I can find out when she's planning to see him next. If he's still there, at least I'll have put some time between when I saw them last." She settled back into the tub. "Has Peter called back about why he wanted to hear the nail techs talking?"

"I called him and asked. He said he wanted to check on a couple of things first, when he got time. He's busy working on the same project I am. He said he'd get back with me."

"So he wasn't alarmed by what he'd heard?"

"Guess not."

Peter was working on the same hot project, huh. That seemed unusual. Of late, anyway—at least since Jonathan had sold him controlling interest. She wondered if Peter had been the one to ask Jonathan to leave the conference and come back to help. He hadn't directly said. Briefly she worried it was business-related, not client related. Surely he would be able to talk about it if it were just business, though.

She put the notion out of her head. "What about Lucas's sister and her accounting firm?"

"What about them?"

"I just wondered if you'd done any investigation."

He paused as if debating what to say, if anything. "You told me Joy'd thought Cayman and Lawman hadn't had the account very long. I confirmed that. They've only had it a year or so."

"Does that mean anything to you?"

"Not really. Tattoo You went from one legitimate accounting firm to another. It's not unusual for clients to switch firms. You know that. My firm's lost and won different accounts over the years."

"But what if the former agency knew something illegal was going on there and decided to resign the account?"

He stood up. "I'm worried that your mind might be working overtime, trying to make connections where there aren't any."

"You've told me before there are loopholes in accounting laws. Could an accounting firm make a client look legitimate without breaking any laws?"

"They could, but I would think an accountant at the firm would have to turn a blind eye to suspicious practices. That would have to be directed by someone at the top."

"I rest my case. Gabriella is a partner. What if the former agency resigned the account for that very reason, and now Cayman and Lawman knows, and what if it cost Gabriella her brother's life?"

Jonathan polished off his margarita. "Charlotte is rubbing off on you. I'll get dinner going. Stay as long as you need in the tub."

"The water's getting cold. I'll be down in a little bit."

She took a few cleansing breaths while she heard Jonathan banging about in the kitchen. She thought about what he'd said. He *was* right. Charlotte was rubbing off on her. The old Charlotte, at least. She wondered about the current Charlotte, seemingly amorous and deep into motorcycle riding. Was she as suspicious of Hank as Francine thought? Would she have the same old enthusiasm for investigating a murder? What was she doing at this very moment? Was Hank still with her?

Later that evening, with Jonathan upstairs in his office working, Francine called her. No answer. Knowing she had no right to pry into Charlotte's affairs, especially after this afternoon's escapade, she left a voicemail message asking to her to return the call when she got a chance.

If she hadn't heard from Charlotte by the next afternoon, she resolved to take drastic measures.

Jonathan crawled into bed very late that night, around 2:30. Francine knew because she'd tossed and turned in bed until then, not really asleep. In addition to her bruises, she was haunted by the idea she would be starting her job at Tattoo You Two the next day and she still hadn't told Jonathan. Did he know something was up? She suspected he did.

Without turning on a light, Jonathan quietly stripped down to underwear and settled into the mattress. She breathed in his scent, a combination of Polo fragrance, now faint, combined with the faded perspiration of a day's worth of activities. She wanted to nestle into his embrace, but there remained a tension in her, generated by his reticence to tell her about his work, and her own uncertainty to reveal the job she'd taken.

She rolled over so she was facing the right side of the bed, which was his. Though there wasn't much light, she could tell his eyes were open, looking in her direction.

"I'm glad you're finally here," she said.

"Did I wake you? I tried not to." In the dimness, she heard him more than saw him. His voice was deep, clear, and after so many years of marriage, comforting. She could feel the tension leaving her body. She scooted up next to him and put her hand across his abdomen, trying to hug him.

"How's the project going?"

"Okay. Not done yet."

"You were up really late. Must be important, especially if both you and Peter are working on it."

He shifted onto his right side and pulled her close. "You want to talk?"

"Do you?"

He hesitated. "What about?"

She kissed him. "About secrets. Mine and yours."

He kissed her back. "I'd rather talk about something else. Or perhaps do something else."

She could feel his passion coming forward. "I don't think this is the right time for that."

"Mmmm. Too bad. I'm afraid the kind of talk you want to bring up would be detrimental for sleep. If we both don't end up satisfied, one or both of us will be awake all night."

"I'm already thinking I might be awake all night."

He kissed her again. And sighed. "I don't want that for you or for me. You start." He rubbed his hand down her back. It was a firm touch, not soft and sexy. Reassuring, in his way.

"Okay." Francine took a moment to compose her thoughts. She'd run through some scenarios earlier in the evening mentally rehearsing how the talk would proceed, but they all involved morning and breakfast. That it was happening now in the dark threw her.

"Here's the thing. I have something to confess. I know you're not going to like it. But I don't like that you're keeping some things from me. So I could just *not* tell you and that would put us in a stalemate. Tit for tat. But it's not good for our relationship, or for either of us, that I feel this way."

Jonathan pulled her close again and gave her a soft kiss. Tender and caring. "I understand and I agree. But I'm not quite ready to tell you what I have going on. When this is over, I promise I'll tell you everything, some of which will likely surprise you. Not in a marriage-jeopardy kind of way—I haven't been unfaithful, nothing like that—but you'll be shocked I'm pretty sure. And I'm okay with you keeping your secret until then. Deal?"

This was totally not going the way she envisioned. She'd just been given permission *not* to tell him that she was working at Tattoo You Two. "You're good with that, not knowing anything about the secret I'm keeping?"

"I'm willing to bet it has to do with Lucas Monet's death, since that seems to be your current obsession. And if it is, it's still okay."

She let out a big sigh of relief. "I can live with that. How long do you think you'll be keeping your secret?"

"Only a few more days."

She wasn't sure if she'd know enough within a few days to be ready to quit her job after revealing her secret, but given that *his* was going to be a shocker—whatever that meant—she figured she could play it by ear. "That soon? I may ask you to go first."

She was close enough to see him grin. "So that you can decide whether to tell me yours?" he said. "No way. You have to reveal yours at that time, too."

She took her right hand from around his waist and put it up to his face. She made a single caress down the right side, feeling the stubble of his nearly day-old beard. "I need you to go first so I can decide *how* to tell you my secret."

"How, not if?"

"Yes."

"I'll go first, then. This must be good."

She smirked. "It might be considered a shocker. Maybe."

"Well, then, we both should sleep good tonight."

Francine's relief at being given permission to work at Tattoo You Two, even though Jonathan had no idea that was it, made her whole body relax. And her heart soar. He was such a good soulmate. "We could do something that would make you sleep very well," she said. "Are you interested?"

He snuggled in close and nuzzled her neck. "Mmm hmm."

In her very best Mae West imitation, Francine said, "Is that a pistol in your pocket, or are you happy to see me?"

"It's a long barrel rifle," he answered.

"So it is!" she said, "so it is."

The next morning there was no talk of secrets, much to Francine's relief and, she guessed, Jonathan's as well. They mostly talked about the weather and dinner plans. Though he said he would go to the office and probably work late again tonight, he also said he'd be home for dinner the next night and that they should go out. Francine suggested one of their favorites, a well-loved local Brownsburg restaurant, Boulder Creek. She said she'd make reservations.

Joy's appointment with Cass Dehoney to get her "Roy" tattoo was at ten o'clock. With school out for the summer, Cass was apparently making some morning appointments. When Joy offered to pick her up, Francine quickly agreed. She'd had enough adventures driving the motorcycle the day previous.

Joy is as perky as ever, Francine thought as her friend drove them to the tattoo parlor. Joy conducted an enthusiastic, in-depth commentary on the latest national news she'd seen on Good Morning America, pausing only for a sip of coffee from a thermal mug. *She'd make a fine morning anchor*, Francine thought. But she also worried Joy's chattiness was covering up an underlying nervousness.

"Have you given any thought as to what you want the tattoo to look like?" Francine asked.

Joy gave her a sideways glance. "I want it to say 'Roy.' How complicated is that?"

Francine thought of all the different typefaces that could be used, but given Joy's sudden defensiveness, she just shrugged. "Not very, I guess." She'd let Cass ask those questions.

The shop had just opened when they arrived. The owner, whom Francine had not yet met, was manning the store. He was short, spoke with a heavy accent, and was dressed in a lightweight tropical shirt with pockets and vertical patterns on both sides. *I'd freeze in this air conditioning if I wore something like that,* Francine thought, glad she'd brought along a summer sweater. If he knew she was the new afternoon manager, he didn't say anything so she didn't either. He'd find out when she came back after lunch. Joy told him they had an appointment with Cass and he ushered them back.

Cass had Joy sit in the chair she would use to do the tattooing. "Well this is excitin'," Cass said in her southern Hoosier dialect. "Here you went and caught the bouquet at my weddin', and now you're gettin' your fiancée's name tattooed on your shoulder. I'm thrilled you asked me to do it."

Joy smiled weakly. "It does seem appropriate, doesn't it?"

Cass had an album of tattoo designs open on the top of a waist-level four-drawer cabinet. Her cubicle was clean and sterile, with no clutter on any of the surfaces. A large framed advertisement for the temporary tattoo business Francine knew Cass had inherited from Lucas dominated the wall opposite the door.

"Y'all got any idea what you want the tattoo to look like? I got a book of designs I've done or would love to do. Y'all are free to look at it if you'd like." She handed Joy the open book. It reminded Francine of the book Snake had been looking at the other day, the one he'd seemed secretive about. Not the same, but similar.

Joy paged through the first couple of sheets. "Thanks, but these are so elaborate. I really just want his name tattooed on my shoulder."

Cass nodded. "Okay. Let's have a look." She rolled her own chair over next to where Joy sat in the center of the cubicle and took hold of the sleeve on her right side. "Do y'all mind if I slip this up?"

"No, go ahead."

She ran her hands over Joy's thin shoulder as though evaluating it. Francine thought immediately of a nurse preparing to give a patient a shot. "I'm hopin' he don't have a long name," she said.

Joy chuckled. "His name is Roy."

"Ah, yes, I remember now from the weddin'." She nodded her head as she said it. "And yours is Joy. How cute!" Then she seemed to rethink that. "Or do you *not* think it's cute?"

"It's never been cute," Joy said. "But that's the reality of it. Those are our names."

Cass moved quickly to something else. "Have you considered addin' a design to the name? I've got some dandies here. Or maybe have both your name and his? Sort of a "Joy-heart-Roy kind of thing? I could give you a deal."

"Ick. No. Just 'Roy.'"

"How about the font you want the name written in?"

Her forehead wrinkled. "I never considered that. Though, I guess without realizing it, I had something in mind."

"Great! Can you describe it?"

"Roy's been in law enforcement all his life. He's from Parke County. I think of him in the way you might think of John Wayne in "True Grit."

Cass cocked her head to the side. "Who? What movie?" She pulled out her phone to google it.

Francine and Joy looked at each other. "Must be that age thing," Joy said.

Meanwhile, Cass pulled up a poster of the True Grit movie. She looked at Joy curiously. "Does he have an eye patch?"

"Let me see that," Joy said. She handed her the phone. Joy looked at the poster. "Okay, I must be thinking of a different movie. He wears a Stetson, though. Didn't have it on at your wedding. I made him leave it in the truck. Thought it wouldn't be appropriate."

Cass laughed. "Well, it would'a been just fine."

"I realized it when we got in, but he was okay without it."

"I'm thinkin' I have a design somewhere with a cowboy hat in it." She took the phone and the design book back from Joy. "Let me find it for ya."

Francine could tell Joy was getting impatient. "Really, I don't want to complicate this," Joy said.

Cass found what she was looking for and showed it to her. "A hat, a lasso, and his name. It's not complicated at all."

Joy's eyes lit up. "I could go this way. But I don't like the font. Looks too much like what you'd see over a saloon. He's not that kind of cowboy, and I'm not that kind of girlfriend. Do you have any other fonts?"

"How about this one?" She flipped the page. "Sort of a vintage

"Wanted" poster typeface."

Joy examined it. "I like it a lot, but I wish I didn't know that font was used for criminals."

Francine laughed. "You have no sense of whimsy when it comes to this."

"If it was going to be permanently on your shoulder, you'd be picky too. What if he doesn't like it?"

"He will love it because it's your shoulder it's on; trust me," Francine said.

Joy turned to Cass. "Can you do it in one sitting, because I don't want to have to generate the courage to come back."

Cass cracked a smile. "Still a bit nervous, huh? Not to worry. It's simple. We can do it in one sittin'. But I may want you to come back so I can check on it."

Joy took a deep breath. "Okay." She twisted her head toward Francine. "You promise you'll stay with me?"

"No worries there."

She turned back to Cass. "Can I take a Valium? Francine can drive me home."

"No." Cass sounded definite about that. "I'm not sure about the health risks with valium exactly, but alcohol and some drugs thin the blood, so I don't tattoo clients who're under the influence of anything. Period. It's safer that way." Cass pulled in a folding chair from another office so Francine would have somewhere to sit.

"Is it illegal?" Francine asked.

"Not illegal, but a reputable tattoo artist won't do it. Lucas, my mentor, taught me not to allow it, which is kind of ironic."

"Ironic in what way?"

"He hated needles. He had a skin condition that made him very sensitive to pain. So he was more sympathetic than me. I think he tended to look the other way. If someone were obviously drunk, he wouldn't, but if they were, shall we say, 'medicated,' he would. He medicated himself on the few occasions he got a real tattoo."

Wait! Francine thought. *Lucas couldn't take the pain of needles? But he was being tattooed when he died. Did that mean he was medicated? If so, who supplied that medication, and how much?*

17

Francine cleared her throat. "It looked to me like Lucas had been tattooed or maybe was even *being* tattooed when he died. So you're saying he must have taken something to stop the pain?"

Cass was at her computer preparing a thermal fax image of the tattoo Joy had selected, but Francine's question stopped her. She sat back in her seat and thought a moment. She looked at Francine. "I gotta say I can't imagine that he *didn't*. Probably a low dose Xanax or something."

Joy tsked. "And here I thought all tattoo artists were heavily tattooed. I guess maybe all I saw were his forearms, but it looked to me like he had a lot of them."

Cass continued to speak hesitantly. "So, here's a little secret about Lucas. He was a really great tattoo artist, but most'a his own tattoos were faked. Very few involved needles. Mostly they involved temporary ink."

Francine went silent as she processed that information. She knew he'd had the temporary tattoo business going, but Cass hadn't told her how that had come about. Now she could guess at it.

Joy, however, was surprised. "Which of the tattoos were real?"

"A few of the ones ever'one could see, like on his forearms. The ones you might expect. 'Cause of the pain, he could only manage a little at a time. I think he was embarrassed about that."

"So how does a temporary tattoo work? Is it like a decal?" Joy asked. Francine wondered if Joy was having second thoughts and might want a temporary one.

"Yep. You have to prepare your skin before you apply it, but then you peel back the design, apply it, wait a certain amount of time, and then pull it off. It only lasts maybe three weeks, but it looks pretty authentic, especially after it darkens. That takes about 24 hours."

Joy was now in reporter mode. "How did Lucas get away with having those temporary tattoos? Didn't his friends notice?"

Cass shrugged. "I dunno how many knew for sure. You can get away with long sleeve t-shirts and jeans most of the year, which he did. He didn't show exposed skin 'cept in summer. Then he'd use the same designs over and over again, reapplying 'em in the same spots. At least, that's what I figure."

"They must have been good temporaries, then," Joy said. "Or else his friends didn't care."

"I can't speak for how many knew, but if there were any, I don't think they cared. You either accept a friend for who he is or ya find other friends. Yeah, in some ways he was a fake, but he was successful, he had lots of satisfied clients, and he was kind. Very kind, especially to me."

"I understand he was generous, too," Joy said.

Francine wondered where Joy got that. Did she know about him leaving the business to Cass? Or did it come from her investigation into his death? Or maybe Roy told her something she hadn't shared yet.

Cass seemed taken aback. "In what way?"

Joy answered quickly. "Maybe I meant it more as a question?"

Cass studied her for a moment and apparently decided not to respond. "Are ya feeling calmer now? Ready to get that tattoo done?"

"Uh, sure. Let's do it."

At first Francine found the process interesting. Cass shaved the area with a disposable razor and applied the thermal fax image to the meatiest part of Joy's shoulder she could find. Next she created a traceable outline of the tattoo. The second the needle was placed on Joy's shoulder, though, Francine got a little queasy. She looked away, thinking about the incomplete tattoo that was on Lucas's forearm. She again remembered the sketchbook Snake had shoved in a drawer in the office he'd taken over from Lucas. She wondered if there might be something there that would tie all this together.

"Joy, you seem to be doing all right, so I'm going to step out for a little bit," she said.

Neither Cass nor Joy said anything, so she beat a hasty retreat into the hallway. She looked around, saw no one near Snake's cubicle, and slipped in. She left the light off in the hopes she'd attract no attention.

The sketchbook was still in the drawer. While the cover didn't have Lucas's name on it, the first section was labeled for temporary tattoo designs. There were lots of those pages.

Francine sat on the edge of the reclining chair for clients and opened the book wide. In the back part of the book someone had placed small orange sticky notes on the top of select pages. A glance back into the drawer revealed a matching pad of sticky notes, leading her to believe it was Snake who'd marked the pages. She checked them first. The pattern was discernable right away. The sketches all started with some kind of hate tattoo, and the progressive drawings showed how Lucas intended to cover them with something beautiful.

She heard footsteps in the hall and panicked. She shoved the sketchbook back in the drawer but it went in whopper jawed and she couldn't get it closed. She scurried out of the office leaving the drawer halfway open. The footsteps turned out to be a woman who saw her rush out but other than looking startled, turned into the hair salon area. Nervous, Francine returned to Snake's office, poked the sketchbook until settled into the drawer, and then nudged the drawer closed. She zipped back out and into Cass's office.

Joy looked up when she entered. "This isn't bad at all," she told Francine. "I can feel it, but it's not painful."

Francine took a seat. She did her best not to look as guilty as she felt, though she was pretty sure neither Joy nor Cass had any idea where she'd been. "I'm glad," she said.

"I guess I didn't need a valium."

"Told ya," Cass said, smiling. "The new tattoo machines make it a lot more comfortable for the clients. No more need to be like sailors, who used to get drunk and then end up with tattoos they regretted."

Francine had thought all along that's the only way people got tattoos. They were drunk and for some reason it seemed like a good idea. She would have to have a *lot* to drink, way more than she ever did, to have those kinds of thoughts.

"So, if a client regrets a tattoo," Francine asked, "can you remove it?"

"I'm gonna switch to a different color ink now," Cass told Joy, pulling back and cleaning the needle. She threw the old ink cap in the trash can. Something about the ink cap caused Francine to stare at it. Then she studied the other ink caps Cass was using. They were all hexagonal in shape. Why had she not noticed that before?

"Erase it, no. These things are fairly permanent. There're ways to "remove" tattoos, but they're actually *more* painful than gettin' a tattoo in the first place. It requires pullin' off layers and layers of epidermis until it's gone. Or at least as 'gone' as it's gonna be. By the time it becomes faint, most people have had enough. Sometimes they cover it up with a different tattoo at that point."

"Could they skip the removal process and just cover a tattoo with a different one?" Francine asked, thinking again about the book she'd just seen in Snake's office.

"Yep. Always an option."

Joy watched as Cass loaded brown ink into the machine. "Do you do tattoo removals?" she asked.

"Removals, no. I saw Lucas do a few."

"Are there artists who specialize in that?"

"I can't think of any. In fact, I'd be hard pressed to think of any artist to send a client to for a removal, at least around here. Now that Lucas is gone." She choked up at the word 'gone,' but recovered.

Francine saw this as an opportunity to get back to what she'd just seen in Snake's office. "Did Lucas do cover ups? It sounds like he was incredibly talented to be able to do so many different things with tattoos."

Cass continued to focus on inking the letters in Joy's tattoo, but she nodded. "Yeah, he did some cover-ups."

The answer was curt. Francine took that to mean she wasn't going to discuss it further. She knew she'd been asking Cass a lot of nosy questions. At least she'd gotten confirmation that Lucas did cover-ups.

The discarded hexagonal ink cap in the trash got her attention again. She decided to risk more questions. "I'm curious about ink caps. Are they all the same?"

"Why do ya ask?"

"The ones you're using just look fancy."

"Well, ink caps all serve the same function, so yeah, they're all alike. The cheapest ones have the same basic round design. I like these hexagonal ones 'cause you can link 'em together."

"Why would that be an advantage?"

"If the design requires a lot of color changes or if the palette has a lot of color gradients, you might want 'em together so you can easily see which one you're usin' and which one you're switchin' to."

Francine pointed to the caps Cass was using. "Are they more expensive?"

Cass scooted back and rolled her shoulders. "Yeah. I probably wouldn't 'a started out on these, but Lucas used 'em. He gave 'em to me for a birthday present."

Francine didn't know what else to say. She'd have liked to go back into Snake's office but wasn't sure her nerves could take a second time.

It didn't take long for Joy's tattoo to be finished. Cass gave her a handheld mirror to see how it looked. Joy's face lit up. "That looks so good! It's exactly what I'd hoped for."

Cass smiled. "It's just the right size for your shoulder, too. Roy should be honored that you had this done for him." She applied ointment to the tattoo and wrapped it in clear plastic wrap.

When Joy went up front to pay for the tattoo, Francine hung back. "In your opinion, could Lucas have been tattooing himself the night he died?"

Cass snorted. "No way. I've heard of a few artists doin' it, but workin' one-handed, ya can't be sure you'd get a good result. And as touchy as he was about needles and pain ..." She shook her head.

"Okay. So it had to be someone else."

"Don't see any way around it."

"Did you get a look at the tattoo that was being put on his arm?"

"The police showed it to me. There wasn't much to go on, I'm afraid."

"So you don't have any idea what it might have been?"

She blew out a breath. "I'll tell ya what I told 'em. I can't describe exactly why it gives me this feelin', but when I look at it, I'd say it was gang-related."

Francine's eyes opened wide. "Was he in a gang?"

"Nah. That's where it gets weird. Not only was he *not* in a gang, he was secretly covering up hate tattoos. For free. Takin' something ugly and makin' it beautiful. When Joy asked earlier about him bein' generous, I thought maybe she knew."

"Knew what?" Joy asked, entering the cubicle from paying her bill.

"Oh, nothin'," Cass said.

"All done?" Francine asked Joy. She nodded in response.

"One last thing before ya leave, Francine," Cass said. "Eric asked me to tell ya Dr. Eisenbarger would be callin'. He has some questions about the night Eric was shot. He'd like to talk about what you saw happen and what you did to save him."

Francine felt her heart thud. That was one call she'd avoid as long as possible.

At lunchtime Francine checked her voicemail and found no response from Charlotte, so she called her again. Charlotte answered but was evasive. Francine wondered if that meant Hank was with her. If he was, had he spent the night? Francine knew she had no right to know and didn't ask. Charlotte suggested she call back later. Francine reminded her she had to go to work in the afternoon. They agreed to talk the next morning.

So Francine found herself eating alone. Not that she ate much. She nibbled on a few crackers and had a bit of cheese with them. The butterflies in her stomach were whirling too much for her to be hungry. *Nervous about starting the new job,* she admitted to herself. It'd been eight years or so since she'd worked her last shift as a nurse. But it wasn't the *start* of the job that concerned her; it was the job itself. She didn't really want it. She had an ulterior motive for taking it. *What if this is all a big mistake? What if it gets dangerous?*

She tried to quell the butterflies. *It's a nail salon and hair studio, for* heaven's sake. Yes, there's a tattoo business the place is named for, but it's clean and sterile. It's not like it's a seedy business. And Cass is a friend—well, kind of—and she's working there. How dangerous could it be?

She tried hard to wipe from her mind the fact that Lucas Monet had been killed there.

Hey, I can always quit, she reasoned.

A box of Girl Scout cookies she'd bought from a neighborhood scout sat on the edge of the bar. Remembering she'd wanted to bring something for the technicians, she picked it up along with her purse. She drove to the Tattoo You Two parlor and gathered her wits before entering. She tried to put on the supreme confident air she'd adopted when she'd come in the day after the murder to get another look at the crime scene. Of course, that had been what had got her into this mess, when she'd been mistaken for a manager and then got an offer from Aretha.

This time, I am a manager, she thought, trying to buoy her confidence.

She took a deep breath and entered. The owner was standing in the reception area looking like he was waiting for someone. Francine took a little more time to study him now. Like the technicians, he was of Asian descent, but whereas their facial features were thin, his were smooth and rounded. She guessed he'd been eating an American diet for some time. She introduced herself and they shook hands. His name was Quan.

"I thought you might be new manager," Quan said, with the stilted speech of someone for whom English was not their native language. "Aretha said you were tall and white and had fingernails in atomic tangerine."

Francine glanced down at her nails and chuckled internally. Her nails had been done yesterday at the original Tattoo You parlor. Aretha must have noticed them when they met briefly.

"She will be here in half hour to teach you duties and show you around. In meantime, I will have you fill out forms." He suddenly seemed to remember something. "Were you not here this morning?" He narrowed his eyes in a puzzled manner.

"I was. My friend Joy McQueen was getting a tattoo from Cass Dehoney, and she needed some support."

He continued to look bewildered. "But Cass is very good, and it not painful."

"My friend knows that now, but it was her first time getting a tattoo."

He nodded mechanically and ushered her into the back room where she'd had her first discussion about the job with Aretha. He took a seat behind the desk and pulled out paperwork. "These are forms to fill out. Government must be satisfied," he said, handing her a pen.

Francine put the box of cookies on the counter and looked them over. Quan gave a puzzled glance at the box. She smiled. "Thought I'd bring something for the technicians. They look like they could use a treat."

Quan scowled at her. "They do not need cookies. Sweets bad for them. Not adjusted to American diet yet." He thumped a finger on the forms. "Please fill these out."

Francine was taken aback but did as he asked. Just about the time she'd finished the forms, showed all the appropriate identifications, and answered his questions about her work history, Aretha arrived.

Quan turned her over to Aretha to finish orientation and hurried out without saying goodbye.

"He's brusque like that," Aretha said. "So's his wife. They always open the place so you'll see one or the other every time you arrive."

She took Francine out into the shop to introduce her around.

As Francine expected, almost all of the employees spoke broken English. The three nail technicians and two hair stylists had taken English names, but Francine couldn't remember who was who.

Cass was there, of course, and the second tattoo artist she was introduced to was Snake.

"He transferred from our Indianapolis studio," Aretha explained. "He has a good clientele and they will no doubt follow him here."

"No doubt," Francine said. "And actually, we've met."

"Yeah, after Lucas died," Snake said, shaking her hand. "I probably won't be here much during the day when you're here. My clientele comes mostly at night."

Aretha was having none of it. "You may be at your busiest then, but contractually you're to be here by 4:30 the days you work."

"Yeah, yeah," he said, "I have a few clients that find it easier to make afternoon appointments. I came in early today to gather up the rest of Lucas's stuff." Francine could see he was sorting items into boxes stacked in a corner.

Leaving Snake's office, Aretha led Francine to the front office. They went over procedures, how to book appointments, how to record payments, and how to manage the flow of customers to the nail technicians. The hair stylists had their own space and managed customers without help, though the hair salon's waiting area could be shared with the clients of the tattoo artists, if there was a backup.

Aretha seemed to have wrapped up all she was going to say. "Let's get you started," she said. "I'll be around if you have questions, but I find people learn best by doing. I won't hover over you, I'm going to work in the back. There's a bit of bookkeeping that needs to be done, so I'll take care of that."

Francine hurried to reply since Aretha had brought up the one thing she was hoping to see—the books. "Is bookkeeping something I'll need to worry about? I'm pretty good with figures, just in case. I'm treasurer for a number of organizations I belong to."

Aretha looked at her suspiciously. Francine immediately regretted bringing it up.

"Perhaps in time," Aretha said dryly. "We wouldn't want to throw a lot at you at once."

Francine interpreted that to mean that they didn't quite trust her yet. *Well, if I were in their shoes, I guess I wouldn't either. I'd want the employee to prove herself first.*

The afternoon flew by. Fortunately there were no troubling clients, which was a blessing. After a few false starts that needed Aretha's help, she was able to record the transactions, most of which were credit cards. The hardest part was keeping everything straight, who was next with manicures and pedicures and which technician they went to.

It didn't take her long to figure out that, just as she suspected, the technicians knew English better than they let on. They still avoided speaking to her unless necessary, and when they did, it was in broken English. But they definitely understood the language, and they understood the business, too. If she asked, they could tell her which customer was next and who among them was next up to provide service.

A phone call came through to make an appointment with Snake. "I need help!" she called back to Aretha while covering the receiver.

"Be there in a minute," Aretha said, but then hustled to the receptionist's desk in half that time.

"What do I do with this appointment call?" she asked. "Do I forward it back to his office or write it down and take it back later?" She held the phone out to Aretha with her hand still over the receiver.

"Sorry, forgot to cover that. We have his schedule on the computer."

Francine spoke to the man on the other end of the line. "Could you please hold? I'm new, and I'm doing this for the first time."

Meanwhile, Aretha's hands flew over the keyboard and Snake's schedule appeared on the screen. The booking was early in the evening. Snake's schedule was light, and while she couldn't fit him in at exactly the time he wanted, she was able to make it work to his satisfaction. He thanked her and hung up.

"So where is his schedule?" Francine asked Aretha. "I didn't see that part." Which was a bit of a lie. She'd been quick to study the procedure. What she had missed and really wanted to know was if Lucas's schedule was there. She was hoping to go through his client list to see if anything unusual popped up. There was also the question of whether Joy was on the schedule for the night he was killed. So far the police hadn't said anything, which would seem to indicate she wasn't, but Francine wanted to know for certain.

Aretha repeated the steps she'd taken so Francine could watch. "The artists and the hair stylists keep their own schedules for the most part, so we have a shared look at their calendar. That's why it's different from the nail technicians."

"Got it. Thanks." Lucas's schedule was not on the menu. Francine wondered who had taken it down, the police or someone from Tattoo You Two.

Her workload started slow but got busier as the afternoon wore on. She started out watching the clock but by 4:30 she was surprised at how fast the time had passed. She had set her personal phone to mute incoming calls, and so hadn't noticed until then that she had a text from Jonathan, reminding her he wouldn't be home for dinner that night. In some ways, she was relieved she wouldn't have to say anything about her afternoon. Because she'd have to lie.

Just after five, a woman entered the shop. She had curly brown hair cut short with a part to one side and was dressed in a tailored gray blouse with black pants. Sunglasses covered her eyes. She removed the glasses when she reached the front desk. Her eyes were red, making Francine wonder if she'd been crying. She looked vaguely familiar.

"Can I help you?" Francine asked.

"I'm Gabriella Cayman," she said, her voice barely above a whisper. "I'm here to collect my brother Lucas's things."

18

For a moment, Francine wondered how she should handle it. There was a resemblance to Lucas Monet in the face, but should she ask for identification? She decided she'd let Aretha handle it.

"Please wait here a moment," she told the woman. Moving into the back room, she leaned over Aretha who was seated at the desk intently looking at the computer screen. "Lucas's sister is here to get her brother's things," she said. "I thought maybe you would want to talk with her."

Aretha glanced up. "Go ahead and take her back to Snake's office. Is he with a client?"

She shook her head. "The client just left."

"That's a relief. Is Cass here?"

"She didn't have any more clients until later this evening and decided to break for supper early."

"Okay. Tell Ms. Cayman I'll join her back there in a few minutes."

Francine nodded and headed up to the receptionist's desk. "Thanks for waiting," she told Gabriella. "I'll take you to his office. One of our tattoo artists boxed up his things for you. He's in there now."

"Thank you." Her voice was still quiet and raspy.

Francine guided her back toward what was now Snake's office. "One of our managers, Aretha, worked with Lucas and would like to talk to you before you leave." Gabriella nodded perfunctorily.

Francine introduced Snake.

"I'm sorry for your loss," he said. "He was a talented artist. I enjoyed working with him." He showed her the boxes and posters.

She looked at them with sadness in her eyes. "So that's it," she said. "A few boxes. That's all there is to show for his career."

Francine wasn't sure how to interpret that, but she guessed it was not meant in an insulting way, like he had underperformed in some way. The comment was delivered with irony.

Snake nodded sympathetically. "He made a lot of people happy with his designs, though."

"He really did," Francine said. "His designs were amazing. Did you know he covered up hate tattoos for free?"

Snake's eyes locked on hers like laser beams, making her look away. She realized right then she shouldn't have said anything, that Cass told her he was doing it in secret. But if it was a secret, how did Snake know? Had he been privy to it because he worked with Lucas, or was it because he was in possession of Lucas's sketchbook?

Gabriella stiffened. "I didn't know it was common knowledge."

"I only just learned of it," Francine said, trying to justify herself. "I was talking with Cass, and she let it slip. She knew, but then, he was her mentor."

Francine looked up and found Snake still staring at her. She decided to challenge him. "Snake, did you know? I mean, before you took over his office and had access to his sketchbooks."

Gabriella seemed to perk up at the thought. "I would love to see his sketchbooks, especially any he'd used to cover up hate tattoos." She looked at Snake expectantly.

He got defensive. "I boxed them up separately. I knew he'd left the business to Cass. I thought they'd probably go to her." He indicated a box separate from the others. Francine noticed it was not labeled with Cass's name on it.

"I won't keep them," Gabriella said. "I'll give them to her. But I'd love to look through them to see the good work he was doing."

Francine moved toward the drawer where she knew Snake had stashed the sketchbook containing Lucas's hate-covering tattoo designs. Had he been true to his word and boxed up all of them, or had he kept that one out? Was that book somehow pertinent to Lucas's murder? She didn't trust Snake. Of course, she wasn't sure she could trust Gabriella either, but at least Gabriella was Lucas's sister.

The drawer was slightly open. She could see it was still there.

Her fingers inched the drawer open a little bit more. She was debating whether she could sneak it out without Snake noticing it, or if she should have her hand "accidentally" catch the open drawer and have the sketchbook revealed for all to see.

Then Aretha stepped into the cubicle.

"I'm Aretha Smith," she said, shaking Gabriella's hand. She apologized for the delay in greeting her and extended her sympathies.

"We were just discussing Lucas's things," Francine said, "particularly his sketchbooks. Snake was just telling us he'd boxed them all up thinking they would go to Cass, but Gabriella has asked if she could have them for a little while so she could look at them. She intends to give them to Cass when she's done."

"Sounds reasonable." Aretha said. She looked to Snake for confirmation.

"Of course," he said.

"I'll help carry them out," Aretha offered, and she bent down to pick up a box. Snake bent down at the same time and they bumped heads.

With no one taking notice of her, Francine slid the sketchbook out of the drawer. Though it was awkward, she hid it behind her back as best she could.

There were three boxes and four of them in the room. Aretha, having recovered from her collision with Snake, picked up the lightest of the boxes. That left two. After some hesitation, Snake picked up the one that looked heavier, though he'd lingered over the unlabeled one, the one supposedly for Cass. It was gapped open a bit. Francine strained to see if there were really sketchbooks in it.

Aretha saw her leaning toward it. She coughed to get Francine's attention. "Would you mind getting the third box for our guest?" she asked.

"Of course," Francine said. She tried to scoot around behind Snake in the small cubicle while keeping her front facing everyone so they wouldn't see the book she was hiding. To the best of her knowledge no one knew she had it.

Snake didn't budge. Francine couldn't get past unless she went in front of him. "Go ahead," she told him. "I'll follow behind you."

Gabriella, who was closest to the door, filed out first. Aretha turned to leave. Snake edged forward. Francine, hoping to somehow sneak the book into the box, bumped the back wall.

She dropped the book. It hit the floor with a 'thunk.' She bent down quickly to retrieve it. Not knowing if anyone saw what she did, she scooped up the book, pulled against the gap in the box, and shoved the book inside.

She looked up. She wasn't sure what Snake had seen, but he was watching her now. He had one eyebrow raised. His eyes shifted from her to the drawer from which she'd pulled the sketchbook. It was still ajar.

She hastily stood and prodded him forward with the box in her hands. If he knew what she'd done, she'd have to deal with it later.

Aretha, Gabriella, and Francine carried Lucas's things out to the car. Aretha asked Gabriella back to her office and she accepted.

Francine bustled to the front desk and resumed working, ignoring any angry glares she might have gotten from Snake as he returned to his office. She knew it was her nature to be suspicious, especially when murder was involved. Was there something special about that sketchbook that caused Snake to want to keep it? There was no way she could look through it again since it was now in Gabriella's car. Before long Aretha walked Lucas's sister to the door, shook her hand and Gabriella left. Francine resolved to avoid Snake the rest of her working day, which thankfully wasn't much longer for her.

Closing the store required a lot of steps and Aretha went over them carefully. The owner had documented the procedures, so there was a page of written instructions to follow. On the computer there was a way to record the closure each day, and they had to check off each of the written steps before they could close out the document. They also had to electronically sign it. Francine made a mental note to go back to the night of Lucas Monet's death and see if the steps had been followed by whoever had closed that night. She also noticed that nowhere was there a mention of security cameras or enabling or disabling them.

The nail technicians left as a group shortly after they cleaned up their area. Francine noticed that a limo came and picked them up, but then she figured they probably didn't have drivers' licenses yet. They didn't seem like they'd been in the country all that long. The hair stylists were a bit behind in leaving because they had clients to finish up and then the floor to sweep, but the limo waited for them. Francine let them out of the shop and re-locked the door behind them.

Cass and Snake both had clients, so Francine didn't have to worry about either. At 7:30 p.m. she and Aretha locked the door for good.

Aretha clapped her on the back. "You did great. I love your attitude. You want to do a good job, and it shows. Have you seen the schedule yet? I don't know when Quan has you working again."

They got back on the computer and found the schedule. The owner had Francine working the entire next week. "I only wanted to work part-time," she said, surprised.

"He regards "part-time" as anything under forty hours/week, even if it's really close to forty. I've had weeks where I was only an hour away from that mark."

Francine scrolled through the schedule. All of the Tattoo You locations were listed. No one had any hours over forty. "They have no full time employees," Francine remarked.

"You catch on fast," Aretha said. "I'm sure there are tax benefits and other federal requirements they're avoiding by structuring the hours the way they do."

Aretha reiterated that Francine had done a great job and added that she didn't think too much more training would be necessary. "In any event, I'll be by tomorrow, but probably not right away. I've got to square everything at the Indianapolis location before I make the trek back over here. It sure is a long way."

"Can I ask, what attracted you to the job?" Francine asked.

That made Aretha chuckle. "What you really want to know is, why am I staying on a job that has no measurable benefits, no advancement and hours that are beyond the part-time work promised?"

"You know how to cut to the chase," Francine said with a laugh.

"And you probably want to know that now before you get sucked into the same thing?"

"It's like you can read minds."

"The unmeasurable benefits," she said, indicating her well-polished nails and styled hair. "Plus, it's good wind-down to retirement. I'm in my mid-fifties. I intend to work at least another five years, but I'm past the career stage. When I go home for the night, I don't want to take the job with me. The only thing this job doesn't have is flexibility. As I'm discovering. So it may not last. We'll see. I figure I can find another job if I need to."

Francine just nodded. She didn't intend for this to last much past a few *weeks*, not years.

Aretha studied her reaction. "I was hoping you might provide some flexibility for me, that when you were trained, you and I might back up each other between Indianapolis and here. But the way you're looking at me, I don't see you in this job long term."

Francine squirmed. She didn't want Aretha to give a bad report to the owner. "Sorry if you mistook my hesitation. I've just had so much thrown at me today. When I'm confident I can handle it, I'd be happy to back you up. Is there much difference between the two locations?"

"We have more distance at the other shop. You've seen it. We have a whole building. So I have very little interaction with the tattoo artists. They're downstairs and their entrance is before a customer reaches me. They pretty much take care of themselves, even more so than here. There's more coordination needed with the hairstylists since they're upstairs, but once you get a client up there, they take care of themselves, too. So it's a lot of the same as here, with the nail technicians."

"I notice they're all immigrants. What country do they come from?"

Aretha suddenly seemed guarded. "Vietnam."

"They look emaciated. Are they not finding American food to their liking?"

Aretha looked at her watch. "I'm sorry to have to run, Francine, but I need to get going." She showed her how to set the alarm. "When I started, they depended on the tattoo artists to do this, but that wasn't working. Now the artists have to disarm the system before they let an evening client in, but it doesn't take a time or two of setting off the alarm before they remember it."

With that, Aretha left. Francine got in her car. Midsummer in Indiana, the sun didn't set until late, so at 7:45, there was plenty of light left. She stared at the storefront and remembered the first time she saw it, when they found Lucas Monet dead. It seemed like she had lived a lot of weeks between then and now.

The next day, Francine was up early, even before Jonathan. She'd tossed and turned all night, alternating between wakefulness and dreams, all devoted to tying together what she knew about Lucas, his tattoo businesses, the Tattoo You and Tattoo You Two parlors, and how they played into his murder. What about Gabriella or Aretha? Then there was Hank. Did he enter into it? And how about Snake? Why had he tried to keep the sketchbook? And what would he do about her stealing it back out of his office? Even the fluidity of slipping in and out of the dream state last night hadn't helped. The facts didn't fit together neatly, no matter how free-thinking she tried to be, like Charlotte.

She sat on a stool at the breakfast bar sipping her first cup of coffee. Maybe it was time for her to insist that Charlotte forget the motorcycle, forget Hank, and help her brainstorm solutions. Charlotte was supposed to get in touch with her today. She heard Jonathan in the shower.

He joined her for breakfast time. His stomach didn't seem to have been affected by the thing he was working on. While Francine chose to have only toast and tea, he scrambled eggs with cheese and ham for himself and topped it off with an English muffin and coffee.

"You're going into work?" she asked him.

He nodded as he buttered half of the muffin.

"Still working on the secret project?" she persisted.

He shrugged. "Yes. And maybe I'll learn today whether Peter's mom has had time to listen to the recording he made and what she makes of it."

"I hope so."

He was out the door by eight o'clock.

Since neither sleep nor talking with Jonathan had helped her any further with the case, she thought exercise might. It'd worked before.

Sometimes forcing herself to focus on something else enabled her subconscious to come up with insights.

However, still sore from the motorcycle incident the day before, she decided stretching would be better. She was dressing in looser clothes when her phone rang. She hoped it was Charlotte.

It was Jud.

"I need to see you. Do you have a half hour?" He tried to sound polite, but there was a certain harshness to his tone that unsettled her.

"Today?"

"This morning, if you can."

She glanced at her watch. If it really only took a half-hour, she'd have time to stretch later. Whatever it was, she'd rather be done with it. But if she had to meet with Jud, she'd prefer to have that discussion with Charlotte first. If she could convince Charlotte to drop everything and come over now.

"I could probably get to the station by 10:00. I presume that's where you want to meet?"

"Yes, and ten would be great."

"Should I bring anything?"

"Joy, if you can."

"Sure. I'm very joyful. I spread joy wherever I go."

He laughed, and the sound of it made him seem like his old self, not the uptight detective he'd been of late. But then he got serious again. "You know what I meant. Joy McQueen. She's not answering her phone. If you have another way to get to her, please do. And invite her to come. We'd like to see her, too."

The whole thing sounded ominous. Of course, Joy might not be answering her phone because she knew it was Jud. If he couldn't reach her, he couldn't question her about her supposed absence at the murder scene or about her on camera reporting about the murder.

Or something might have happened to Joy. Francine didn't want to think so, but Joy was involved in something she was reluctant to share with any of the Bridge Club members. That often meant she was getting ready to report obliquely on one of their weird Bucket List accomplishments, but they hadn't done one in a while, not one worth reporting on. Besides, she was pretty sure it had to do with her ongoing story about Lucas Monet's death. If Joy didn't want to go, she could say so. Francine should check on her one way or the other.

Joy answered her cell on the first ring. "I'm glad you called, Francine. Jud's been trying to reach me. He calls every half hour. Do you know anything? What's he want?"

"I can honestly say for sure I don't know. But he's asked to see me and he asked me to try to get hold of you."

"What are you going to do?"

"I've agreed to meet him at 10:00."

"For coffee? At your house?"

Francine almost laughed. It seemed like everyone had been coming to her place to meet lately. But this would not be that way. "No, at the station."

There was a pause, and Francine was sure Joy was weighing it in her mind.

"I'll go. If I have to meet him sometime, I'd rather have you there with me."

"Can you come by here first? I'm going to try to get Charlotte here, too. We need to talk ahead of seeing Jud."

"I'll be there in a few."

Francine called Charlotte next and was relieved when Charlotte answered.

"I'm glad you called Francine. I was debating whether you were up and ready to receive visitors."

"How long have you known me, Charlotte? Do I ever sleep past seven o'clock?"

"I suppose you're right."

"Can you come over right away? Jud called. He wants to see me and Joy at 10:00 in his office."

"Sounds ominous."

"I thought you might want to come along. It's time you told the police about the ink cap you stole from the crime scene."

"Stole is such a harsh word. It's not like I took it on purpose. I was startled when the police showed up and I hid it in my pocket. I intended to put it back but everything happened so fast after that I forgot."

"You can explain that to Jud. The police might need it! It may be their best clue to solving the murder. Did you know Cass Dehoney uses the same style of ink cap?"

"You think she did it?"

"Not really, but it might help the police figure it out if they knew everything."

"Yeah, and it might land me in jail, too. Especially if Chief Turner finds out. But you're right. I need to do something about it. Especially since they haven't solved the case yet."

"And neither have we."

"I … also learned something about Hank last night."

There was a mixture of discovery and disappointment in Charlotte's voice. It caused Francine's eyebrows to shoot up.

"Then please get over here as soon as you can."

19

Joy's "be there in a few" turned out to be more than a few. Charlotte arrived at Francine's house first. In many ways, Francine was relieved. It gave her time to question Charlotte about Hank without having to catch Joy up on any of the recent craziness, like the motorcycle riding escapade that had ended up going viral. Though, given how much Joy was into media, she probably already knew of it.

Charlotte, however, came through the front door with a question. "BTW, we're not having Bridge Club tomorrow night, are we?"

Francine had a sudden panic. Had she forgotten about Bridge Club? It would be affected by her having to work until 7:30. She checked the calendar on her cell phone. "No, it's a week from tomorrow," she said, relieved. While her phone was out, she made a note to make sure she didn't get scheduled to work on Bridge Club night. If she was still working there.

Charlotte seemed reassured as well. "Good. Mary Ruth wants to double date with Hank and me, and we're talking about doing it tomorrow night."

Now that was a twist Francine hadn't seen coming. Mary Ruth usually asked her to be the wingman, not Charlotte. Plus, she had hoped Charlotte was having second thoughts about Hank. "Is Mary Ruth's date that Tyler guy she met at the scone class?"

"Yeah, the pushy one, the one she doesn't have much in common with."

"Why is she having another date with him if they have nothing in common?"

"She told me she feels like she owes him a date since they had to flee the last one when she pushed Garrett Stone's face into the scone dough. She wants to get the date over with so she can break up with him. She told me it would be so much easier if another couple was involved. But not you and Jonathan. A dating couple, not a married couple."

Since she hadn't put the phone away yet, Francine checked to make sure they didn't have to rush to the police station. 9:15. They had a little time. But where was Joy? "Just curious, who's pushing for the date to be tomorrow?"

"What do you mean by that?"

"Is it Mary Ruth's idea? Or Tyler's? Or maybe it's yours or Hank's?" She brought Tyler's name up because it suddenly occurred to her that perhaps Tyler was being pushy for a reason. A nefarious reason. What did they really know about him?

Charlotte paused. "I guess it's a combination. Mary Ruth doesn't want to put this off too long. She wants my opinion on Tyler just in case I see something she's missing. Anyway, when I suggested it to Hank, he pushed for us to have a double date soon."

"Does Hank know Tyler?"

"I don't think so. Although I might have mentioned his name when I talked about the double date."

Francine's doubts about Hank overrode her usual hospitable nature. "Mary Ruth's wondering about Tyler. I'm wondering about Hank. I thought you said you had discovered something about Hank."

"I have. And we probably need to sit down."

That sounded worrisome. Yet, Charlotte had spoken about having further dates with him. Francine decided sitting down was probably the right thing to do. "Then let's head into the great room."

Once Francine and Charlotte were settled, Charlotte said, "I, uh, got Hank out of his shirt at my house," Charlotte said. "It gave me the chance to check out his tattoos."

Francine's eyes widened as she thought about how this shirt shedding incident likely took place. Charlotte caught her worried look. "It's not what you think. I jostled Hank's wine glass and he spilled some wine on his shirt. I washed it out."

Francine was relieved, but she didn't want Charlotte to think she was obsessing over it. Plus, she wanted Charlotte to get to her discovery. "And?" she prompted.

"Full of hate tattoos. Hank is a white supremacist."

"Whoa."

"Yes. Whoa."

"And you want to continue dating him?"

"What I want to do is figure out his connection to Lucas Monet's death. You know how he made suggestions about what was being tattooed on Lucas's forearm when he died?"

Francine thought back to what Hank had said. "He thought it might be some kind of letter. A "P" or a "Z," I think."

Charlotte nodded. "That's what he said, and it was a good way to move us in the wrong direction. But when I saw a tattoo on his back, I recognized the pattern. It wasn't either of those letters. It was a stylized 'S.' As in SS bolts. As in the symbol used by German special police and by concentration camp guards. It was in the upper part of Hank's back, between his shoulder blades. Unless his shirt's off, it's not noticeable."

Francine realized she was holding her breath. She exhaled, her mind reeling from this new information. "I don't like what it says about Hank. But what does it say about Lucas?"

"Depends on if Lucas wanted that tattoo or not."

"I don't think he wanted it." Francine filled Charlotte in on what she and Joy had learned from Cass about Lucas's super sensitive skin and his need to be medicated to be tattooed. "But Cass suggested he would have taken a low-dose Xanax. That would *not* have put him under like he was."

"Or made him sick."

"Plus, Cass told us that Lucas covered up hate tattoos for free. It was something he didn't tell many people about. He was as good at creatively reimagining tattoos as he was at creating original tattoos."

"So he very likely wouldn't get a hate tattoo, unless he was leading some kind of double life."

Francine was about to admit to stealing Lucas's sketchbook of hate tattoo cover-ups from Snake's office when Joy came through the front door. "Francine?" she called.

"In here!" Francine called back. "Charlotte and I were catching up on what we've each learned about the case. I was just talking about our visit to Cass."

Joy found them in the living room. She was dressed casually in stretchy jeans and a tee, though Francine was pretty sure both were a Ralph Lauren brand. Joy stopped short of the leather recliner Charlotte was in. She stared at her, momentarily speechless. Then her tongue loosened. "Your hair!" she said.

Charlotte grinned and shifted her face into a model-like pose. "What do you think of it?"

"It's black!"

"Yes, and it's also straighter than it was."

"It looks ... well, actually, it *looks* like you."

"Thank you," Charlotte said.

Francine wasn't quite sure Joy meant it as a compliment. Joy sat on the couch next to Francine and kept making covert glances at Charlotte.

Francine cleared her throat. "As I said, I was catching Charlotte up on our visit to Cass yesterday."

"Did you tell her about Lucas's lack of real tattoos?" Joy asked.

"And the reason why," Francine said.

Charlotte added, "And she just finished telling me how he covered up hate tattoos for free." She went on to explain about Hank's "SS" tattoo.

The revelation caused Joy to lean forward. "Surely you're not going to continue to date him!"

"Only until I figure out if he had anything to do with this murder."

"That's dangerous! Francine, tell her it's dangerous."

Francine looked at Joy. "It's only dangerous if he's really involved in the murder."

"That and the possibility of dying of second hand smoke," Charlotte cracked. "I've never seen evidence of him smoking, but his hands sure smell like tobacco."

Joy narrowed her eyes at Charlotte. "Tell me again how you got him to take his shirt off?"

Charlotte coyly avoided her glare. "A lady doesn't kiss and tell."

Francine drummed her fingers on the arm of the couch. Though she also wanted to know, she wasn't sure it was something to be discussed right then. She planned to bring up again later in a private conversation after she'd had time to think about how best to pry the answer out of Charlotte.

Francine crossed her arms over her chest. "Joy, it's time for you to come clean. You keep telling Jud you're not investigating the Lucas Monet death, but you were going to see Lucas about something. What is it?"

Joy nudged her right shoe aside so she could rub a spot under her heel. It meant she wasn't looking them in the eye. "I was going there to get a tattoo. You know that. We met there. You and Charlotte were going to help me through it."

"There's something more you're not telling us." Francine thought back over their conversation the last time she visited. "Does it have anything to do with your station being sold? You're not trying to scare up some kind of big story to justify the new owner keeping you on, are you?"

Joy became incensed. "Why would you think that? I don't need that kind of justification. If I were doing a story, and I'm not saying I am, but if I were, it wouldn't be for that reason. It would be because there was a story that needed to be told, and I was the one to tell it." She looked at her watch. "And we need to get going. We don't want to be late for our meeting with Jud. By the way, I found out they're having a press conference about the Lucas Monet murder at 11. I don't know if they want to talk to us ahead of it for any particular reason, but I thought the timing was interesting."

"Wait a minute," Charlotte said. She reached down for her purse and pulled out a pair of exam gloves, then removed a plastic bag containing the ink cap she'd had in her possession all this time. "We haven't discussed the ink cap yet. Do I give it to him? How do I do that without admitting I've been withholding evidence?"

Joy brightened at seeing it. "That's the hexagonal kind. Cass uses those. She showed us yesterday."

"Francine told me on the phone this morning. I find it intriguing. Why would one of Cass's ink caps be in Lucas's trash can?"

"We don't know that it was Cass's," Francine said. "And besides, Cass told us that Lucas used them, too. That's how she got started. He gifted her some. She said they were expensive compared to the circular kind and she wouldn't have had them otherwise."

The news momentarily deflated Charlotte's excitement. "So this is probably Lucas's." She put it back in her purse and pulled off the gloves. "It might not have anything to do with the case. I may not have to worry about it."

Francine shook her head. "Maybe, maybe not."

Charlotte stood up. She picked up the purse. "I know I don't have to go with you. Jud didn't ask to see me. But I can't let the two of you have all the fun. I'll go and we'll play it by ear."

Since the press conference would be after their meeting with Jud, Joy insisted on driving separately. Francine wondered aloud if they couldn't all stay around for it, but Joy was adamant that press conferences were for the press.

Which made Francine unhappy. Nerves usually make Joy chatty, and she hoped to glean some insight into Joy's thoughts. Instead, Francine drove Charlotte, who questioned her about the tattoo Joy had received.

"This is a sudden thought," Charlotte said, "but doesn't it seem odd to you that Joy originally wanted to get her tattoo late at night because she was afraid she might be spotted and Roy would find out, but you and she waltzed in yesterday in broad daylight and she got the tattoo from Cass?"

Francine puzzled over that for a moment. "Maybe because of the murder, she now has an excuse for visiting the place. If anyone mentioned it to Roy, she could easily invent a vague reason for being there."

"I suppose," Charlotte said, but she didn't sound convinced.

The Brownsburg Police Station wasn't far from their Summer Ridge subdivision, so even if all three of them had been in the car, there couldn't have been much talking. Just before Francine turned into the parking lot off Main Street, Charlotte said, "Do you think that nasty Chief Turner will be there?"

Francine grimaced. "Hadn't thought of that. I was focused on Jud. But I wouldn't be surprised. I'm confident he's still interested in making sure we stay out of this."

They entered the station together after the receptionist guarding the entry buzzed them in. Francine, Joy and Charlotte each introduced themselves through the bulletproof glass and showed identification. The receptionist then contacted Jud.

"You're in the conference room," she advised. "It's ..." but Jud appeared at the doorway and led them down the corridor.

"Glad you could make it, Ms. McQueen," he said pointedly. "You must be busy. I couldn't seem to get through to you on your phone."

Joy reacted coolly. "I've had to put the cell on silent to get any work done. Too many calls."

Jud nodded.

"Good to see you, Jud," Charlotte said.

He smiled weakly. "Thanks, Mrs. Reinhardt. You are Mrs. Reinhardt, aren't you? I almost don't recognize you with your new hair style."

"Of course it's me. I thought it was time to get a new look. Whaddaya think?"

"I think it was good of you to accompany your friends here today."

"Nice dodge, Jud," she said.

"So what's this about, anyway?" Francine asked as he led them into an empty conference room. There were fifteen seats around the oblong table.

He directed them to sit in the chairs at the middle of the table which faced away from the door. "Just hoping to straighten out a few things. Chief Turner will be joining us shortly."

"Are we being recorded?" Joy asked. Francine realized it was a smart question to ask, particularly since she was a member of the press.

"No, this is all off the record. Are you recording us?"

Joy pointed to the pad she had sitting in front of her. "I brought a notebook."

"Please put it away," said a gravelly voice. They turned toward the door and found Chief Turner standing there. He was in his regulation

Brownsburg police uniform but without the jacket. His Police Chief badge was pinned to his chest. His receding hair line made his high forehead glisten in the fluorescent light like a black eight ball in the hot light of a pool tournament camera.

Joy slid the notepad a few inches away from her right hand but still accessible. If the chief was annoyed that she hadn't fully complied with his request, he didn't show it. He took the seat immediately to Joy's left. Because the chief had a large frame and the muscle to match it, he filled the chair and seemed to take the air out of the room.

Jud took a seat opposite all four of them on the other side of the table. Since he seated himself last, Francine found herself looking at him. Jud was in civilian clothes, not unusual for a detective. But he sat stiffly in the chair, not at all at ease. She once again felt sorry for him, as she was sure Turner was not letting him have the freedom he'd been used to.

Joy fiddled with the pen she'd brought. "I'd like to know what this is about."

"And I'd like to know why you're still the reporter on this assignment," Turner said, "since we know you were present when the body of Lucas Monet was found."

"Have you proof of that?" Joy was nothing if not stoic, Francine thought. Her voice had wavered only slightly when she answered.

"We're giving you the opportunity to prevent compromising your position with the station by resigning this assignment before we do anything."

Joy narrowed her eyes at Jud, then Turner. "I'm going to need more than that."

"So, are you denying that you were there?" Turner asked, sitting up.

"You're the one accusing me of being there. I'm not confirming it or denying it. I'm asking you to prove it."

If they really have proof, Francine thought, *they wouldn't be doing this.*

Jud interrupted the momentary stalemate that quietly settled in. "We might be willing to suppress this information if you could answer some questions for us."

Good cop, bad cop, Francine thought. She was glad Jud was the good cop, although it was the only thing that made sense since they'd known him most of his life.

"What makes you think I have answers?"

"We found your name in Mr. Monet's appointment book," Turner said, playing the bad cop again. "For the night he died. At approximately the time he died."

Joy air-doodled on the table with the non-engaged pen. "You know that my friend here, Charlotte Reinhardt, decided to take that appointment instead of me."

All eyes turned to Charlotte. "Yep," she said. "I was there for that reason. Already stated that."

"Yes," Jud admitted, "but past experience tells us that you are sometimes ... unreliable in how you remember facts. We would rather have Joy answer our questions."

The chief leaned forward and peered at Joy. "For instance, why didn't you get the tattoo? Was he already dead when you arrived?"

Joy maintained her cool. "I never said I was there that night."

"Why didn't you go, then?" the chief asked.

"I admit I was a little afraid of going under the needle. I was having second thoughts. I admitted it to Charlotte, and she said she'd always wanted to get a tattoo and offered to go rather than me miss the appointment."

"So did you then go to see how it would be, but he was dead, and so you left quickly?"

"You keep pushing me to admit I was there."

"And you have not denied it."

"This is not a court of law," Joy sputtered. "Am I being officially questioned? I don't believe I have to answer to anything."

The air was tense. No one said anything. Francine decided to change the line of questioning. "If this is all about Joy," she asked, "why am I here?"

When the two policemen turned to look at her, it occurred to her that she was a witness to anything Joy said. They weren't recording it, but if for whatever reason this became a matter for the court, would she have to testify that Joy lied? Joy stated that Charlotte had taken her place at the tattoo parlor, which she, Charlotte and Joy knew wasn't really true.

"As for you, Mrs. McNamara, I'd like to know why you are still investigating this matter when I thought you had agreed not to," Turner said. His voice stayed neutral but his eyes were anything but.

"In what way am I investigating?" she asked.

"In the past several days you, Charlotte and your husband have been in and out of two of the Tattoo You parlors," Jud said, tripping over his tongue. Then he chuckled at the mess he made. "You try saying it," he said. It made Francine smile.

The chief cleared his throat and tried to put tension back in the meeting. "Yesterday," he said, turning to Joy, "you and Mrs. McNamara went to the Brownsburg location and got a tattoo."

"Well," Joy said, interrupting, "that only goes to prove that I really *did* want a tattoo."

"And I went just to provide emotional support," Francine added. "I didn't get a tattoo."

"She's a good support person," Charlotte chimed in. "It's why she was with me the night Lucas was killed."

The chief spoke slowly and deliberately. "And now, Mrs. McNamara, we understand that you are working at the Brownsburg shop."

Francine was incensed. "How do you know all this stuff? Have you been spying on me? Following me?" She stood up. "Listen, I was a child of the sixties. I don't appreciate my rights being trampled. Police sometimes overstep their bounds and this is clearly one of those times. And Jud, I'm surprised at you, putting up with this. Unless you're in favor of it. Are you?"

Jud turned red. "Please sit down. I can assure you, you are not being followed." His eyes pleaded with her to follow his instruction.

Joy, however, took this opportunity to jump up as well. "I can't believe this. The Brownsburg Police putting a tail on a perfectly innocent citizen who had nothing to do with the murder of Lucas Monet, just because she happened to find him. Do you want this to go on the air? I think you owe her, us, an apology."

"I don't think any of us really want this going on the air," Turner said calmly. "Please have a seat. Let's discuss this like the reasonable human beings we are."

Joy was just getting wound up. "I'm not so sure what reasonable is. Are we being held here? Are you going to arrest us? We came voluntarily, and unless you want to accuse us of some kind of crime, we're going to leave."

20

Turner stood up and came just shy of invading Joy's personal space. Francine's first thought was that he was trying to intimidate them. "What I want more than anything," he said, "is to protect you. Lucas Monet was murdered. Let that sink in. Murdered." He paused for effect. "That means someone killed him for a reason. Whoever that is, he won't spare you if he thinks you could be a danger to his identity."

"So it's a he?" Joy asked. "A man?"

"We have no reason to suspect it's a man over a woman," Jud answered, jumping in quickly. "I'm sure the chief used the male pronoun because he'd used a singular antecedent."

Turner narrowed his eyes at Jud, confused. "What are you talking about?"

"You said 'some*one*,'" Charlotte said. "So that means a single person. Used to be, people used the male pronoun 'he' to go with a singular indeterminate antecedent, so you were correct. I used to be an English teacher in high school."

Turner looked even more confused.

"Never mind," Jud said. "Sorry I brought it up." He indicated Charlotte. "She was one of my teachers in high school. I haven't gotten over it yet."

Charlotte smiled. "Why, Jud! That may be one of the nicest things you've ever said about me."

Turner tried once again to regain control. "Can we all please sit down?"

Joy was having none of it. She looked at the chief. "Nonetheless, it's probably a 'he,' isn't it? Most murderers are male, aren't they?"

He sighed. "It's true that men are more likely to commit a criminal act than women, but we haven't jumped to ruling out half the population."

Jud put his hands out as if to stop everyone from getting any more crazed. "Let's all calm down. I think the chief's earlier words are what we need to focus on. Our goal is to solve the crime and keep our community safe. We are especially worried about the two of you because it appears to us that you are looking into the murder."

For a moment, it appeared Joy might bolt. But Francine decided to trust Jud. She eased back into her chair. After another tense moment with Joy clenching and unclenching her fists, Joy did likewise. Charlotte followed suit.

Everyone took a deep breath.

"I have to use the restroom," Charlotte said. She picked up her purse.

"You know where it is?" Jud asked.

"I've been here a few times," Charlotte said, cracking a smile. "It's down the hall from your office, correct?"

"That's right."

She left the room.

Joy immediately went into defensive mode. "Look, I have an obligation to the station and to the viewers, particularly those in our town, to follow this story. It's a murder, and it's in the community of Brownsburg. While Indianapolis might see a homicide or more a day, it's rare in Brownsburg to have one a year. Why are you so upset? Is it that it's me doing the reporting? The other stations are around, too. Are you having individual meetings with them warning them off, or am I the only one?"

"None of the other stations had a reporter who was there or whose friends were there," Turner said. "The more you look into it, the more danger you might be in."

"I understand that," Joy said. "I have from the start. But it's really my decision, isn't it? I haven't gotten in your way, and I'm being honest here when I say that I don't have any information you don't have about who killed Lucas Monet."

The chief's expression said he didn't believe her.

"I'm doing other investigating as well as providing updates on this murder," she insisted. "The station and I are counting on *you* to solve this crime, and I'll happily report that, too, when you do."

The chief leaned back in his chair, seemingly confused over Joy's choice of words. Francine found herself thinking about that, too. What was Joy investigating, if not this murder? And was she really *not* investigating the murder? That was what she had implied. But she'd asked a lot of questions of Cass yesterday. Or did Joy not consider that investigating? Francine was tired of all the game-playing going on. And she supposed she was as guilty of it as Joy.

"Francine?" Jud asked. "I mean, Mrs. McNamara?"

It broke her out of her thoughts. "What?"

"Your investigation," Chief Turner said. "It needs to stop before you're in any more danger."

"Any more than I am now? Am I in danger? Because that's what you're saying."

The chief narrowed his eyes at her. "Have you not been listening to anything we've said?"

"Every word." Francine nodded for emphasis. "And I will not place myself in any more danger than I am in now."

The chief cocked his head to one side. "That doesn't sound like much of a change."

"Well, look, if you're asking me to quit my new job at the Tattoo You Two parlor, I think that's a bit unfair. I just started it yesterday, and it's an establishment I've patronized for over a year now. They recruited me. It's not like I sought the job."

Jud looked at the chief. Turner gave him a scowl. Jud shrugged. "Best we've got," Jud said. "She's a private citizen and we can't control what job she takes."

Joy, who was still a little hot, wasn't satisfied yet. "And I'd still like to know how you found out she took that job if you aren't following an innocent citizen around."

Turner ground his teeth. "If we find out any of you are getting in the way of our investigation or withholding any information you come across, I will personally do everything I can to show obstruction of justice. Do you understand that's a serious charge? If we can prove it, then we can arrest you. If you're convicted, you could face jail time, and of course you would have an arrest record. Those are all dangerous things, as dangerous to your way of life as taunting Monet's murderer to come after you."

The thought of actually being arrested weighed heavily on Francine's mind. She blew out a breath. "When you put it that way ..."

"So you finally understand?" Turner asked.

"I think so. You've certainly made your point."

"Good. Because we've got this. Without your help."

Charlotte returned from her bathroom break. The room was silent. "Why so quiet?" she asked.

The other four shifted in their seats. Francine thought the sudden sound of their shuffling revealed their discomfort over the whole discussion.

Chief Turner finally answered her. "We've reached an agreement, haven't we, ladies?" He glared at Joy and Francine.

"Of sorts," Joy responded, her tone still defiant.

"Well, that's a happy thought," Charlotte said. "Since we find ourselves in agreement, perhaps you can shed a little light on something. How did Lucas die? Was it poison? We think so, based on what we saw that night, but you've been slow to release anything. Was there any ...umm, evidence of that?"

"We have a press conference shortly," Turner said. "We intend to cover that then."

"Surely you can give us a preview," Joy said. "Just that one question. I promise I won't go on the air with it until after the news conference."

Turner rubbed the stubble of short hair on his head, seemingly annoyed by the endless questions. "Jud will see you out."

Jud escorted them out of the conference room while Turner made a beeline for his office. They trailed Jud like little ducks down the hall toward the door leading to the lobby. Charlotte was immediately behind him. "C'mon, Jud," she said. "Poison or not?"

"We went through the open bottles of ink we believe were used for the tattoo he was receiving, but there were no traces of poison. Nonetheless, the coroner insists it was poison that killed him."

"What kind of poison?" Joy asked.

Jud studied her. "That's more than one question. You asked for *one* question."

"Okay, it's a related question. Please just answer it."

Jud smiled. "Nicotine. And that's all the questions we have time for now." They arrived at the lobby door, which Jud opened with a flourish. "I'm sure I'll see you at the press conference, Joy. Francine and Charlotte, thanks for coming when I asked. I really appreciate it. And please, watch your back. The chief wasn't exaggerating that you could be in danger. You, especially, Francine."

He let the door swing shut, and they were back out in the lobby.

Joy looked at her watch. "Fifteen minutes to the press conference. I'm going to go ahead and scoot over there." Press briefings were held in a large public meeting space in the same building, but down the hall away from the side where the police were stationed. She scurried away clutching the notebook she'd carried in.

Francine and Charlotte walked out the front door. It was warming up already. Francine slipped out of the lightweight summer sweater she needed for the arctic conditions office buildings seemed to have this time of year. She draped it across her forearm. "So did you leave the ink cap in Jud's office?"

Charlotte's mouth almost dropped open. "Was I that obvious? I hoped not."

"It's hard to keep stuff like that from old friends, but no, I don't think anyone else will know but him, when he finds it."

"I left it on his chair, so it won't be too noticeable to anyone passing by. No one saw me go in or out. I left it in the plastic bag with a typewritten note I printed at the library explaining what it was. No fingerprints on anything."

"He'll know it was you."

"I'm hoping he'll be satisfied just to have it. He doesn't necessarily need to tell anyone how he got it. I'm not even sure they need it at this point. They already know how he was poisoned and what the poison was. They probably know both he and Cass have those hexagonal ink caps, but that won't lead them anywhere because they're readily available from any store that supplies that kind of equipment."

Francine unlocked the doors to her car. "So you think you're in the clear?"

Charlotte had a glum look on her face. "Time will tell."

After she dropped Charlotte off at home, Francine drove back to her house. She found herself anxious to start work—anxious and apprehensive—after the troubling meeting with Jud and Chief Turner. Jonathan was at work, so she assembled a salad and ate alone.

She thought about the nail technicians. *I need to befriend them, but how best to do it?* Then she remembered a thought she'd had at the salon the other day when she'd gotten the free pedicure, that she would bring them cookies. She still thought it was a good idea, despite Quan's warning. She'd just wait until he left. *Sweets are kind of universal, aren't they? But what kind?* She knew peanuts were used in some Asian cultures. Googling it, she found they were widely used in Vietnam. Coincidently, she had some frozen Girl Scout peanut butter cookies in her freezer that she'd bought in the spring. She found the box and transferred it to a grocery sack to take in the next day.

Francine arrived in the Tattoo You Two parking lot fifteen minutes early. Assuming Aretha wouldn't be there until later as she'd mentioned the day before, and wanting Quan to see her as a responsible person, she went in right away. Not that she cared about the job; she really only wanted it to last a little while. *How long will a little while be*, she wondered?

"Good afternoon, Francine," Quan said. He held the door open for her. The gesture, while noble, startled her. *He must have seen me through the picture window out front*, she thought.

"I am glad you are here. And early. I must be off. I need to get to other shop at once. You know how to close up? I believe Aretha showed you yesterday."

Francine nodded. "She did. She said she'd be back today, though, so I'm hopeful she can review the details again when she gets here."

His eyes darted back and forth. "That may not happen. You have the sheet with instructions?"

"I do." She was glad she'd remembered to put it in her purse before she left the house. She snapped the purse open and held the sheet up to show him, folded as it was into quarters.

"Good." He nodded profusely and headed toward the back. Within seconds, she heard the heavy outer door close with a clunk.

"Okay," Francine said to herself. She put her purse and the sack with the cookies in the bottom drawer of a file cabinet as Aretha had instructed her and locked the cabinet. She put the key in the pocket of her jeans. "Let's see what we have going on today." She glanced at the white board that had the names of the employees on it. She saw that Snake would be there around 4:00. Cass had the day off.

The nail technicians and hair stylists were also checked in. Francine chuckled at the Anglicization of their names. For some reason it hadn't struck her as comical the day before when Aretha introduced them. Maybe it was because today she felt more nervous, and nerves sometimes made things funnier than they really were. She would have to get over it before she talked to them. She was confident there was no way the technicians could have been named "Judy," "Dorothy," and "Patsy" at birth.

Wandering around, she discovered the hair stylists were busy with multiple clients and the nail technicians all had customers. She checked the two back cubicles where Cass and Snake worked. The lights were off in both. She did a brief walk-through of their work areas but didn't spot anything suspicious, so she quickly returned to the front.

The business hit a slow spot around 3:00. Francine decided to go check on the nail technicians. She got the cookies out of the file cabinet still hidden within the plastic grocery sack so they wouldn't be obvious to the clients that were there.

Patsy was working on a pedicure and Dorothy on a manicure. Judy had just moved a client to the drying area to finish her pedicure, so Francine approached her. Judy was the tallest of the three, but that wasn't saying much. The brown-skinned woman was barely five feet, making Francine feel like she had a lead role in "Land of the Giants."

"Hello, Judy," she said, "how are things going today?"

The woman trembled and averted her eyes. "They are fine."

Francine worried the height difference between them might be intimidating to the smaller woman. She stepped back. "Good. I would like to be friends since we will be working together." Francine found herself unintentionally mimicking Judy's speech pattern of not using contractions. She didn't know if it came across as patronizing or an attempt to make herself easier to understand.

Judy gave no clue that she thought either way. She didn't respond affirmatively or negatively. Mostly she quivered. Francine noticed that Judy looked up *toward* her but never quite *at* her.

She plunged on. "I notice you three leave together in the evening. Did you all work at the Indianapolis location before you came here?"

The woman bowed slightly before answering. "Yes. We were all taught there."

"Where did you come from before that?"

"Come from?"

"Country?"

"Oh," she nodded. "Vietnam."

"How about Dorothy and Patsy?"

This time Judy tilted her head as if she didn't understand.

"Dorothy and Patsy," Francine repeated. "Did they also come here from Vietnam? Did you know each other from there?"

Judy rocked in place. "I must get my next client," she said.

"Wait a minute," Francine said. "I brought you something. Are you and the other technicians able to eat cookies?" She held the bag open for her to see what she had in there.

Judy's eyes danced. "Cookies!" she said. She looked over at the two other technicians that were working. "Yes, can eat cookies. Thank you."

Francine handed her the sack. The little woman bowed several times.

"We will eat them all this afternoon," Judy said.

There were quite a few cookies in the box. "You don't have to do that," Francine said. "You can take them home with you."

Judy gave a faint smile. "I must get my next client," she repeated. "Thank you." She placed the bag containing the cookies in a drawer at their station, treating it like a sacred object.

Francine puzzled over that on the way back to her front desk. *Hmph, so much for Quan thinking they don't want them.* She resolved to bring them a treat every day. *There should be a break room for them to sit in when they don't have a customer, too.*

Charlotte showed up at 3:15. She was back to wearing her white wig. Francine gave her a puzzled look and pointed to her own hair. Charlotte smiled in recognition. "Helmet hair from motorcycle riding," she said. "This covers it up."

"Yes, but it's shocking to see your hair go from black to white."

She lifted her hands up by her side in a "what else to do?" gesture.

Francine leaned across the front desk so only Charlotte could hear. "What are you doing here?"

Charlotte glanced around the room as if they were being watched. "What's wrong? Can I not show up? Am I on some naughty list I didn't know about?"

Francine drummed her fingers on the desk. "I guess it's okay." She kept her voice low. "Any word from Jud yet about the ink cap you left in his office?"

"Not a peep."

"He has to know it was you. What other civilian was in the station this morning and so close to his office?"

"I'm telling you, I got lucky. They know he was poisoned and how the poison was delivered, even if they can't find the ink source. There's nothing more to get out of that ink cap."

"And if you're wrong?"

She shrugged. "Then he'll come after me and I'll get arrested. But I really don't think they'll arrest me."

"Maybe you should think about getting a lawyer, just in case."

Charlotte brightened. "Jonathan's got a law degree!"

"Yeah, but his specialty was business law, and he did that only because of the accounting firm. He's not experienced in trial work and he wouldn't want you or me to be his first."

"Does he know someone?"

"I'm sure he knows a lot of people."

The front door opened and Snake came in. He was wearing ripped jeans, a black t-shirt with the "Tattoo You" logo on it, and a colorful do-rag covering his hair. Over the tee he had a ragged denim vest with a couple of chains attached. Upon closer inspection of the do-rag, Francine realized that it was of an impressionistic painting, though being folded and twisted around his head she couldn't be sure of what. If she had to guess, she would have guessed Monet's *The Garden at Argenteuil*.

Monet?

Francine glanced at the clock. "Three-twenty," she said aloud.

Snake glared at her. "Yeah, so I'm early. No big deal. I got a call from one of my regulars who needs to come in early, but he couldn't say what time. But he's a regular, so I'm here."

"Oh, I didn't mean I was surprised," she said. She closed her eyes and tried to figure out how to make it right. She opened them and said, "It's my first full day on the job. It just feels a little slow."

Snake looked like he didn't believe her, but he shrugged. "Well, I'm here now, so if anyone comes in, you can send them back. I don't expect my guy to be in real soon, probably closer to four."

Charlotte spoke up. "I'm Charlotte. I'm thinking about getting a tattoo. Can you show me some designs you think I might like?"

Snake eyed Francine. "A friend of yours?"

"Is that a problem?" Francine asked. Her eyes sparkled mischievously. "Worried you might get a reputation as the tattoo artist to the geriatric generation?"

"To the skinny-dippin' grandmas!" Charlotte corrected.

Snake gave Charlotte the once over. "Not concerned at all." He motioned her to follow him. Okay, c'mon back. You got any special ideas? I have a book of tattoos I've done and ones I'd like to do, if that helps."

"Yep. I think that would help."

"If it's a simple one, I could probably fit it in today."

"We'll see. It might take me a while to figure out what I want. I really have no idea. Could I schedule it for later when I find something?"

"Later today?" He thought a moment as if he were running through his calendar. "It'd have to be way late. I've got customers through 10 o'clock."

"That late?" Charlotte said. "I've not had the best of luck showing up after dark."

"Change your mind about the tattoo you were going to have Lucas do? That was why you were here that night, wasn't it?"

So Snake is not fooled, thought Francine. *He knows who Charlotte is.*

"Decided it would be bad luck to try that one again," Charlotte said. "Yep. I'm seeking a whole new concept for my first tattoo. I'd like to see what you've got."

Francine blew out a breath. She hated to leave her best friend alone with Snake. Not that she thought he would harm her in a public place during the day, but she didn't trust him. She walked back with them and stayed until Charlotte was in the chair and looking at Snake's book of tattoos.

"I won't hover," she told Charlotte, "but I'll be back to see what tattoo you settle on."

She hoped that would at least put Snake on notice.

21

On the way back to the receptionist's desk, Judy stopped Francine. She handed her the sack that had contained the cookies. "Thank you," she said, bowing. "You are most kind."

The sack was empty. Had the women eaten all of them in so little time? Either that or they had hoarded them for later.

She returned to the receptionist's desk, angry that the women might not be getting enough food. She decided to order Vietnamese food for them to have for dinner. Brownsburg had an Asian restaurant that covered Vietnamese as well as Chinese and Thai cuisines. Francine knew it'd be an Americanized version of Vietnamese food, but she hoped that the women would at least see things they recognized.

Only problem was, they would need to be able to finish it before the car picked them up. If dinner arrived about 6:45, she decided it would work, especially if she helped them clean up between 7 and 7:30. She looked up the phone number for the Imperial Asian Wok, placed an order, and arranged for the food to be delivered at 6:30. Not wanting it to come in through the front door where clients could see it, she told the restaurant to deliver through the back door, which she would leave unlocked. She set an alarm on her phone for 6:00 to remind her to unlock it early.

Fifteen minutes later Charlotte showed up at the front desk and tugged at her elbow. "C'mon back. I want to show you the tattoo I've picked out."

Relieved to see her, Francine followed her to Snake's cubicle.

"Nice," was all Francine could say when she saw it. It was an anchor, smallish, which Charlotte indicated she was going to have put on her right hip. "You know Philip was in the Navy before he went to college. Used his GI benefits to get his undergrad degree and then went to law school."

"You sure you don't want me to do that now?" Snake asked. "It won't take long. If my client shows up before we're done, I can push him off a little later to finish it. He'll wait."

"Nope," Charlotte said. "Let's stick to the schedule we established. Tomorrow afternoon."

His tone was friendly, but he pressed. "I'm just sayin' that people who wait sometimes decide to chicken out. Better to get it done now."

Charlotte turned to Francine. "He doesn't know me very well, does he?"

She might be the daring type, Francine thought, but she still wouldn't put it past her friend to change her mind before tomorrow. Nonetheless, she defended Charlotte. "She's nothing if not brave," she told Snake. "If she's committed to doing this, she'll be back."

Snake wrinkled his brow. "If you say so." Still, he gave it one last parting chance. "Don't forget that I'll be here until after ten tonight," he told her. "I'm fully booked, but I'd stay later to fit you in if you change your mind."

Charlotte was nonplussed. "Past my bedtime, but thanks."

He spun out of his chair and put his book of tattoo designs back on a shelf. The women left his office together.

"He's got creepy eyes," Charlotte whispered. Francine's head bobbed. It wasn't the only thing creepy about him, but it was as true as anything.

Charlotte hung around the front desk as Francine took care of checking customers in, directing them to their proper places, and handling payments for those checking out. When it finally looked as though no one would be around to hear, Charlotte said, "So, what can you find out about Snake?"

"He's your boyfriend's tattoo artist. Didn't you think to ask him?"

"Couldn't do that without raising suspicion.

"Well, you were back there with Snake just now. Didn't you ask a lot of questions?"

"As many as I could get in. But he gave a lot of one-word answers, and heaven knows how many of them are actually true."

"How do you think I'm supposed to get them out of him, then?"

"Don't you have employment records back there you can check?"

Francine glanced into the back room to the file cabinet where she kept her purse. She hadn't really explored that cabinet, but it was wide and deep and was the only one that had a lock. "I might know where those records are kept," she said, but the thought of doing something like that made her sweat.

A customer walked in. Francine greeted her, checked her in, and walked her over to the waiting area for the nail salon. After making sure the nail technicians saw the woman, she returned to Charlotte. "I'll check on it later. Maybe after I close."

Charlotte looked at the clock on the wall. "That's over two hours from now!"

Francine put a hand on her hip. "Not all that long. Until you came in, I hadn't even thought of it."

Charlotte huffed but she left. Out of idle curiosity, Francine checked Snake's schedule. He'd put Charlotte on there for the next afternoon, just as he'd said. She reviewed the rest of his evening and discovered he was fully booked from six to ten. She was glad to see he'd at least been honest with her in that regard. What she didn't see was who this regular client was who'd caused him to alter his schedule and come in earlier than normal.

The remainder of the afternoon buzzed by. Francine found it steadily busy, and by five o'clock there seemed to be quite a few customers around. She worried that if the trend continued, she would forget to leave the door unlocked for the Imperial Asian Wok delivery. She wondered if it wouldn't be better to unlock it now, though that could be bad, too. On a whim, she went back to take a look and see if there wasn't some other way to handle this.

She was surprised to find the back door already unlocked.

The door was immediately adjacent to Snake's cubicle. She peered around the corner to see if he had a customer. He did. The chair normally used for sitting had been reconfigured for the client to lie down on. In this case, the man was lying face down and Snake was tattooing his back. His client hadn't come in through the front door, so Snake must have let him in the back. It made her wonder if Snake didn't want her to see the client. Of course, that made her even more curious.

The client's back looked like some kind of design had already been created on it and Snake was adding to it. Francine thought this might be comparable to how a sleeve was done, in sections because it was so intricate it would take multiple appointments to complete, with time in between for healing before the next section was started. Snake stopped to switch to another color, and when he did, she got a look at the client's upper back. The 'SS' mark was there.

Even though she'd tried to stop any noise, a squeak still came out. It made Snake look up.

"Oh, hi!" Francine said. "Sorry to bother you. I was just checking the door and found it unlocked. My first day on my own, you know, I'm just nervous about things." She felt like she was babbling, but she hoped it wasn't coming off that way.

The man being tattooed turned his head to the side. "Francine McNamara?"

Busted.

"Hank?" she asked, though she had already suspected who it was.

He rolled up slightly so he could see her. "Did I hear you say you were working here? I had no idea you were into tattoos."

She laughed nervously. "No, no tattoos. I'm working as a manager here. First full day."

"Ah. Got it," he said. "What kind of hours are you working?"

"It's part-time," she said. "Afternoons to closing. Not every day, of course."

Snake growled. "Now that you two have become reacquainted, perhaps we can get back to the tattoo."

Hank eased himself back onto his belly in the fully reclined chair. "Always the temperamental artist, aren't you, Snake? Nice to see you, Francine."

"Likewise. I'll be getting back to the front now."

She backed out of the office, but she had no intention of bolting to the receptionist area. She gave a little cough while tromping down the hall so her retreat would be unmistakable, then she tiptoed back to Snake's cubicle. She stood quietly outside the door and listened. Her back was flat against the wall and her ear was trained on what was being said inside. She hoped the nail technicians wouldn't peer down the hall and find her eavesdropping. Or worse, the hair stylists stepping out of their large space across the hall and saying something about her suspicious behavior. Fortunately the openings weren't directly across from each other, or they'd be able to see exactly what she was doing.

"How do you know the new lady manager?" she heard Snake ask in his rumbling deep voice.

So Snake hadn't been aware before this that she knew Hank.

"She's friends with the old woman I'm dating, Charlotte." Hank's voice seemed a bit muffled from his prone position. Francine had to do her best to block out the noise from the air conditioner, the chatter of the clients drifting down the hall, and the whirr of the blow dryers from the hair salon area.

"How much longer is that going to go on?"

She heard Hank groan. "Go easy with that needle, okay? You stressed about the new manager complication? Don't be. It'll all be okay."

"So you say. But you still haven't answered my question."

"Not much. I got Charlotte to tell me everything. The police have warned them off. McNamara seems to be the only one we might have to worry about. I need to get a handle on why she's working here. I'm hoping it's nothing but a crazy coincidence."

"Doubt that," Snake grumbled.

Francine had to bite her hand to keep from yelping. Hank was clearly suspicious. So was Snake. And she was right there in the shop with them. But she still didn't know what was going on.

Across the hall, a hair stylist walked out with one of her clients. Spotting Francine, she said to the woman, "Here's our new manager. She'll check you out and make your next appointment."

Francine's face immediately reddened. She glided up the hall a few steps before answering. "Please come this way," she said, giving a fake smile to the woman.

At the place where the hallway met the front part of the store, Francine let the patron go first so she could look back down the hallway. She could see Snake's head sticking out of his doorway. He was watching her. It made her gulp.

Unsure what to do, Francine pretended she hadn't seen him and continued to the desk. She collected the client's payment, logged onto the appointments calendar and booked her again in four weeks. After that, Francine stayed behind the desk in the office area as much as possible hoping to keep Snake from getting any more suspicious than he already was.

Although she wanted to avoid Hank as well, she braced herself for it. Unless Snake collected his own fee, Hank would be out after Snake finished whatever tattooing he had planned for that session. Given Hank's curiosity about her working here and asking about her schedule, she was sure he'd want to ask additional questions.

What was going on here? How were Hank and Snake connected to Lucas's death?

Hank approached the front desk about forty-five minutes later. Francine was almost relieved to see him. She just wanted to get it over with. "What did you have done?" she asked, working to keep her voice as neutral as possible. "And what were the charges?"

He gave her Snake's billing slip and paid by credit card. "So how's the first day going?" he asked.

"Business has been up and down," she said. She looked at the clock. "I was hoping the manager from the Indianapolis location would be here by now so I could ask a few questions. She mentored me. But the owner said it might not happen."

"Aretha trained you? When was that?"

"Yesterday." Francine wasn't clear whether he was just making conversation to keep them talking or if Aretha was another concern of his. Earlier he'd said that Francine was the only one they might need to be concerned about. "You know Aretha?"

"Yeah. Until Snake moved over, I went to that shop to get my tattoos. I was just surprised because it doesn't seem like she's been there all that long, either."

"It doesn't matter one way or the other. She knows what she's doing more than I do."

"I'm sure," he said. He looked down at the counter, and Francine got the impression he wasn't going to leave anytime soon. "I mean, since you've only been doing this for one day."

Francine tried to snatch a calming breath. She wanted him to leave. "Do you need another appointment?" she asked.

"Snake has me on his schedule. But thanks." He continued to stand at the counter. "I have to confess I'm surprised to find you working here. I mean, not just here, but anywhere. Charlotte gave me the impression you and your husband were pretty well fixed for money."

Does he really expect me to confess why I'm here? "That's kind of a personal question," she said, hoping to embarrass him.

He stood resolutely at the counter and showed no signs of discomfort. "Just seems like after a death here and you being one of those that found the body, this is the last place you'd take a job."

How to answer that one? At least she could say honestly how she found out about the job. "Aretha recruited me. Guess she must have liked me in spite of what happened. You know, sometimes it's not about money. It's about having a job to do."

The words no sooner left her mouth than she regretted them. Why had she used that phrasing? She should have said, "it's about *wanting* a job to *go to*." But the former was clearly more accurate. She had a job to do. A murder to solve, another puzzle to figure out.

Hank didn't react. He said a few pleasantries and left the shop, leaving her to wonder what he'd taken away from the conversation.

At 6:00, the alarm on Francine's phone went off, jangling her nerves. She remembered she'd set it to alert her to unlock the back door. She didn't remember resetting the lock after the Snake and Hank incident so she went back to check. After making sure no one was watching her, she found it was still unlocked. She went back up front.

At 6:15, Aretha burst in through the front door, startling Francine. She jerked up out of her chair.

The concern on Aretha's face softened after seeing Francine. Glancing about the shop, she seemed to take comfort in that it all looked normal. Everything about her entrance slowed down. "Hi,

Francine," she said. "Glad I was able to make it before you closed up."

Francine's heart rate calmed. "I wasn't sure you were going to be here. Quan said something about not being sure you would make it this afternoon. Is anything wrong?"

"No, not at all," she said. "Why would you think that?"

Francine smiled and tried to look reassuring. "No reason. I feel like I have everything under control."

"Good."

The two women looked at each other.

"Anything I need to go over with you?" Aretha asked.

Francine lifted the lockup procedure sheet from the desktop where she had been reviewing it. "I think I'm good. Are you planning to be here until then?"

She gave an affirmative nod. "We can do it together again today. Or maybe, if you want to leave, I could lock up today for you."

Francine's cell phone buzzed with a text. She pulled it out of her pocket. Jonathan.

"I'm at home. Want me to start dinner or do you still want to go out?"

The way things were turning weird all of a sudden, she decided she wanted Jonathan here, despite the fact he didn't know she had taken a job Tattoo You Too.

"Sorry," she told Aretha. "I have to take this."

"I'll go check on the nail technicians," Aretha said.

Francine was retreating to the office when she passed by the front window. She saw Quan marching in from the parking lot, and he did not look happy. Whatever is going on, she thought, I don't have much time. She went into the office and closed the door.

"Don't judge. Taken job at Tattoo You 2. Something going down. Help!"

She'd barely hit the 'send' button when the owner pushed open the office door and confronted her. "Where's Aretha?" he demanded.

22

Francine tried to think quickly. Should she answer honestly? She didn't really trust Quan all that much, but she didn't know Aretha well either.

"Is everything okay?" she asked.

Quan touched the small of his back. "It is fine. Is Aretha here?" he repeated.

Francine slowly let out a breath. Clearly everything was not fine. She let honesty win out in answering, but only marginally. "She's around someplace, I think."

The little man nodded. He touched his backside again. She'd not seen him have that kind of nervous habit before. It didn't take but a second before it hit her. *He's carrying concealed.*

He might have read her mind. "Please put your phone down and come with me," he ordered.

She'd texted Jonathan that she needed help. He couldn't possibly know how soon she wanted that help to come. Like right now.

Francine put the phone in her pocket.

"No," Quan said. "On the desk."

What should she do? *There are no doubt clients with the hair salon stylists and the nail technicians. Surely he won't do anything with all these witnesses.* She decided to do what he asked.

He nodded. "Good." He stood to one side and motioned for her to go ahead of him. She did, and he followed closely behind.

Does he have a gun trained on me? she thought. And then she had another. *What was Aretha up to? And who was in the right? Or were either in the right?*

They hadn't gotten very far when Francine heard a patron's voice. "Well, I never!" said a woman. She had no trace of accent, so Francine was sure it was not an employee. "It is absolutely ridiculous that I should have to leave before my pedicure is finished."

The owner quickened his steps to where the voice had come from. Aretha was standing next to the woman. "I'm sorry," Aretha said. "There's been a bit of an emergency here. We're going to need to clear the shop. You won't be charged for your visit. We hope this will be over soon and you'll be able to return."

She stiffened when she saw Quan walking behind Francine.

The patron put her hands on her hips and looked at the owner questioningly.

He gave a brief bow. "It is best if you leave so we can deal with this."

She gave a brief, "Hrmph," gathered up her shoes and purse and marched out wearing the temporary flip-flops, her toenails still wet with an apple red polish.

The technicians clustered over at the last station farthest from the door. Huddled together, they had alarm written all over their faces.

The other two clients with whom the technicians had been working seemed more panicked than upset. They shoved their half-finished pedicures into their sandals and scurried out, grabbing their purses on the way. "I'm never coming back here," one said to the other.

The front door shut, leaving the clustered technicians, Aretha, Francine, and the owner, who now pulled out his concealed gun. "You tell them what?" Quan asked, waving it after the patrons who'd just left.

"Same thing I told the first one, that we had an emergency and needed them to leave," Aretha answered. "I also told the hair stylists to hurry and finish their work."

"Good." He glanced at his watch. "Car already called for. We should be forward of police. Good thing we got tip."

Francine stood open-mouthed when she heard this. Her mind raced to put it all together. Human trafficking? The Vietnamese women were surely being exploited in some fashion. It all fit, the hunger, the tattoos they had, the extra hours they put in, the grunt work in closing after hours. How had she not seen this before?

But how did it tie into Lucas Monet's death?

From down the hall, she could hear the hair salon busy with hair dryers going. She wondered if those stylists had any idea what was happening – or if they would be affected by what was happening on the nail side. She wondered what Snake was doing. She was glad Hank was gone. Or was she? All she knew was that he was a white supremacist. Didn't mean he couldn't be handy in a fight. But then, if this was over immigrants, whether they were legal or not, she doubted he would be on the side of the Vietnamese women. Or hers.

Aretha told Quan, "If you take them out front, you can escape quickly once the car gets here." She gestured to the back offices. "No one else needs to know. We won't have to endanger anyone else." Then she gripped Francine on the shoulder. "I'll handle this one."

"No," the owner said. "We go together. You, me, her." He pointed his gun at Francine. "I do not trust you or her."

Aretha took quick, shallow breaths. She was clearly nervous. "Why not? I've known about your operation practically since I started. I could have turned you in long before now."

"From start you have too many questions. We knew you knew. Had it been me, we would have gotten rid of you then."

"I didn't tell anyone, though."

Francine's hands tightened into fists. "Why did you want me to work here if you knew there was something going on?" She said it through gritted teeth.

Aretha started to say something but Quan interrupted her. "It was not her. It was me. I want to find out what you know. And get rid of you if you knew too much. It is easy to make employee disappear. As you will see."

The words chilled Francine. Her eyes widened. She glanced from side to side, searching for a way to escape. She noticed Aretha doing the same. Had Aretha figured out her days were numbered, too? Francine wouldn't bet on either of them surviving if the car picked them all up.

She glanced up at the clock on the wall. Six twenty-five. Something about six-thirty tickled her brain. Then it hit her. In five minutes the Imperial Asian Wok food was scheduled to be delivered.

Could she take advantage of that? Could she use that distraction to get away? Or would the car arrive before the food? There was no guarantee the food would be on time. What would Quan do to the delivery driver? Had she put his life in danger, too? And where was Jonathan?

A patron came out of the hair salon office. Quan moved the gun behind his back. The patron had a questioning look on her face as she approached the trio standing in the entrance to the hall.

The owner nodded. "Aretha will check you out," he said.

Aretha smiled and led the woman to the front desk. Quan shuttled himself and Francine behind her keeping Aretha in full view. She couldn't try anything.

Aretha took the payment. It was a check. "Do you need a receipt?" she asked.

"No."

"Another appointment?"

"Already taken care of." The woman kept eyeing the owner and Francine, who remained to one side of the desk. She glanced at them before she left.

They could see the parking lot from the big picture window. The woman got in her car and drove away, but not before another car pulled up and parked. Francine recognized the car. It was Joy's.

Joy opened her car door and climbed out. She reached into the back and pulled out a book, her phone, and her purse. She started toward the door.

Quan grabbed Francine roughly by the arm and marched her to the front door. "Lock it," he said. "Before she gets here."

Francine did as she was told.

"Turn 'open' light off," he told Aretha, who was still at the desk.

Aretha did.

Joy got to the door. The owner waved her off and pointed to the light Aretha had turned off. "Emergency," he said, mouthing the words so she could see his lips move even if she couldn't hear him. "We will reschedule you."

Joy's eyes widened with concern. She searched for Francine through the glass. Their eyes connected. Francine did her best to communicate how scared she was. She hoped Joy couldn't miss it.

Joy rattled the door as if to open it so she could argue, but Quan held firm. Giving Francine a last glance, she stomped back to her car.

Quan let out a breath. He showed his gun to the women. "No more interruptions before car comes," he declared.

Francine turned to look back at the nail technicians. She had hoped the women would use the distraction to run out the rear door and escape. But they didn't. Quite the opposite. They had made themselves even smaller by hunkering down at the far station and holding on to each other. She guessed they were too beaten down to try anything. Or they had nowhere to go. They didn't know American society, probably didn't trust the police, and probably feared for their lives either way. A no-win situation.

A car drove past the front. It had a lighted sign at the top that read "Imperial Asian Wok." It turned to go around the back of the building. Francine knew where it was headed, but she hoped Quan would assume it was on its way to some other place.

A dark limo pulled up out front. Francine recognized it as the car that had taken the Vietnamese women away the day previous. How could she not have had at least a suspicion they were victims of human trafficking?

Quan nudged her to unlock the front door now. She gulped. He pushed the gun into her side. Her hand trembled, but she reached up and did it.

Still holding Francine by the arm, he growled something in Vietnamese to the nail technicians. They jumped from their hiding place and scurried to the door.

And then everyone turned at the noise coming from the rear of the shop. It sounded like the rear entry door opening and then thudding closed. Footsteps came down the hall.

"Lock the door again," the owner said, grumbling. His grip on Francine's arm tightened. She threw the lock.

The delivery man came around the corner of the back hallway. He looked at them from under a ball cap that had "Imperial Asian Wok" and the logo on it. Quan was poised to shoot at him but didn't.

Then Francine recognized who it was: Hank.

"Your order?" he said, waving a large bag of food at Francine.

Quan growled at him. "Why are you here?"

"Covering your ass and mine." He put the food down on the floor and pulled out his gun. "I've got Snake emptying the hair salon of clients. They're leaving out the back." He used the gun to point to Francine. "She knows about your operation and she knows what happened to Lucas Monet. She met with the police this morning. She's the one who tipped the feds off."

"That's not true," Francine said. "I didn't know if you were doing anything illegal until just now, and I still don't know what happened to Lucas. I did meet with the police this morning but they were the ones who wanted it. I didn't tell them anything because I couldn't. I don't *know* anything."

Snake marched the Vietnamese hair salon stylists to the front and joined them in front of the door. He brandished a knife but didn't have a gun that Francine could see. Quan glanced out the front window. The driver of the car sat in his seat, waiting for them. "We do not have room for everyone in the limo," Quan said.

"No problem," Hank said. "Snake and I'll take Francine and Aretha out the back. We'll take them to my place and hold them until you come to get rid of them."

Snake held up his hands. "Hey, don't volunteer me to do your dirty work. I helped you with the Lucas Monet problem, but that's as far as I'm going. I'm gettin' out of here before the feds raid this place."

Hank grabbed him by the upper arm. "You are up to your tattooed neck in our dirty work! Don't think you can escape now." He gave Snake a shove. The force of it surprised Snake and sent him off balance careening toward Aretha. She ducked the knife and hit him hard in the stomach with her fist. He tumbled to the floor but yanked her down with him. Before she could get any leverage he had the knife at her throat.

"Get up," he hissed, still out of breath from her punch. "Carefully. Or I will cut and gut you."

Hank trained his gun on Aretha so she wouldn't try anything else. Francine would have liked to help Aretha, but with two guns against her and so many innocents at risk of being shot, she could only grind her teeth. She hoped she could make them pay later.

"You take Aretha out the back," Hank said. "Put her in my Wrangler. Good thing I drove it instead of my bike." He tossed his keys at Snake.

Snake snatched them with his free hand. He slid them into the pocket of his torn jeans. "What about Francine?"

"I'll bring her out once Quan leaves and I lock up the place."

Snake tried to move Aretha but she resisted. He dug his fingers into her shoulder and made her wince in pain. He managed to tug her about a foot before she resisted again. Snake stopped and put the knife tight against her windpipe. Her eyes got wide but she didn't look like she was panicked. To Francine it looked like she was waiting for an opportunity. She admired that coolness.

Quan bent down to pick up the bag of food from the Imperial Asian Wok. "Smells good. We will take it with us." He turned to Hank. "What happened to delivery man?"

"I'd been watching for Francine to leave so I could intercept her. Then I saw Aretha, and then I saw you, and I figured something bad was happening. When the food guy arrived, I paid him off and came in. Didn't know if he knew anything, but there was no point it risking it. Hell, it was worth the $20 tip to see your reaction when I came in under that cap."

"Maybe you should not have let him go. Maybe he was in on it. Maybe now he is calling police." Quan turned to Francine. "Why did you order food?"

"Because you're starving these women. They deserve better treatment."

"Thanks to you, they will now be treated worse."

Meanwhile the driver out front became impatient and came to the door. Francine saw him out of the corner of her eyes. He had his driver's cap pulled down so far it nearly covered his face. She could see that he was tall and black. Her eyes widened in hope. Chief Turner.

He tried to open the door. It was still locked.

Quan twisted at the sound. He caught sight of the tall man pulling on the door. "That is not our driver!" he said, startled.

Judy, one of the Vietnamese women, kicked him hard in the knee. He buckled but stayed on his feet. Judy threw herself at the door and went for the lock. Quan whipped toward her, striking her with the gun and knocking her to the floor before she could unlock the door. He pointed the gun at her but the other two women jumped on him and pulled him to the ground.

Francine thought this might be her chance. She tried to join the fray, but Hank put the gun to her head. She froze immediately.

Snake resumed yanking Aretha to the rear exit, his knife already causing little droplets of blood to show against her dark skin. "Don't even think about trying to help," he told her. They disappeared into the back hall.

Hank put his left arm around Francine's neck, his right still holding the gun to her skull. He began dragging her backward into the hall. She watched helplessly as the Vietnamese women bit Quan and scratched at his face with their nails. They screamed like they had years of pent-up frustration they were releasing. Perhaps it was exactly that.

Patsy stomped on Quan's gun hand and lurched for the door. Francine never got to see if she successfully unlocked it, though. Snake had her so far into the hall she'd lost her view. Had Turner been able to get in the door? She hoped so.

They were halfway down the back hall when Hank stopped pulling her and turned her around. Snake, his knife still threatening Aretha's throat, had stopped short of the back door.

"What the hell are you waiting for?" Hank growled at Snake. He thrust Francine past Snake and Aretha, propelling her toward the exit with his body so close to hers she could feel his shoes touching the back of hers. His gun barrel was between her shoulder blades.

As she passed the door to Snake's cubicle, she caught a brief glimpse of someone in there, but she was moving too fast to get a good look. She pushed against the bar that opened the back door and they burst out into the evening sunlight.

She took a dozen small steps forward before Hank pulled her back. They turned around and faced the door.

No Snake, no Aretha. They waited for what seemed like a long minute. Still no one came out.

Hank exhaled noisily. "Damn," he said.

The back of the retail center had only a few parking spots for employees and a Jeep was backed into one of them. *Must be Hank's,* Francine thought. She took brief glances around without moving her head, hoping to find some way to escape. She could hear the traffic of the busy intersection nearby, but behind the center no one could see them. Even if she could escape his grasp, she didn't spot anything to use as a weapon. Plus, the leaden feel of the gun barrel against her back kept reminding her she could be dead any moment. The sour smell of trash from the seafood restaurant two storefronts over nauseated her, and she hoped it wouldn't be the last thing she smelled.

Hank maneuvered her toward the Jeep Wrangler. Francine resisted as best she could. As he forced her closer, she expected to hear the sound of the vehicle's door unlocking. But nothing. He pushed her a few more steps. Still nothing. And then she knew why.

"Snake still has your keys," she said. "You can't get away."

Hank didn't seem perturbed. "I find Brownsburg to be a very safe place to leave a car unlocked," he countered. "Which I did. And as for keys, there's an extra set under the front seat. Get in."

23

Francine briefly wondered what would happen if she just refused to cooperate. Would Hank really shoot her? He had to know at this point that while he might escape the immediate vicinity, every officer in the county would be looking for him within the hour. There was no way he would get away with killing her—but if he had been the one who killed Lucas, he might think he had nothing more to lose.

The backed-in Jeep's driver side door faced them. If he made her get in the passenger seat, he'd have to aim the gun through the windshield as he went around to the driver's side. The windshield wouldn't stop a bullet, but could she do something to frustrate him before he could get in? Maybe hit the lock button from the passenger side? He didn't have keys—he'd already said they were under the driver's seat.

He pushed her into the driver's side. "Get in and slide across," he said. "I'm following you in. The gun will still be pointed at you, so don't try anything."

So much for her plan. She got in but the console made it difficult to slide from the driver's seat to the passenger's seat. "This is tough," she said. "I'm an old lady."

"No, you're not. You're as agile as someone half your age. Keep going."

"You know you'll never escape, even with me as a hostage. Whoever took care of Snake inside is going to be out here in a minute. Or contact the police. Probably both."

"Shut up. I don't have to kill you to make your life as ugly as possible from here on out. A few well-placed bullets and your life will be miserable. Do you really want to risk that?"

Francine was on her knees trying to bridge the chasm between seats. "You may think it's easy to get across, but it's not."

Hank shoved her onto the passenger seat, piled in after her and slammed the door. She rolled as best she could but her legs were still astride as she hit the door on her side. While she was disoriented he grabbed the keys from under the seat, switched the gun to his left hand and started the Jeep with his right. Francine realized her feet were in a good position to kick him in the face. He pointed the gun barrel directly at her eyes, making her realize he saw it too. She pulled herself into a seated position. She wouldn't give up searching for a way out, but for now she was going to wait.

The exit door to the building opened and two people rushed out.

Aretha and Jonathan. Both had guns. Both took aim at the Jeep.

With the Jeep going, Hank moved the gun to his right hand, keeping it focused on Francine. He used his left to power the window half-way down so they could hear him. "Shoot me and this woman is as good as dead."

"I'm a federal agent," Aretha said. She flipped out a badge with her left hand. "We have your accomplices captured. Don't make this any harder on yourself than it has to be."

"Don't try to stop me." He put the Jeep in first and pulled out of the parking spot. Francine could tell he would head out from the rear of the shopping center and into the main parking area. If he could clear that, he could exit onto 56th Street. The police would no doubt come after them, but a high speed chase could kill them both.

He hadn't gotten ten feet away from the parking space when three cars pulled up and blocked his escape route. Francine knew immediately whose they were. They belonged to Joy, Alice, and Mary Ruth. Her heart swelled. There was no way for Hank to get around them.

He had just reached for the gear shift when a motorcycle skidded to a stop immediately behind them. The driver of the motorcycle wore a pink helmet and had a WWI aviator scarf wrapped around her neck. Charlotte. But the motorcycle was bigger than Francine remembered. Then she realized it wasn't Charlotte's. It was Hank's. In a surprisingly quick move, Charlotte dismounted the bike and left it at the rear of the Jeep. She moved to the side and took off her helmet.

"You can back over your ride if you want Hank, but I think it'll damage the Jeep," she said. "And it's gonna kill any chance you have to escape."

Hank seethed. Francine eyed the gun warily. He couldn't concentrate on everything happening at once, and she needed to get him off balance so she could deflect the gun away from her. She edged her left hand toward the gear shift. It was a manual transmission, and the Jeep was still in first gear. Hank's left foot was on the clutch keeping the transmission disengaged. She hoped she could use this to her advantage.

"It's over!" Aretha yelled at him. "Throw the gun out of the window and come out slowly with your hands up!"

Francine saw that Jonathan was no longer next to Aretha. He'd made a semi-circle around the rear of the Jeep and was now crouched five feet from her side, but behind her. If Hank looked at her, he wouldn't see him. She hoped Hank hadn't seen the move.

"It ain't over," Hank said.

"Yes it is!" Francine screamed, hoping her fury would take him by surprise. She threw the gear shift into reverse with her right hand while knocking his gun hand with her left. Hank's foot came off the clutch in surprise and the Jeep bucked backward. It jerked as it plowed into the motorcycle with a loud crunch. The force sent Francine and Hank lurching forward, then backward. Francine was ready for it. Hank wasn't. She grabbed at his flailing gun hand with both her hands and twisted it upward. The Jeep stalled. Jonathan rushed from the right, Aretha from the left.

Francine kept a tight grip on the gun but Hank was stronger. It was all she could do to keep the gun pointed away from her. Their arms waved wildly in the space between them.

Jonathan threw open the passenger side door and tried to take aim at Hank but with Francine still grasping at the gun he didn't have a clear shot. Aretha had a clearer shot through Hank's half-open window. She brought her gun up inches away from Hank's left eye. "Drop it," she said.

Francine felt the tension leave his arm. She gained control, pulled the gun from his hand and threw it onto the floorboard on her side of the Jeep. Jonathan snatched it up and disarmed it.

Francine started to shake. She turned to her right and grabbed for her husband. He hugged her fiercely and let out a breath.

"Help me out!" she pleaded.

He did. Then they wrapped their arms around each other and held on tightly, hardly noticing the heat and the smell of the trash and the noise of the sirens as emergency vehicles pulled up.

Aretha ordered Hank out of the Jeep, and when he didn't comply right away, yanked him out.

Joy, Mary Ruth, and Alice moved their cars out of the way so the emergency vehicles could get to the scene. They hurried toward Francine.

"Thank you all for coming to my rescue," she said, numb from the shock of what had just happened. She blinked back tears.

"We may be wrapped up in our own activities," Alice said, "but that doesn't mean we won't drop everything when one of us has a gun to her head."

"How did you know to come?"

"It was me," Joy said. "I knew the human trafficking issue was coming to a head and I was worried about you working here, so when I got here before the police, I came to the door. One look at your face through the locked door was all I needed. I knew it was time to call in the troops."

"Group hug," Mary Ruth announced.

The ladies hugged her and Jonathan.

Charlotte sauntered up to Hank. "You can forget about our double date tomorrow night," she said. "I'm officially breaking up with you. And here's the key to your motorcycle. Not that it will do you a lot of good right now. I think it needs to be repaired, much like mine did when you arranged to have me run off the road a week ago. Good luck with that."

And with that, Charlotte became the last to join in the Summer Ridge Bridge Club group hug.

Aretha moved them back inside the Tattoo You Two studio. Chief Turner had Quan and Snake in handcuffs, and a state policewoman with a name badge that read "Jade" was speaking to the technicians and hair stylists in their own language.

Francine presumed they had been reassured they were safe. She figured they would be put in touch with a group that helps victims of human trafficking.

"I told them you were going to take them to the police station, but that they were not in danger or under arrest as long as they cooperated," the officer told Chief Turner. "I also told them I would go with them as the interpreter. They seem agreeable."

Joy, Mary Ruth, Alice and Charlotte were separated by the police and their statements were taken. Chief Turner asked Francine and Jonathan to accompany him to the police station to get their statements.

"Can we drive ourselves?" Jonathan asked.

"No," he said, "you can stay together but I want you with me. You're not to discuss anything until we have your individual statements."

Francine longed to talk to Jonathan, but all they could do was hold each other's hand. She found herself shaking again when they got in the back seat of the police car, but having Jonathan there was soothing. She snuggled in close and wondered how they'd allowed him to become part of rescuing her. Or maybe they hadn't. Maybe it would have taken too much time to disarm him. Or maybe he'd freed Aretha from Snake's grasp, and she couldn't stop him from moving on to saving his own wife. She was still shocked to discover Aretha was a federal agent.

Finally, she wondered what, if any of this, had to do with Lucas Monet's murder. Was the human trafficking issue related to the murder, or had the two just come to a head at the same time?

Turner assigned Jud to take Francine's statement. She was relieved he was involved in her questioning process. Glad the worst of the ordeal was over, she told him everything that happened over the last two days as it related to the human trafficking case. She stayed away from admitting she'd been prying into the Lucas Monet murder, although she conceded it influenced her decision to take the job.

Jud frowned at her. "I think Chief Turner made it clear that we did not need your help in the investigation, that we already had it covered."

"Did you?" she asked. "Was that because of Aretha? All this about human trafficking is certainly important, and I'm glad you stopped it. I was oblivious to it until just today. But does it have anything to do with the murder? Do you know who killed Lucas?"

"I'll let the Chief debrief you on that. He wants to see you and Jonathan together before you leave."

"Did Jonathan save Aretha? How did that happen? Why did she allow him to help save me? Don't get me wrong. I'm glad she did. But she's a federal agent. I would have thought an agent ..." Her voice drifted off.

At this Jud smirked. "That is definitely something you will need to take up with your husband. The answer is probably not at all what you expect. Trust me when I say that it surprised me, but I suspect it will shock you."

Shock me? she thought. She remembered back to the promise Jonathan had made to her in bed, that when it was over he would come clean about everything. He said then it would surprise her. *I'm ready to hear it,* she thought. *No more secrets.*

The ordeal in the station took two hours. The police had been kind about it being over the dinner hour. They'd rescued the Vietnamese food she'd ordered for the workers and set it up in a conference room. Though the emaciated salon workers went first, there proved to be enough to share with everyone who'd been brought to the station for questioning.

It felt like forever before she and Jonathan were reunited. The next time they saw each other was when they were hustled into the chief's office. Aretha was there as well.

Chief Turner gave Francine a stern glance. "First, let me say I'm glad you're still alive. This could have taken a far worse turn than it did. Lord knows we tried to keep it from escalating. After our small tactical team stopped the limo several blocks away, I took over being the driver in the hopes we could bring this to a conclusion without there being hostages involved. Between taking over the limo and knowing the back door was open after Hank took the food through it, we thought we had a good chance. Fortunately it worked out. You do know I could arrest you for obstruction of justice, don't you?"

She gripped Jonathan's hand. "But you aren't going to do that, are you?"

"No. We were working on the Lucas Monet murder case when the human trafficking was pushed ahead of it by Homeland Security. We suspected Snake was involved but didn't have the evidence to arrest anyone. If you hadn't been there pushing everyone's buttons we might not have gotten to the truth about why Monet was killed. Or it might have taken us longer. At any rate, I hope the threat to your life will be punishment enough. Jud, however, says he's not so sure you won't do something stupid like this again in the future."

"I hope I won't be involved in something like this for a long, long time."

Turner wasn't satisfied with that answer. "When I told you we had it under control, I meant it. You were wrong to keep prying. I have enough trouble keeping older people safe without them playing Miss Marple or Jessica Fletcher. Like," he said, with a trace of exasperation, looking at Aretha, "my own big sister."

"Marvin," she said sweetly, "I may only be part time now, but I'm still an investigator. I can't help it if I see a situation like this one, where these women were being exploited, and decide something needs to be done. It was sheer circumstance that a murder happened a few months into the job."

He cleared his throat, annoyed. "We'll get into it later. Mother will no doubt have something to say to both of us about it, too."

Something funny struck Francine. "Aretha and Marvin? As in Franklin and Gaye?"

Aretha smiled. "You see the connection. Our mother was—and still is—a Motown music fan."

She didn't know if it was some kind of emotional release now that she was safe and finding out the truth, but it gave Francine the giggles. She struggled to regain her composure. "What about the murder?" she asked. "Why did Hank do it?"

Now it was Turner's turn to grin. "Speaking of music, Snake has started singing. He's doing everything he can to save himself jail time. He says that Hank was in a gang of white supremacists who learned Lucas Monet was 'reimagining' hate tattoos for free. At least one of their members had quit and had gone to him to get the hate tattoo redesigned into something more beautiful. The gang member 'disappeared' after visiting here and we're still trying to figure out if the gang killed him or if he outmaneuvered them, changed identities and moved away."

"I hope it was the latter," Francine said.

"We do, too," Aretha said. "Gabriella, Monet's sister, gave us the book of Lucas's designs that shows his sketches for the redesigns. We believe Hank's gang decided to teach Lucas a lesson and send a message to other artists in the area not to do it. Snake agreed to provide entry to the tattoo parlor and the supplies they needed, but he claims he told them he wouldn't do the tattooing. So Hank did, though he didn't have any experience. Apparently Hank didn't realize how quickly the nicotine in the ink dye could act. Lucas died before the tattoo was close to being done, and then you showed up soon afterwards."

Francine's brow furrowed. "There was no connection between the human trafficking and the murder?"

"Actually, there was," Chief Turner said. "Lucas had befriended the Vietnamese women and knew the truth. He had tipped off a reporter to what was going on. All along we suspected it was Joy McQueen, but we had no proof, and you and Charlotte protected her alibi."

Francine gulped.

Chief Turner continued. "Lucas had confided in his sister Gabriella. Her accounting firm bid for the Tattoo You account in the hopes of finding a way to shut them down without Lucas's identity becoming an issue. In the days after he died, she turned what she had over to a Treasury agent, who in turn contacted Homeland Security. Treasury didn't know we were already investigating. But the connection was a fortunate one."

Francine turned to Aretha. "So are you a Treasury agent or a Homeland Security agent?"

Aretha paused as though she wasn't sure what to say. Turner, however, seemed happy to fill the silence. With no hesitation, he said, "She's Homeland Security. But we do have a Treasury agent here." He turned to Jonathan, who'd been unusually quiet during the debriefing. "Agent McNamara?"

24

Francine sucked in a breath. "*Agent?*"

"This isn't the time or the place I would have picked to tell you." He sounded irritated as he held Turner in his gaze. "I did that kind of work for the Treasury department before we got married. I couldn't tell you at the time. Then after we married, I went to work for an accounting firm. I continued to do forensic accounting for Treasury every now and then but had to keep it a secret. I never fully stopped being an agent."

Francine shook her head in disbelief. She had such faith in Jonathan that she had trusted him completely. Technically, her trust had been well-placed. She recognized that he hadn't lied to her or betrayed their marriage or anything like that. He'd just kept silent. "Why didn't you tell me?"

Jonathan lowered his head. "It's an agent thing. We'll talk about it later."

Everyone else in the room sat silent, watching them. Francine began to think Chief Turner *wanted* them to continue discussing the personal issue. She took the initiative to move on.

"Do you know who tipped off Quan?" Francine asked.

"There has to be a leak in one of our organizations," Turner answered. "We're trying to track that down."

"What will happen to the Vietnamese women?"

"I can answer that," Aretha said. "It will largely depend on them. Most times the women clam up and won't admit to the forced labor. They worry about what will happen to their families back home if they confess. But they can't stay if they don't have a job. If they're here on a green card, they'll be returned to their families overseas."

Francine knew trafficking was an issue, but she mostly associated it with prostitution, like 'Chinese massage parlors.' "How did they get into this?"

"Any number of ways. They might have responded to an ad in their home country for a waitressing job or a 'glamorous' job in the beauty industry, and got caught up by a fake agency that confiscated their legal documents and shipped them overseas. Sometimes they do it willingly, either due to lack of jobs in their country or because they become convinced that something good will eventually come from it, that they'll earn immigration status, or make a lot of money or something like that. Sometimes their families will sell them at an early age because they can't afford to feed them or keep them."

"That's sad. How did you figure out what was going on?"

"Prior to involving Homeland Security, I had gotten manicures and pedicures at the original Tattoo You parlor downtown. I always leave cash tips, just out of habit, because you never know at a small place like that if the girls are really getting the money. I saw how they treated it, how they nearly worshipped it. So I became suspicious. I shared my suspicions with my bosses at Homeland Security, and we approached the fire department to do an inspection."

Chief Turner took over. "Our fire department found money stashed in odd hiding places. That's a telltale sign. If the nail technicians didn't hide the cash given to them as tips, they'd never see it again. So they hid it from their handlers. When the fire department inspector found the money, Homeland Security started working on it."

Francine shook her head. The story was all twisted up in itself. "How did you manage to get yourself hired, Aretha?"

"I wheedled my way in. I convinced them I could make them money with better management. Once I got hired, I did everything I could to gain Quan's trust. But owners like him keep a tight rein on their businesses. He'd convinced the women not to talk to me, told them I was worse than he was. I thought Lucas might know something, though. The women were enamored of him. But then he requested the abrupt transfer to Brownsburg. I think it was because he felt threatened and hoped he was safer out here. I didn't know what it pertained to, though. Obviously he wasn't safer."

Francine tried not to glare at her husband but she still couldn't get over that he was a Treasury agent. Now that she thought about it, that explained his annual trip to Washington, DC for a "conference." As far back as she could recall, he'd never offered to take her along and she'd never heard him talk about anything accounting-related when he'd returned. It must have been for some kind of annual training. Hence his skill with guns.

But when had he learned there was something suspicious going on at Tattoo You Two? He'd kind of encouraged her investigation—had even gone with her to the original tattoo parlor and gotten a pedicure. That was probably to protect her, though.

Or did he realize, she was forced to admit, that it wouldn't have mattered if he'd told her it was dangerous without any proof? She could be stubborn and willful, and she wondered if she wasn't getting worse in that department.

Jonathan must have mistaken her glare as a prod for more information from him. "With Gabriella's help, we started a forensic audit and figured out they were hiding money from the IRS. Their original shop had generated so much cash they'd opened a second location in Brownsburg. I was working overtime to prove it. You were making it tough, though, because I felt I had to go along to protect you. Doing one slowed down the other."

So she was right. He knew he couldn't stop her from prying into things unless he'd had some kind of proof of the danger she was putting herself in. She wondered if it had worked out differently and he'd ending up telling her what was going on, if he might have violated some kind of Treasury agent rules. It sounded like he would have done whatever it took to keep her safe. That was certainly reassuring.

And she knew this: his training as a federal agent had saved her and saved Aretha.

The next few days were troubling for Francine. Despite the fact that everything had gone as well as it could have, she couldn't stop thinking about the moments when it almost didn't. She especially had trouble sleeping.

Jonathan recognized the need to take her away, and *not* to their new cabin in Parke County. That, he told her, might only bring up new issues given the recent break-in, and her worries about De Leon's Desire and the waters it produced. He flew them instead to the Kansas City area where they stayed in a hotel, visited with their son Craig and his family, played with the grandkids, and decompressed. When she was sleeping easily again, they returned.

After the women of the Summer Ridge Bridge Club had come together to save her, Francine noticed they'd had a renewed sense of camaraderie. There were no more cancelled or delayed bridge sessions. Alice had made peace with Mary Ruth over their catering business, and Alice herself was cutting back a bit on the real estate business. Joy, having broken the story of human trafficking at the Tattoo You and Tattoo You Two parlors, seemed to be more relaxed about her journalistic chops. She and Roy had set a date, and that gave her a new focus. Charlotte said she gave up motorcycles and dating as being too dangerous, but Mary Ruth told Francine she'd seen Charlotte put up a profile on Ourtime.com, so she wasn't sure about that. Mary Ruth dumped Tyler and, of all things, must have made peace with her evil nemesis Garrett Stone because they were now dating. He'd initiated it, apparently unembarrassed over the scone dough incident. Maybe he liked her spirit.

And Francine had stopped serving them tea made with the special spring water. Whether that had anything to do with the changes or not, she wasn't sure.

"I want you all to be in my wedding," Joy announced. "Roy has two brothers and two sons, and he wants them all on his side of the wedding party, so it made room for me to have all of you in mine."

They were gathered at Alice's home for bridge, but it was taking a backseat to the chatter about Joy's wedding plans. Knowing Joy would be dishing out the details, Alice had hustled them into the living room where she'd set up a party atmosphere. Mary Ruth had contributed a strawberry cake, Joy's favorite, for the event. The three tiered cake looked sculpted with a white Italian buttercream icing covering it, and on top was a replica of the "Roy" tattoo Cass had created on her shoulder. It also had #26 on it, the bucket list number that had been checked off Joy's list by getting the tattoo.

Charlotte noticed the number on the cake. "Did I mention—I got a tattoo too! It wasn't on my bucket list, but we can celebrate our tattoos together."

"I can't believe you actually went through with it!" Francine said. "I thought you were only doing it to pry information out of Snake."

"I was, at first. But then I kind of liked the idea. Cass did it. I think the rest of you should get one."

Alice brought in a tray that held five champagne flutes and a bottle of the sparkling drink already uncorked. She poured champagne into each of the flutes and Mary Ruth passed them out. "Actually," Mary Ruth said, "I don't need to get a tattoo because I already have one."

"You don't really," Francine scoffed.

"Oh, but I do. It's a small one. So many chefs on Food Network and Cooking Channel have them, and I decided, why not be one of the gang? It's of my catering logo." She set her glass on an end table and rolled up her sleeve for all to see. The others admired it, but Francine found it hard to like. She still didn't think tattoos looked good on anyone.

"I guess maybe I should admit that I have one now, too," Alice said. "I was inspired by what Mary Ruth did, and so I got my real estate firm's logo on my shoulder." She unbuttoned the top button on her blouse and pushed her bra over an inch. Once they'd checked it out, they all looked at Francine.

"Sorry," she said. "I don't have one, and I don't *intend* to have one."

"We'll see," said Charlotte.

Anxious to move away from that topic, Francine proposed a toast. "To another Bucket List item checked off!"

"And another mystery solved!" Charlotte added after they'd all had a sip of the champagne. She held up her glass.

Francine drank to Charlotte's toast along with the rest of the group, but she made a silent addendum before she did. "And may it not be too soon before we see another one."

25

In the weeks following their return from Kansas City, Francine made a concerted effort to avoid answering any phone calls from medical facilities she knew Dr. Eisenbarger was associated with. She further ignored whatever messages he left on voicemail. But when the doctor showed up at her front door, she knew she had to be courteous. He wasn't going to go away until she allowed him to confront her.

Still, she stared at the young doctor through the peephole several seconds too long trying to decide what to do. Daniel Eisenbarger was in his thirties, the same age as her son Chad, who'd played against him during high school football seasons so many years ago. *The years of being a doctor must have taken less of a toll on him than most*, she thought. *He seems not to have lost that youthful look. I wonder if he's married or has kids?* The pause caused him to ring the doorbell a second time. She steeled herself and opened the door.

"Hello, Daniel," she said. "Sorry I haven't had time to return your phone calls."

"If you have time now, perhaps I could come in?"

She stepped back. "Okay."

He was slightly taller than her, she noticed, maybe 5' 11," but still built like the running back he'd been—a low center of gravity with short, powerful legs and a muscular torso. His hair was jet black and trimmed close to his head. He had a full beard and mustache now, also close-cropped. Between the beard and penetrating deep brown eyes, he looked sinister.

She was glad Jonathan was home, though he was upstairs in his office. "We'll go into the great room," she said. He followed her and when she indicated for him to sit on one the upholstered chairs, he did.

Not uncomfortable, but not too easy to sit in, she thought. *Maybe it'll encourage him to leave sooner rather than later.*

Francine sat on the couch which was way more comfortable. "You have some questions?" she asked.

If he was nervous, she couldn't see it. He nodded. "About what happened the night Eric Dehoney was shot."

Francine shrugged. "I think I've relayed this over and over again to the doctors who treated him, but what do you want to know?"

"What you did, exactly. How you stopped the bleeding, how you performed CPR. His rapid recovery was nothing short of miraculous."

"So I've been told. But I'm not sure what you think I had to do with that. I'm just a nurse. I worked on him like I was trained to do."

She went over the events of the evening, telling him exactly what she'd told everyone from the EMTs who arrived first on the scene to the doctors at the hospital who'd supervised his recovery. She'd rehearsed it often but she always tried to make it sound off-the-cuff, like she was recalling it as she told it. Of course, she left off the part he was after, that she'd given him a concoction made from the spring water on her property in Parke County. Spring water that was reputedly the fountain of youth.

"Hmmm," he said. "So there's nothing out of the ordinary that you did."

"Not that I can recall."

"Eric seems to have a hazy memory of drinking something you gave him."

"Eric and I have talked about that, too. I think he must have been delirious from the gunshot and loss of blood."

Eisenbarger nodded. "That's certainly a possibility. There are others." He stood. "Well, I guess we might never know how his body has developed this remarkable ability to repair itself. Pity. Think what medical advances could be made if one could replicate that."

"It's a once-in-a-lifetime thing, I guess," Francine said, which was true in more ways than one, since she couldn't duplicate the formula that had been left behind by her ancestor Zedediah Matthew, aka Doc Wheat. There had been one ingredient she had no idea how to find.

She walked him to the door. As he was leaving, he snapped his fingers as though he almost forgot something. He stared at her again with his piercing eyes, and she felt he could almost see through her. "One more question. Do you by any chance have a cousin named Dolly Falkes?"

Chills ran up and down her spine. Did he know something or was he guessing?

"Dolly was married to my cousin William, so yes, in a sense, she's my cousin."

"She's in jail for arson and for murder, isn't she?"

"In the Rockville women's prison."

"She's been telling my brother, who serves as a doctor to the inmates, a remarkable story about some special kind of water she and her husband discovered on land that I understand now belongs to you."

Francine faked a chuckle. She hoped it was convincing. "Oh, yes, the 'Pluto water' of Parke County. It's a bit of a long story, but basically Dolly and William wanted to bottle and sell mineral water from the property, claiming it had special qualities. He thought it could be the next 'Pluto Water' like they sell in French Lick. The man I inherited the property from, Zedediah Matthew, wouldn't give him permission to do that. I won't either. It's a gimmicky thing. I won't go in for giving people false hope or taking advantage of them."

"I see." Eisenbarger never let his eyes waver from hers. She was afraid to shift her glance away from him. She didn't want him to think she had anything to hide, but his stare was creepy.

"Were you aware she claims it's a fountain of youth?" he said.

Francine feigned a wan smile. At least she hoped it looked wan. "Now really, Daniel. You don't believe in that sort of thing, do you?"

His eyebrows lifted. "Oh, I don't know. My brother has run all kinds of tests on her. She seems to sincerely believe it."

"And there are people who sincerely believe in UFOs, in Bigfoot, and in zombies, for whatever reason. It doesn't mean those things really exist, does it?"

He paused before answering. "I guess not. If I have any more questions, may I call you?"

"You can," she said. "But if it's along these crazy lines, I may choose not to respond to them."

She watched him get in his car and drive off. He did not look the least disappointed in his visit with her, almost as if she'd confirmed his speculation instead of denying it.

She went upstairs to give Jonathan a rundown of the meeting.

Francine was in the laundry room folding towels when her phone went off. She didn't recognize the number, but it had an "812" exchange, which could mean it was coming from Parke County. Given the issues they'd had with the house, she answered it.

The woman on the other end identified herself and said she was calling from the Rockville Correctional Facility and asked to speak to Francine McNamara.

Francine felt her heart skip a beat. "I'm Francine."

The Facility contact asked a few questions to verify Francine's identity, then said, "I'm sorry to inform you that Dolly Falkes has passed away. As her next of kin, we wanted you to know. We're terribly sorry."

Even though Dolly and William had been estranged from her well before William's death a couple of years ago, it still hit her hard. Francine left the laundry room and went to her office in case she needed to take some notes. "How did it happen?"

"The coroner believes she ingested a poison of some kind."

"Deliberately?" Francine plopped onto the desk chair.

"We're not sure. That has yet to be decided. She had a visitor earlier that day, and we're not sure if he had anything to do with it. The coroner is investigating."

"A visitor?" Francine felt a smidgeon of guilt that she had never been to the prison to visit Dolly. But who had?

The woman continued with information about what the prison would do in the interim until she decided what to do with Dolly's remains.

"And I'm her only living relative?"

"You're listed as her emergency contact. We have no way of knowing beyond that."

Francine knew that Dolly at one time claimed to have a sister, but then discovered she was using that as a ruse for covering up some illegal activities. If she truly was the only living relative, it would mean she'd have to figure out what to do about the funeral and begin the legal process to settle the estate Dolly shared with William, her cousin.

Francine fumbled around in the desk drawer until she found some paper and a pen. She recorded the information the Alice, recognizing that Francine was receiving distressing news, got her a pad of paper and a pen so she could record the information she needed.

When Francine hung up the phone, she was saddened by what she'd learned. But she couldn't help wondering who this mysterious visitor was, and what his purpose had been in visiting the prison to talk to Dolly.

Two immediate suspects jumped to mind: the person who broke into her house in Parke County, and Dr. Daniel Eisenbarger.

Or might they be one and the same?

TO BE CONTINUED

A NOTE FROM LIZ AND TONY
(THE ELIZABETH PERONA TEAM)

We hope you enjoyed *Murder in the Tattoo Parlor*, book #4 in our Bucket List mystery series!

If you have a moment, please review the book … anywhere is good and you can find all the review links at www.elizabethperona.com/the-bucket-list-mystery-series-review-page.

All authors appreciate honest reviews. It gives us a chance to see our characters and our plots through your eyes, and that kind of feedback is priceless. And if the review is a good one, it's like having our birthday, Christmas, Easter, and Fourth of July all rolled up into one! (Okay, maybe we're exaggerating, but it really does make our day!)

Francine, Charlotte, and the rest of the Skinny Dipping Grandmas return in *Murder at the Karaoke Bar*, book five in the series. Please read on for a sneak preview of what's ahead for them …

SNEAK PEEK

Murder at the Karaoke Bar
Bucket List Mystery #5

Murder at the Karaoke Bar

A Bucket List Mystery
ELIZABETH PERONA

1

Even Francine McNamara had to admit that her study looked cluttered when she was working on a project. Papers important to that project needed to be at hand but also needed to be spread out so she could see each one—or at least each category—at a glance. In consequence, her work was spread out over her inherited antique secretary's desk, onto the surrounding oak hardwood floor, and up against the wood-stained quarter round and baseboard to one side. Her mess hadn't quite reached the wall on the other side.

The project she was working on was not particularly pleasant, but the sooner she got it over with it, the sooner she could move on to other things. She heard someone coming up the stairs and presumed it was her husband Jonathan. She braced for him to make a snide comment about her organizational skills. It was a point on which he often teased her. She always responded that she knew where everything was, so it wasn't disorganized. He was just witnessing a deconstructed file cabinet.

The footsteps didn't sound right, though. They were plodding, deliberate. Jonathan's were quicker, more energetic. She listened for the squawk on the third stair from the bottom, which Jonathan always hit, but it never came. The steady footsteps labored on. Just when she was beginning to feel a small panic building in the back of her mind, her best friend Charlotte Reinhardt entered the room.

"Jonathan said it was okay for me to come on up," she said, "but he didn't tell me you were barricading yourself in with paper mache. When do you start pasting everything together?"

"You're hilarious," Francine deadpanned.

Charlotte tiptoed through the maze of paperwork until she reached an antique chair that was the only other place in the room for her to sit.

She daintily extracted the three sheets of paper that covered the seat and eased herself into it. Leaning back, she tilted her head upward so she examine the papers through the bottom lenses of her white framed bifocals. "Is this related to your cousin's death?"

Francine nodded. "This is some, but not all, of the paperwork I have to go through. Since there was no will and William and Dolly were childless, the prison tracked me down as the only living relative."

William had died a few years back. Though he'd been shot for trespassing on someone's property and ended up in critical condition, his death in the hospital had actually been linked to a substance Dolly had given him that turned out to be poisonous. The police also concluded Dolly killed a resident in one of the nursing homes she and William had owned. Dolly went to prison after that.

"Does that mean you'll be inheriting their nursing homes?"

"She didn't own at the time of death. They were profitable enough that some of her competitors were interested in buying them. In fact, even from prison she was able to arrange for the sale of virtually all of her assets. The only thing left she refused to sell was the house."

"I guess she planned to live out her sentence and get back to it?"

"That must've been it. I was told several people made offers to buy it."

"Was that the house out near Montezuma?" Charlotte asked. "The one that looked like the Victorian mansion from the "The Munsters" tv show?"

Francine gave her a wry smile. "And considering how many years of neglect it's seen since she's been in jail, it probably looks even more like it than the last time we were there."

"I gather you haven't been by since then."

She shook her head. "No reason to. I was never very close to William, and certainly not to Dolly. I never expected to inherit anything from them, although I suppose I should have considered it a possibility, given their lack of family."

Charlotte stared into a corner of the room and ran her hand over her chin, ruminating. "We were there tracking down William's car, weren't we? I remember that it was dark and that mansion gave me the creeps."

"We drove out there from Rockville when we were helping Mary Ruth at the Covered Bridge Festival …"

"… and they had those terrible arson incidents," Charlotte said, finishing Francine's thought.

The two grew quiet. Memories of that time period were difficult for Francine. She learned too much about her ancestry and William's, and especially about the 300-acre farm property that had been in her family. Though she valued the farm and the vacation home they'd built on it, the inheritance from Jedediah Matthew had come with a 'treasure' that had put her in a quandary.

"What are you going to do with William's house? Surely you don't want it."

Francine made a face. "Of course not. My goal in getting control of the estate is to make sure Dolly's body gets a decent burial and she ends up with William in the family cemetery."

"Noble of you." Charlotte glanced at her watch. "But I'm here to help you with a different goal."

"Oh?" Francine said, raising an eyebrow, "What goal is that?"

"Helping you check another item off your Bucket List."

The smirk on Charlotte's face told Francine there was probably a twist to this she wasn't going to like. "I don't recall asking for any help."

"Oh, come on, Francine. We've all noticed that you haven't done anything on your list in quite a while."

"But I've helped the rest of you!"

"And now we're going to help you. You don't think your Bucket List items are going to check themselves off, do you?"

"Well, no."

"Then let's get on it. You're not going to live forever, you know. It's not like you get a choice."

Ah, but what if I did? Francine thought. The quandary of what to do with DeLeon's Desire, the spring on her property in Parke County, filled her mind. But then conflicting feelings about it overwhelmed her. She shoved the looping debate over what to do with her spring into the background.

"Very well," Francine said, crossing her arms. "What Bucket List item are you proposing helping me with?"

"#19, sing karaoke."

Francine sighed. She leaned forward and gave Charlotte an earnest look. "Oh, Charlotte, I just put that on the list as a lark. You know I can't sing on key."

"We're all of the opinion that you can carry a tune if you try. Even Alice feels that way, and you know she's quite musical. She did musical theater when she was younger." Alice, the real estate broker of their group, had done musicals in high school and college and continued that after graduation doing community theater in Indianapolis. She had a strong enough voice to have had some leading roles, including Dolly in "Hello, Dolly!"

"Alice thinks that? She's never said anything of the sort to me. In fact, I remember her advising me to sing softer when she sat next to me in church."

Charlotte looked away. "Well, I might have misconstrued what she said. I know it was something about how many voice lessons you would need to carry off a karaoke song. I thought that was positive! I mean, voice lessons imply that you could actually do it. Isn't that right?"

"If it was anything less than five hundred voice lessons, that would be generous." Francine waited until Charlotte looked back. She made eye contact. "I'm not going to do it."

"What's the point in having on your Bucket List if you're too afraid to try it?"

"I'm not into embarrassing myself."

"You won't be alone. We're all going to be on stage together."

Francine sat up straight. "Wait! You've already arranged it?"

"It's for a benefit, one of those endless number of charity things Joy gets invited to because everyone knows her as a news reporter. They wanted the Skinny Dipping Grandmas to perform a song. We all thought it would be a hoot, so we said 'yes.'"

"I never heard anything about it, let alone agreed to it!"

Charlotte tsk'd. "See? I told them you would react this way. That's why we've hired a vocal coach to help you."

Francine frowned. She was getting ready to launch another protest when, unexpectedly, a wave of optimism overwhelmed her. Maybe a vocal coach was exactly what she needed. She'd never tried it. Perhaps a vocal coach could help her make a connection between her voice and her ability to hear and sing a note.

But then her experience of 72 years set in. "Promise me that if this experiment fails, you won't make me do it."

Charlotte fidgeted. "We won't be the Skinny Dipping Grandmas if you're not there."

"Not true. Chicago is touring with only three or four of the original members, and they still call themselves 'Chicago.' When is this benefit?"

"In three weeks."

"Three weeks? I can't unlearn how to sing off-key in three weeks. I need months! And Jonathan and I are leaving for a week in Rockville tomorrow. If you think I'm driving back here to meet with this vocal coach …"

"Relax, relax," Charlotte said. She put her hands out in front of her as if to restrain Francine's outburst. "I knew you were going to be in Rockville, so I talked to Alice, and she found a vocal coach who lives out there."

"This coach knows I can't sing?"

"I believe Alice went into detail about that."

"And she still thinks she can teach me?"

"It's kismet, but apparently she's known for that sort of thing."

"She must be an alchemist then."

Charlotte clapped her hands. "Alchemist or not, are you in?"

Francine thought about that. *Oh, well, at least if I embarrass myself it'll be in front of a teacher instead of a whole room of catcallers.* "Only if you promise that if the vocal coach agrees I can't be taught to sing, you'll let me out."

"Can you lip sync?"

Francine nodded. "Like a boss."

"Then we have a potential solution. But we won't need it because it won't be a problem. You'll conquer this and everything will be fine. And you'd be happy, wouldn't you, if you could learn to sing?"

"I would be elated. But I remain skeptical. Have you picked out a song?"

"We have!" Charlotte said. "'I Will Follow Him,' the finale from Sister Act. Remember that movie? Whoopi Goldberg was the lead."

"Was that the one where she was the lounge singer and saw her mobster boyfriend commit murder, and then she got hidden in a convent until the trial, but she really doesn't stay hidden because she ends up turning their choir into a sensation?"

"That's the one."

"Then I find it encouraging there was a murder in Sister Act."

Charlotte wrinkled her forehead. "Why? That doesn't seem encouraging."

"It's the connection."

"A connection to murder?"

"Yes. If anyone can murder a karaoke song, it's me."

Charlotte laughed. "Good one," she said, aiming a finger gun at Francine. "Let's hope no murdering takes place."

"I've hoped that before," Francine said, "and been disappointed."

"I sense you're not just talking about your singing."

"We've come across more than a few dead bodies of late."

"Pshaw," Charlotte said. "This is between you and a vocal coach. What could possibly go wrong?"

Francine declined to respond. She hoped Charlotte hadn't just jinxed them.

Liz and Tony hope you enjoyed this sneak peek of
Murder at the Karaoke Bar
#5 in the Bucket List Mystery Series

Please visit our website at www.elizabethperona.com to sign up for our newsletter, learn more about our upcoming releases and to purchase copies!

ABOUT THE AUTHORS

© *Ellen Joy Photography 2021*

Elizabeth Perona is the father/daughter writing team of Tony Perona and Liz Dombrosky. Tony is the author of the Nick Bertetto mystery series, the standalone thriller *The Final Mayan Prophecy* (with Paul Skorich), and co-editor and contributor to the anthologies *Racing Can Be Murder, Hoosier Hoops and Hijinks,* and *Trick or Treats: Tales of All Hallows' Eve*. Tony is a member of Mystery Writers of America and has served the organization as a member of the Board of Directors and as Treasurer. He is also a member of Sisters in Crime.

Liz Dombrosky graduated from Ball State University in the Honors College with a degree in teaching. She is currently a stay-at-home mom and serves as an administrator for her church. Like her father, she is a member of Mystery Writers of America and Sisters in Crime.

Learn more about the Elizabeth Perona duo, their latest books and short stories, and sign up for their newsletter at www.elizabethperona.com.

Books by Elizabeth Perona

Please visit us at www.elizabethperona.com to purchase copies of our books!

The Bucket List Mystery Series
Murder on the Bucket List
Murder under the Covered Bridge
Murder at the Male Revue
Murder in the Tattoo Parlor

AS TONY PERONA
The Nick Bertetto Mystery Series
Second Advent
Angel Whispers
Saintly Remains
The Final Mayan Prophecy (with Paul Skorich)

SHORT STORIES
"The Land Grab"
(appears in *Racing Can Be Murder*)
"Snowplowed"
(appears in *Hoosier Hoops and Hijinks*)
"The Santa Cause"
(appears in *Homicide for the Holidays*)
"The Missing Ingredient for Murderous Intent"
(appears in *Mystery Most Edible*)
"The Ear Witness"
(appears in *Murder 20/20*)
"Three Simple Rules"
(appears in *Trick or Treats: Tales of All Hallows' Eve*)

Made in United States
Orlando, FL
19 November 2024